In five minutes, her sister would be gator chow. She looked back to the spot where she had last seen Pearce. Her sister was swimming for all she was worth, with the gator hot on her heels. Pearce was a good swimmer.

As Fay watched her sister make a valiant attempt to stay ahead of the gator, she recalled an observation Charles Darwin, the evolutionist, had once made: "He who hesitates is… lunch."

Fay grabbed the remaining speargun and prepared to swim to her sister's aid. Just as she was about to leap from the boat, she spotted a shark. A giant bull shark hovered about three feet back and about five feet below the boat's stern. Pearce was heading directly away from the gator's jaws into those of the waiting bull shark.

Were these two creatures working this area together? The gator herded Pearce toward Jaws Junior, and fish and reptile would split the profits? Out of the frying pan and into the fire, as they said – or in this case, out of the fire and into the inferno.

Fay needed to think fast. She pointed the speargun at the shark. After shoving the gun into the water, she fired. She must have hit the fish, as the speargun ripped from her hands and disappeared into the water. This was not a good move on her part. Now there was an angry alligator, a wounded bull shark, and a blood trail in the water.

Praise for Norm Harris

"… complex and well crafted, and you'll immediately invest your emotions in these vivid characters. The dialogue is some of the freshest I've encountered…. As a novelist myself, and now as a fan, my hat goes off to this guy… Larry Brooks, author of psycho-logical thrillers (including Darkness Bound, Pressure Points, Serpents Dance and others),

"Norm Harris is a talent to be reckoned with. Good, exciting, inventive read."

~ *Wendell Wellman, actor, producer, screenwriter-*
Clint Eastwood's Firefox,
The House in the Canyon, and Sail Away.

Arid Sea

by

Norm Harris

*Spider Green Mystery Thriller
Series, Book 2*

This is a work of fiction. Names, characters, places, and incidents are either the product of the author's imagination or are used fictitiously, and any resemblance to actual persons living or dead, business establishments, events, or locales, is entirely coincidental.

Arid Sea

COPYRIGHT © 2022 by Norman A. Harris

All rights reserved. No part of this book may be used or reproduced in any manner whatsoever without written permission of the author or The Wild Rose Press, Inc. except in the case of brief quotations embodied in critical articles or reviews.

Contact Information: info@thewildrosepress.com
Cover Art by *Diana Carlile*

The Wild Rose Press, Inc.
PO Box 708
Adams Basin, NY 14410-0708
Visit us at www.thewildrosepress.com

Publishing History
First Edition, 2022
Trade Paperback ISBN 978-1-5092-4132-3
Digital ISBN 978-1-5092-4133-0

Spider Green Mystery Thriller Series, Book 2
Previously Published, 2021 Amazon KDP
Published in the United States of America

Dedication

For my son, Kristopher-Kent Herbert Harris, with love and amazement.

IN MEMORY

Josephine Hindman, Gladys Richardson, Nell Gelis, Eunice Harris, and Jack Brix.

Acknowledgments

Many thanks to those friends and associates who made this book happen, be it for your technical advice and moral support: Jeanette Lundgren, Navy Captain David Meadows, Carolyn Starr, Alexis Singletary "Attorney at Law", and Sheriff Jack Gardner. A special thank you goes out to Kathleen Jackson, and to Mom and Dad. Thank you all for both your inspiration and valued friendships.

A special thank you to Carolyn Shafer for her superb editing and proofreading.

Chapter 1

Present day, Homernic, an eastern border town in the Czech Republic

Her lower lip trembled. She drew the blade across her wrist, then let it fall from her fingertips. The razorblade cut deep into her upturned right wrist, grasped tightly in unsteady fingers. Her heart pounded, and she struggled to keep tears from obstructing her vision—falling tears mixed with blood.

With trembling lips, she mumbled, "Deliver me. My Lord, please forgive me."

With her black leather-bound Holy Bible clutched to her chest, she reclined on her bed, resting her head on a pillow. A smile formed on cracked lips; she closed her eyes to wait in welcome for the inevitable.

Kristi Larsson would be the typical young woman imported from Ukraine - if she were from Ukraine. Kristi was different. Like a growing number of abducted teenagers, she was an American citizen. A prostitute plucked from an American street and sold, as a sex slave, to the Russian Mafia. One of a million women serving ten men each night in the many brothels of the Czech Republic. Her ordeal had carried her far beyond the precepts of degradation. She now stood at the threshold of her self-destruction, weeping softly, her heart and soul bound up in total despair.

She was a missing person to her family and friends—a runaway. To anyone else, she was just another prostitute. A girl who had vanished one day from her Phoenix, Arizona home, never to be heard from again.

****

Same day, Citrus Tree, a retirement community near Pensacola, Florida

Alvin Joe inhaled the cool Floridian evening air as he passed through the plate glass patio door leading to the backyard swimming pool. "*Cariño*," he called to his wife, Lyza. "I'm going to swim."

"Supper will be ready in forty-five minutes, Al. I must run to the market. Be back in twenty minutes."

"Will you turn on the pool lights on your way out? It's dark out here."

****

Two days later, The Officer's Club, Pensacola Naval Air Station, Pensacola, Florida

The white wrought iron patio chairs, giant turquoise umbrellas, matching tablecloths, and napkins, she assumed, were to blame. Or the attractive servers in pressed white shorts and teal short-sleeved shirts who drew her back to this place. Still, the humidity, the damp pool deck, the chlorine-scented breeze, and an annoying kid shouting, "Watch me, Mom! Watch me!" as he proceeded to belly flop into the pool, reminded her why she had often promised not to return. Did she care? No, not really.

A sporadic summer breeze playfully ruffled her shoulder-length flaxen hair, perfuming her damp neck with the sweet scent of Southern magnolia. The faint love song of a lonesome mockingbird lingered on the tepid wind, underscored by the soft clinking of dinnerware, the muffled conversations of dinner guests nearby and the merry children frolicking in the swimming pool. This was a most perfect moment.

Faydra Green glanced at her father across the table. Making sure she had caught his attention, she smiled and held his gaze in intimate solitude. "I love you, Dad," she whispered through subtly curved lips.

He acknowledged her with a comforting smile.

It was easy for her to know why her mother's world had revolved around this man. Despite his seventy years, former United States President Bill Green had remained fit and trim. His once blonde hair was now faded to silver gray. Beneath his Florida sun-bronzed skin and the stoic diplomat's rugged, boyish good looks lay the compassionate father she loved. And the one she had missed during the long time they had not spoken to each other.

The evening started at noon in the South; any meal served past noon was dinner. She and her guests had ordered dinner.

A server approached with a phone in hand and an apologetic expression on his face. "Call for Commander Green."

"That would be me. Thank you." She smiled and took the phone from his extended right hand. Who could be calling? Who even knew she was having dinner at the O Club?

"Hello," she said, hesitation evident in her voice.

"Faydra," came a familiar voice. "This is Vern."

Mystery solved. Her boss, Navy Judge Advocate, Captain Vern Towsley, was calling her from her home in Bremerton, Washington. His voice brought a broad smile to her lips.

"Well, hey Vern! How ya doin'?" Fay responded.

"Doing fine, Commander. And before you ask, your cat is doing fine too."

She had left Barnacle Bill, her cherished pest, in the captain's capable hands. She knew Vern disliked the cat, but she had no faith in Bill being with anyone else. Fay also suspected Vern and her cat got along better than both let on. In fact, she secretly hoped Vern would become attached to the cat and would decide to keep it.

"It's good to hear from you, sir," Fay stated.

"I'm sorry to interrupt your lunch - and your leave - but I'd like you to do a favor for me," the captain told her.

"Sure, sir. Name it."

"You remember Alvin Joe, don't you?"

Initially unable to match the name with the face, Fay replied, "No, sir. Oh… uh, wait… yes, I remember now - Admiral Alvin Joe. Yes, sir, I do now recall the gentleman. He has a wife. A gracious woman, as I recall. Miss Lyza, I do believe her name is? Admiral Joe and his wife are your good friends."

"Alvin retired last year, but yes, he is a dear friend. I've known him a long time." The captain paused. "I received a disturbing call from Miss Lyza this morning. Her husband has been missing for two days."

"No!" Fay gasped in surprise. "Sir, any details? I mean, the man up and vanished?"

"From what I gather, she last saw him heading for the swimming pool and hasn't seen or heard from him since."

"Mercy." She sighed. "I reckon Mrs. Joe must be frantic. Has she contacted the police, sir?"

"She called them right away. A sheriff's deputy came to the house. There's no evidence a crime was committed, so the local sheriff can do little," the captain explained.

"Sad." As the dinner was served, Fay placed her hand over the phone and spoke to her companions. "Y'all go on and eat now. I'll be with ya in two shakes of a lamb's tail."

Fay removed her hand from the phone's mouthpiece. "What can I do?"

"The Joes live near Pensacola. A small town called Citrus Tree. Do you know where it's located?" the captain asked.

"No, sir. But hold on. I'm having dinner with Dad, my bubba, and JP. One will know where it's located."

She again placed her hand over the phone. "Pardon me. Any y'all know where Citrus Tree is?" Fay asked her tablemates.

"It's a suburb of Backwater. Down the road from us, in Hicksville County," came the reply.

Fay smiled. "Thanks."

She returned to her phone conversation. "Miss Pearce says it's over near Backwater," Fay told the captain.

"Backwater?" Towsley's skeptical voice clued her in.

"I think she's pulling my leg. Hold on, sir." Fay glanced at JP, her face conveying a look of mock disgust. "She looks like she's going to tell me."

"Citrus Tree's at Choctawhatchee Bay's east end," Pearce informed her.

Fay flashed her sister an appreciative smile. *Funny girl. I'll club her upside the head later*. "Citrus Tree is between Pensacola and Panama City. At Choctawhatchee Bay's east end," Fay reported to Towsley.

While she spoke to Vern, Fay admired her half-sister, Petty Officer J. Pearce, a striking woman, willowy and blessed with both her parents' best features. Along with her father's long legs, JP also had his caring and inquisitive, sky-blue eyes. She had her biological American Indian mother's dark skin and raven hair, now styled in what Fay referred to as a "China Chop." Fay had always considered her sister to be an exotic-appearing woman, despite the scar running the entire length of her left cheek, which was the result of an automobile accident. The crash had killed Fay's mother, who had adopted JP following her biological mother's death.

"Say what? Chocta-who-chee?"

Fay chuckled at the captain's humor. "Choctawhatchee, sir."

"Chocta…whatever. Citrus Tree is not too far from you?" he asked.

"Not far, sir. Do you want me to call Miss Lyza?" Fay queried.

"I'm sure she would appreciate the call."

"No problem. Anything else?" Fay hoped not.

"No, Faydra. You've done enough. Oh, and by the way, when are you coming home? We miss you around here," the captain said.

"We, sir?"

"Your cat and I. His mom and my ace lawyer are on leave." The captain chuckled. "I'm pulling double duty to cover her workload."

"Why, sir, this sounds like this would be a good time

to ask for a promotion!" Fay exclaimed.

Towsley laughed. "Nice try, Commander. We promoted you not too long ago. You're going to have to wait awhile for your fourth stripe."

"I know. I thought I'd give it a shot. Hold on, sir, let me get a pen and paper." Reaching under the table, Fay located her pocketbook and removed a pen. She snatched a paper coaster from beneath a water glass, much like she would do if she had met an interesting man in a bar.

"Okay. I am ready for the Joes' phone number." Fay wrote as Captain Towsley dictated, before then confirming the phone number.

"Thanks, Commander. And give my regards to your lunch partners," Towsley said.

"I will, sir. Have a nice day now."

Clicking off the phone, Fay said to the others at the table, "Sorry. It was Vern Towsley. He said to say 'hey' to y'all."

"Did Vern make admiral yet?" her father asked.

"No, Daddy. The Pacific Northwest has captured the man's soul, I'm afraid. He seems content. I do believe he thinks if the Navy promoted him, he'd have to leave what he calls 'God's country.' 'To trade it all for a desk buried deep within the Pentagon's impersonal walls would be a fate worse than marriage,' as I recall him saying. I can't say I disagree with the gentleman either," Fay remarked.

"I heard you mention a disappearance?"

"Yes, Daddy. It seems Vern's dear friend disappeared. A fellow named Alvin Joe. He wants me to call Mrs. Joe," Fay explained.

"The police aren't offerin' any help, I presume," Pearce said.

"A sheriff's deputy went by the house, darlin', but

for now they do not suspect foul play. What can they do?" Fay replied.

"Why don't you call her right now?" Bill Green suggested.

Fay wanted to eat her dinner. "Permafrost is setting in on my French fries," she said, but then, a sense of duty overcame her. "If y'all don't mind, I do believe I will."

Clicking the phone back on, Fay punched in the phone number for Mrs. Joe.

The phone rang three times.

"Good afternoon. Joe residence. Callie speaking," a woman's voice picked up.

"Afternoon, Callie. This is Faydra Green calling for Mrs. Joe."

"One moment, Miss Faydra. Miss Lyza's resting," Callie said. "She's expectin' your call, ma'am. I'll go fetch her."

"Are you the housekeeper?" Fay asked.

"Yes, ma'am."

Callie's phone introduction told Fay that Mrs. Joe was a Southern belle, which was what Southern folk called them. Southern girls evolved from Miss when they were small to Mrs., if they married, back to Miss again - married or not.

"Good afternoon, Commander Green," Mrs. Joe said a few minutes later. "Thank you for calling."

"Afternoon, Miss Lyza. Please call me Fay."

"Thank you, Fay. Vern said you might be calling."

"My pleasure. How can I help?" Fay asked, thinking to herself, *Mrs. Joe sounds so sweet*.

"My husband has disappeared." Lyza paused for a moment. "It's not like him to wander off. I don't know what to do."

Fay could sense the sadness, frustration, and worry in Miss Lyza's voice. "Ma'am, I'm up the road in Pensacola. May I call on you this afternoon?" She was unsure what she would say or do but would figure it out by the time she arrived.

"Oh, yes… if y'all wouldn't mind. A sheriff's deputy dropped by the house yesterday. I asked them to file a missing person's report and begin a search for Alvin, but they seem reluctant. I didn't know what to do, so I called Vern…" Lyza's voice trailed off.

Fay glanced at her wristwatch. "I can be there by…"

Will, who had been listening to the conversation, held up four fingers.

Fay gave her brother an appreciative nod and said to Mrs. Joe, "I can be there by four, ma'am."

Fay finished the call by getting Lyza Joe's Citrus Tree address, clicked off the phone, and asked her sister, "Should I send these fries back for a reheat?"

"It sounds like our foursome has become a threesome." Will chuckled.

Will, a colossal bear sized man with short blonde hair and rosy cheeks, was a nurse by profession. Fay often wondered if her younger brother's size tended to unnerve the patients in his care.

Bill Green shifted his gaze from Will toward JP. "More than likely a twosome, son," he clarified.

"If you don't mind, Daddy," Pearce cut in, "I'd like to tag along with Spider."

Her dad seemed disappointed. "As a make up, can I take you to dinner before I leave? Just you and me?" he asked.

A broad smile graced her father's face. "You got yourself a deal!"

Fay's nickname was Spider, much to her chagrin. According to her father, she had been all arms and legs as a child, with long spider monkey-like fingers and toes. Her long, spindly arms and legs, which seemed to be a family feature, would periodically cause her to lament: *I must have been hideous*. She loathed arachnids; she despised her nickname even more. Still, because JP called her "Spider" often, she had gotten used to the nickname.

"I think Will and I can manage a twosome this afternoon." Bill Green turned back to Will, with a sly smile on his lips and a twinkle in his eyes. "You know what this means, don't you?"

"We get to smoke the Cuban cigars I've heard so much about?" Will asked eagerly.

"You bet, son."

"Daddy! Yuck!" Fay mildly protested. "Filthy, smelly, damn cigars. Besides, Cuban cigars are illegal. I'm gonna call the cops on you guys."

"Hey! Those cigars were a gift to me from the Cuban Ambassador," her dad good-naturedly protested.

"Oh, and that makes everything all right?" Fay teased. "In my opinion, the Cuban Ambassador is a greasy leering little man, much like his nasty cigars."

Both men laughed.

"You sure you want to come with me, Precious?" Fay asked her sister.

"Yeah, and I tend to agree with y'all regardin' those cigars," JP replied.

Fay's father owned two cars. The one he used for everyday driving was a retired Pensacola city cop car. Fay suspected her dad was, more than likely, a multi-millionaire. Although she had never seen any evidence, she supposed any former U.S. president was likely to be one.

Fay had long held the opinion that her father was also a multi-tightwad. He had bought a used cop car, repainted it himself to save money, and driven it around until the fenders fell off. His other car was a 1967 Camaro, a perfectly restored red roadster. For years, she and her siblings could not even touch the car, much less entertain the idea of actually driving it.

Now, Fay faced having to drive over to Citrus Tree in a boring old used cop car, which still looked, despite the new paint job, like a boring old used cop car. The whole concept of two proper Southern girls sporting around town in a used cop car was beyond tacky.

Pearce verbally mirrored Fay's concerns. "Daddy," she said in her sweetest Southern drawl, "y'all think that old car will make it on over to Citrus Tree and back?" She did not let him answer. "Aah mean, we won't have no trouble with that old thing now, will we?" She, again, did not give him a chance to answer her, but instead, went for the jugular. "Why, aah took notice, the other day, the front taars were as bald as the guy who invented chemo-therapy. Wasn't that brand of taars the ones they recalled, or—"

When she and JP had left the South and moved north across the Mason Dixon line, Fay had attempted to leave her drawl behind her, in the South where it belonged. Now, she only lapsed into a Southern drawl when with close family or friends. On the other hand, her sister had packed her Southern accent along with her to Washington State. For a reason known only to her and the Lord God Almighty, JP personified the South. Often, Fay believed an interpreter would be handy when JP got to going on about something.

"Okay, okay... enough." Bill Green threw up his arms in mock surrender. He knew J. Pearce would eventually get her way. "Take the Camaro."

By 15:00 hours, the two sisters were blasting down Highway 98 in the bolero red Camaro on their way to the Citrus Tree Retirement Community. By Fay's standards, they looked pretty good in the car. They had the roadster's top retracted while the wind whipped their hair around. A bright afternoon Florida sun warmed their faces, and they had their sunglasses on.

To show respect for Mrs. Joe, Fay had deemed it appropriate that they call on her wearing their white dress uniforms. The uniforms spoiled the total effect of two hot chicks cruising the highway in the hot car.

Fay had a second motive for wearing the whites. She wanted the Cartman County Sheriff to meet her at the Joes' home. By doing a quick background check on Sheriff Virgil Gus, she had learned he was ex-Navy. Gus, a Shore Patrol Lieutenant Commander, had retired from the Pensacola Navy base. He had settled in Cartman County, then hired on as a deputy, eventually working his way up the food chain to land the job as head of the Cartman County Mounties. The sheriff was also a Republican. This was all she needed to know about the man.

As Pearce drove them toward Citrus Tree, Fay called the sheriff's office on her cell phone. He was out.

"Gone fishin'," the lovely person who answered the phone informed her.

She asked for his cell phone number and was told, "I'm sorry, I can't give out Sheriff Gus's number."

But when Fay mentioned the Justice Department,

low and behold, she got the number.

Actually, she had a third motive for wearing the white dress uniform. Fay secretly harbored a theory regarding blondes and how people evaluated said blondes' ability to comprehend complex thoughts. Being legally blonde all her life, she had noticed there were far more blonde jokes circulating throughout society than any other, including lawyer jokes. Significantly, Polish jokes had fallen from favor when the Pope had ceased to be Italian. She had yet to hear a blonde lawyer joke, which seemed odd to her.

General George Washington had said, "When we assumed the Soldier, we did not lay aside the Citizen." Fay had changed this to, "When we assumed the Blonde, we did not lay aside the Airhead." When she met Sheriff Gus, she needed him to do a few things for her, and she wanted to be sure he took her seriously.

Fay called Sheriff Gus on his cell phone.

Three rings. "How'd ya come by this phone number?" a voice asked.

Not even a "hello?" Fay wondered to herself. "How's fishin', Sheriff Gus?" she responded out loud.

"How'd ya get my phone number?" He repeated, apparently annoyed.

"Sheriff, would y'all meet me at Admiral Joe's home?" Fay requested.

Before he could ask any more repetitive questions, Fay told him who she was. She reminded herself that he was, at one time, a commissioned officer in the Armed Forces Police. She knew he would understand her naval rank's significance as a Navy Judge Advocate and her present duty assignment with the Naval Criminal Investigative Service. NCIS investigators, or agents, were referred to as "Terminators" because they had a reputation for staying with a case until it was resolved.

Fay closed the deal by pointing out, "Sheriff, you're aware Cartman County's voter base is predominantly retired military. Therefore, they are predominantly Republican in their voting habits, correct?"

Virgil, being an elected official, understood her point. "I'll pull up anchor," he agreed. "There's a marina about two miles downriver from the Citrus Tree Retirement Community. I'll have a deputy meet me at the marina and drive me on over to the Joes'."

He estimated he would arrive there by 17:00 hours.

"See ya at five," Fay responded before hanging up. She calculated she and JP would arrive at Mrs. Joe's by four. This would give her an hour to chat with Mrs. Joe before Gus and his posse showed up.

It was ten minutes to four when the two women arrived at the Citrus Tree Retirement Community's main entrance gate. They stopped at a small guardhouse and waited while a security guy made his way from the guardhouse to their car.

"Afternoon, ladies," the guard greeted them, bringing his right hand to his cap's brim. "How can I help y'all?"

"We're here to see Admiral Joe," Pearce replied. She smiled and winked at the guard, a fit man who was easily in his fifties.

Fay did not know why her sister was busy winking at the man.

The guard returned the smile. He had obviously noted the women's white dress uniforms. "Navy business, Petty Officer?" he asked.

"Yes, sir. You ex-Navy?"

"Yes, ma'am." By now, the man was beaming. "Twenty years, Fire Control Technician, U.S.S. *David Ray*."

Fay assumed the man would have attained Chief Petty Officer's rank after twenty years. The hot afternoon sun and high humidity were causing the poor man to perspire and breathe heavily. She could tell he needed to get back into the air-conditioned shade of his little guardhouse before he either melted or developed sunstroke.

To be neighborly, Fay called, "Hey, Chief."

The guard must have noticed she was a naval officer, because he stiffened and snapped a salute. "Ma'am. You must be Commander Green."

"That would be me," Fay confirmed.

"We've been expecting you, ladies," the guard informed her. "Mrs. Joe left instructions to let you in when you got here."

Fay grinned. "Would you direct us to the Joes' home?"

"Right on Oak Street, right on Sycamore Street, left on Bark Street," he replied.

"Right, right, left? Got it. Thanks, Chief."

They had named all the Citrus Tree Retirement Community streets after trees, except for the road on which the Joes lived. The Joes lived at 471 Bark Street. Fay assumed it was "bark," as in tree skin, as opposed to "bark," as in the sailing ship.

The bucolic community's two hundred and eighty-three homes were on the Citrus Tree Golf Course's eighteen various fairways. As the car rolled slowly past the large and immaculate homes enclosed by magnificently landscaped yards, Fay breathed in the scent of Southern magnolia. What so awfully terrible could ever happen in a place like this?

On the way from Pensacola, Fay and Pearce had discussed several ideas. They had suggested marital issues, Alzheimer's disease, or kidnapping as possible reasons behind Alvin Joe's disappearance. But the debate about why the Admiral had vanished had been short-lived.

Pearce had delivered a fourth viewpoint: "I'd presume an alien kidnapping if we were in the FBI *X-Files*."

Chapter 2

By the time Fay reached the entrance to the Joes' home, she was perspiring. She took a deep breath, straightened her skirt, patted the dew from her brow with a scented handkerchief, and rang the bell.

After a few moments, Mrs. Joe opened the door. On seeing her, in an instant, Fay recognized the lovely and petite Filipina woman. Lyza Joe conveyed a warm smile, but her eyes appeared sad. Already slim, she now looked weary and frail.

"Faydra!" Mrs. Joe greeted her. "I'm so glad y'all could come! Please… come in!"

Mrs. Joe held a little dog in her arms. Fay called them "shit-zoos." She understood Shih Tzu meant "lion dog" in China or Tibet, or wherever in hell those arrogant little fur devils came from. All she knew was that they barked a lot and crapped all over the place, and when she tried to be nice to one by petting it, she usually got bit.

Okay, perhaps this yapping monster is why Mr. and Mrs. Joe live on Bark Street? Fay joked to herself. Her twisted humor needed a little fine-tuning. She likened the little dogs to human babies. Babies cried a lot, crapped all over the place, and when she tried to be nice to one by holding it, she always got peed on.

Fay took her chances and patted the little mutt on the head as she said, "Miss Lyza, how nice to meet you." She introduced her sister, saying, "This is JP, my sissy," and they all went inside.

She did love dogs. But Fay did not trust the sneaky small breeds. She also dearly loved children, the minute the diapers came off for good.

Mrs. Joe had done a remarkable job decorating her elegant home with furnishings from her native country, the Philippines. Fay recalled Admiral Joe's Cuban ancestry. Still, she did not see evidence of anything Cuban in Mrs. Joe's decorating, except for a rich cherry wood humidor loaded with Cuban cigars. She looked to be sure. In her mind, small dogs and cigars were but two of the Devil's many sick jokes.

She took a moment to admire Mrs. Joe's many hand-carved teak and mahogany woods, both in the furniture and in the knickknacks, which graced both the walls and halls - oh, and Mrs. Joe's dress. She wore a knee-length, crimson silk, oriental style dress with a high Mandarin collar and a Suzie Wong style slit running up the left side from hem to hip. The dress was simple, elegant, rich, and perfect.

"Miss Lyza," Fay said, "I must tell you. Your dress is precious. The dress would be hard to wiggle into, but once the job was done, the dress would slide off like butter on a hot knife."

"I'm thinkin' the same thing," Pearce added. "That dress should be classified as a strategic weapon."

A warm smile came to Lyza Joe's lips. "These come from the Philippines. My family makes them."

Fay's eyebrows arched. "There's more than one?"

With a sly smile on her lips, Lyza asked, "What sizes do you girls wear?"

It sounded to Fay like there were soon going to be two hot new dresses in her and her sister's wardrobes.

Each woman eagerly volunteered her dress size. Lyza smiled and thanked them. Fay was not sure if Lyza was thanking them for readily confessing their dress sizes, or if she was thanking them for not being so bloated that her family tailors would have to visit the Manila Tent and Awning Company to have these dresses made.

Lyza made a comment that placed her at the top of Fay's all-time favorite people list: "Oh, you girls are so thin! You should eat more food."

In Fay's mind, the Filipinos were much like the Italians. It was always with the food. If one was trying to diet, they should not accept an invitation to dine with them. Mrs. Joe was adorable.

Lyza handed the little dog to Fay, pointed toward the swimming pool, and said, "You girls go on out to the pool. I'll meet you there in a minute."

"Nice doggie." Fay affectionately rubbed the dog's head. She whispered to her sister, "I swear to God if this little dustmop bites me or pees on me, I'm going to kick his shaggy-assed tail from here to the pool. And I dearly hope doggie knows how to swim." She had yet to determine if the little dog was male or female.

Fay handed the dog to her sister, thus avoiding an unfortunate accident, and they proceeded to the pool.

The Joes had a nice set-up. The yard surrounding the pool was landscaped in a traditional Japanese garden style. At the edge of what Fay assumed to be the property line was a low fence with an unlocked gate which opened onto the golf course's fairway. Beyond the fairway flowed the Sawsashaw River.

Like Fay's home in the Pacific Northwest, Florida was loaded with many places bearing interesting Native American names. Near Fay's summer home on the Hood

Canal were the Hamma Hamma, the Duckabush, and the Skokomish rivers. She understood Sawsashawneetah to mean "beautiful river, beautiful friend." Over time, the river's name had been shortened from its original name, Sawsashawneetah, to Sawsashaw. Locals simply called the river "Old Saw." That's what she had been told, anyway.

Like the word "Sawsashawneetah" had been shortened over time, the word "Choctawhatchee" had also been trimmed. These days, most folks referred to the bay as Choctaw Bay, and even more recently as simply "The Choc." On the one hand, one might take a lazy paddle down the Sawsashawneetah River to Choctawhatchee Bay in one's canoe. Or one might blast down the Saw to the Choc in one's high-powered cigarette boat.

Fay, being an old-fashioned Southern girl, preferred things as they were. She loved the way the old name sounded. *Saw-sa-shaw-nee-tah*; the word, like the river, seemed to flow pleasantly along.

By the pool, the two women found four tangerine upholstered chairs placed around a large, white, glass-topped wrought-iron patio table, complete with a matching tangerine umbrella. They made themselves comfortable and chatted for a spell. Pearce was adamantly holding onto her opinion that Admiral Joe had been abducted. Fay was about to explore the notion with her when Mrs. Joe returned.

Fay could not believe her eyes. In Lyza's hands, she carried two dresses. "Mercy, that was fast!" Fay exclaimed. She assumed Mrs. Joe must have a drive-through sweatshop in her house. Apparently, her hostess had a good inventory of those beautiful dresses.

Lyza smiled as she placed a sexy silk dress in each sister's lap, before asking, "Would anyone care for iced tea?"

"If it wouldn't be too much trouble for you," Fay replied.

Pearce responded with an agreeing nod. "I do believe, in passing, iced tea would be right served even in a blizzard."

Mrs. Joe smiled again. "Excuse me." She scurried off to her kitchen with the small dog yapping at her heels.

"How could anyone put up with the yapping?" Fay wondered aloud. "What do you think, sis?"

"Small dog go through life with same tact as tornado." JP's pearls of wisdom had resulted from her watching far too many old Charlie Chan movies. "Oh…I don't know. Either he left here under his own power, or he left here under someone else's power," JP continued, once again speculating about the Admiral's fate.

"His disappearance makes no sense, JP," Fay pointed out. "Look at this place. Admiral Joe has a lovely home, in a great neighborhood…a darlin' wife."

"Too much to up and walk away from."

"My sentiments exactly," Fay whispered.

Mrs. Joe returned with a pitcher of iced tea, glasses, sliced lemons, and deviled eggs. To serve iced tea without deviled eggs was considered, by most Southern belles, to be tacky. She set the tray on the table and said in a melodic voice, "Here we go." She poured three glasses. "Alvin and I love to sit here in the late afternoon and sip tea."

Southern girls drank nothing; they sipped—a lot.

"Miss Lyza," Fay said. "I have a delicate question to ask."

"Are Alvin and I having problems?" Lyza guessed.

Lyza had asked the question she was going to ask. "Are you?" Fay wondered.

Fay did not take notes, like most lawyers or detectives did. Instead, she relied on her sister's brain, which worked much like a word processor. Whatever went into Pearce's ears ended up embedded in her brain's hard drive. All Fay had to do was ask, "What did so and so say about such-and-such?" and Pearce would feed it back to her—verbatim. Although her sister got it screwed up occasionally, Fay could usually put the correct spin on it. When Fay did take notes, they were copious. The problem was, her notes were so copious it took her hours to find what she was looking for in them. Since her sister was a copious listener, Fay depended on her sister's copious brain to provide copious feedback.

"We've never been happier, Faydra," Lyza explained. "Alvin and I often travel; we have two homes... this one and one in the Philippines. Our bills are paid... no marital problems." She sighed. "Alvin is my soulmate." She looked at Fay. "Where is he, Faydra?"

What could she say in reply? Fay was as mystified as everyone else was. "I don't know. But we will find him," Fay promised.

Pearce was right. There were two reasonable explanations for Alvin Joe's disappearance. Either he had walked away, or he had been carried away. Since Mrs. Joe had received no phone calls demanding ransom money, Fay was of the notion that he had walked away.

"Miss Lyza, would you mind if JP looked around the house? We don't have a warrant, and this is not an investigation. You can say no, but we may be able to learn what may have happened," Fay requested.

"Please, Miss Pearce, be my guest." Lyza gave them permission.

Pearce interjected, "Miss Lyza, do y'all have a den or an office where Alvin spends his time?"

Pearce's instincts were good. Admiral Joe's home office would be the place to begin a search for clues.

Mrs. Joe directed her to the den. Pearce took her iced tea and headed there.

The doorbell rang. The little dog began yapping. *Do I have a diazepam in my pocketbook?* Fay silently wondered.

Mrs. Joe went off to answer the door. Fay presumed it would be Sheriff Gus. She was correct.

Lyza returned moments later with Sheriff Gus, a deputy, and the little dog in tow. Unfortunately, the little dog seemed to have taken a liking to Fay. Much to her annoyance, the dog started jumping into her lap. It would squirm around for a minute or two and attempt to lick her face, only to jump off.

Fay stood to meet Sheriff Gus and was at once struck by his good looks. She had seen her fair share of handsome men, but this man was gorgeous.

She could often tell a man's disposition by how he dressed. Sheriff Virgil Gus had come from a fishing expedition, so she would excuse him for his fashion faux pas. Had Fay spotted him, say, at the mall, for example, dressed as he was, she would have been duty-bound to call the fashion police.

His faded blue jeans, black motorcycle boots, a T-shirt, sunglasses, and a motorcycle brand ball cap suggested: redneck. Faydra could not help but notice the round, silver dollar-sized, worn spot on his jeans' right front pocket. Created, perhaps, by a chewing tobacco can resting therein?

"Sheriff Gus, this is Commander Faydra Green," Mrs. Joe said.

Fay smiled and extended her hand. "Sheriff. Good to see ya." Being a former First Daughter, she had met so many people over the years, she could not possibly remember them all. Not to risk offending people by not recognizing him or her, she had adopted what she referred to as her "tofu" greeting. The folksy "good to see ya" greeting, like tofu, went with every occasion.

Virgil removed his sunglasses with his left hand and firmly shook her hand with his right in one smooth motion. "Howdy, ma'am." He turned to his deputy. "This here's Deputy Doug."

Good Lord! Virgil Gus had the most dazzling eyes... deep sea green... much like her own. Mercy!

Fay turned toward Doug, smiled, and offered her hand. "Good to see ya, Deputy."

Was Doug the man's first name or his last? His name badge read "Doug," so Fay had no clue. She remembered Deputy Dawg, the TV cartoon character from her childhood days, and grinned at the reference.

If Sheriff Gus was a hillbilly and a redneck, he was also a cowboy. He wore big iron on his hip. Fay knew most sheriffs were elected officials. Many had never served as peace officers before taking the office of sheriff. They were managers or administrators. But the .44 Magnum hanging in a black leather hog-leg holster at Gus's hip suggested otherwise.

As Fay watched, the Sheriff unbuckled his gun belt and draped it over his left shoulder. She wondered if the weapon might not have another use. Like for clubbing or shooting fish? In a pinch, the long barrel could substitute as a fishing pole.

They all sat down. Fay needed Sheriff Gus to do a couple of things for her. This was his investigation, not hers, but until now, he had been moving slower than a three-legged swamp turtle. She had not yet determined how she was going to motivate him. Perhaps when her sister returned from her search of Alvin's home office, Fay would have a better idea how to proceed along those lines.

Fay glanced at the river. "Miss Lyza, is it possible Alvin could have taken a swim in the river?" she questioned.

"It's possible, but I doubt it."

"Why?"

"His towel and robe were draped over a deck chair when I got back from the store. I would assume he would have taken them with him if he had planned on swimmin' in the river," Lyza explained.

"One would think," Fay said.

Pearce returned, and Fay could tell by the anxious look on her sister's face she had urgent information. So, Fay excused them both.

After checking for golfers, the sisters took a stroll across the fairway toward the river. Fay was uneasy about leaving Mrs. Joe alone with Sheriff Gus. Under the circumstances, Lyza needed an excellent lawyer.

"What did you find?" Fay asked.

"You mean the handsome man?" Pearce quickly glanced back over her shoulder as they walked and turned back around.

Fay frowned at her. "Cut it out. I meant, what did you find in Alvin Joe's office?"

"Sorry. I think there might be secret information stored on his computer hard drive," Pearce told her.

"You searched his computer?"

"I found several files," Pearce confirmed.

The two women found a wooden bench placed near the riverbank and sat down.

"Anything else, Pearce?" Fay asked.

"The Admiral had recently increased his life insurance policy. And I found an airline ticket."

"One ticket?"

"Yeah." Pearce nodded. "A single fare ticket from Pensacola to Manila, in Mrs. Joe's name."

"Was there a gun, a knife, a candlestick... a lead pipe, perhaps?" Fay joked.

"A gun. But it had not been fired." Pearce snapped open her pocketbook, reached in, and withdrew a small photograph. "Here." She handed the photo to Fay. "Admiral Joe's photo."

Fay accepted the photo from her. After studying it, she handed it back to her sister. "Thanks. That's the fellow I met on the U.S.S. *Abraham Lincoln* when I... well, it was a while ago. But that's him alright."

Fay looked over her shoulder. She observed Sheriff Gus and Mrs. Joe as they chatted near the pool. "We must get Miss Lyza a lawyer," she decided.

When the women returned from the river, the little dog ran out onto the fairway to greet them. It was yapping and jumping at Fay like he/she/it had forgotten her entirely from the first time it went through this drill.

"Hey, little dog," Fay said in a soothing voice. "It's only us." This, of course, encouraged more yapping and jumping.

"It's a different dog," Pearce pointed out.

While a child, Pearce had spent significant television watching hours tuned into the animal channel. Fay believed her to be a quasi-authority on animals and animal behavior. Pearce's favorite program had been reruns of *The Crocodile Hunter*, starring an alligator hunter-type guy with a "kid in the candy store" attitude. Whenever he had discovered a creature, be it a wombat or a sugar glider, he had gotten excited.

"Another dog?" Fay asked.

"Yeah. I spotted another one of them little critters in the house when I was searchin' Alvin's home office," Pearce confirmed.

"Holy shit-zoo, Batman, there is another little dust mop?" Fay exclaimed.

As the women neared the others seated poolside, Sheriff Gus and Deputy Doug rose from their chairs. Their gentlemanly act impressed Fay. When it came to manners and rednecks, Fay believed most rednecks considered it polite when they offered a woman the last swig from their beer, or when they put their old coon-dog in the back of their truck for their gal to sit beside them.

After being greeted, they all sat.

"Miss Lyza, is your husband consulting during his retirement?" Fay asked. Fay knew many retired military people did this. *Listen up, Sheriff Gus, note my question and what Mrs. Joe is about to say,* she thought.

"Alvin has a degree in aeronautical engineering. He's working with a defense contractor on a project. BASS? Although, he never discusses his projects with me," Lyza replied.

Fay noted Mrs. Joe had said "has" and "is" rather than "had" and "was." This was a subtle reference, yet an important one. Her connection to her husband in the present tense indicated she believed he was still alive. A murder suspect would tip their hand by referring to the victim in the past tense rather than in the present tense. Fay knew that once the Sheriff discovered the life insurance policy and the single airline ticket, Mrs. Joe would become a prime suspect.

This was where Fay had to get Sheriff Gus active and involved in the case. This was not her investigation, but she would take it upon herself to call the shots for now.

"Sheriff, I believe Admiral Joe may have stored classified data on his computer hard drive," Fay spoke up. "The BASS Mrs. Joe spoke of is an acronym for the Navy's new Bismarck Anti-Ship System. I don't know a whole heck of a lot about BASS, but I know it's a missile that can be launched from a ship as small as a frigate… or from a boat, a boomer, or a fast attack submarine. Yet, it can find and sink a ship as large as the largest aircraft carrier from six hundred miles away. I think we need to get the FBI in here, post-haste, to secure the computer."

Star Trek, The Next Generation's Jean-Luc Picard, the starship Enterprise's captain, had the most extraordinary way of delivering an order. He simply said, "Make it so." In that regard, Sheriff Gus was even more remarkable. He did not say a word, merely pointed at Deputy Doug, and Doug "made it so" by springing to his feet. Last Fay saw, the deputy had disappeared through the patio door, headed, she presumed, toward his car and a phone.

FBI special agents took their work seriously. In less than thirty minutes, federal agents would arrive, and Sheriff Gus would be involved with the FBI in launching a search for the missing retired admiral. The FBI would likely believe he may have disappeared with top-secret military data.

Mrs. Joe needed a talented lawyer. Fay knew a trial lawyer up Tallahassee way, Kramer Shock, a dear friend. They had met at the University of Texas at Austin School of Law during their first semester. It had been a classic meeting. It had been raining. As Fay had passed through the entry door to her civil law class, she had slipped on a puddle of water. She had gone down, her books and study notes scattered. Her classmates had laughed, but it was Kramer, the timid guy from the back row, who had bolted from his seat and come to her rescue. From that moment on, they had been friends and had kept in touch since.

As soon as she could get Mrs. Joe alone, Fay would encourage her to retain Kramer Shock.

In the meantime, Fay was curious to learn more about Sheriff Gus. He had referred to the swimming pool as the "cee-ment pond" three times.

"What do you call your boat, Sheriff?" Fay asked him.

"Mountin' Mama," he responded.

Mercy. Fay gathered the man was proud of how he felt towards his wife, sexually, or he was from the hills. An Ozark Mountain Daredevil, as she called them. "How you spellin' that, Sheriff?" she asked.

Virgil chuckled. He had caught her drift. She sensed Virgil Gus to be a bright man.

He spelled it out for her, "M-o-u-n-t-a-i-n." He repeated the name, "Mountain Mama."

Pearce and Mrs. Joe had tears of laughter in their eyes. Considering the gravity of the situation, Fay believed the levity to be therapeutic for Mrs. Joe.

Mrs. Joe noted that the little dog was sitting on Fay's lap. She stood, and with a stern look on her face, she took the little dog from her lap, thank God, and placed it outside. The dog was yapping and hopping up and scratching on the glass door, trying to get back out.

When Miss Lyza returned, she said, "I'm sorry, Faydra. We have two dogs, but if I let them both out together, they tend to get a bit out of control."

She sounded pretty sincere when she apologized. Fay smiled. She considered it may have been the little dogs who had eventually forced Admiral Joe to flee his home to preserve his sanity. But she was still curious about Sheriff Gus.

Fay asked him, "Y'all a mountain boy, Virgil?"

"Yup. West Virginie," he confirmed.

Well, take me home country roads and skin me a possum. She had gotten her mountain range wrong, but the man was a genuine hillbilly. He was even more remarkable than she had first imagined.

They all chatted for a while until the FBI showed up. The two Special Agents introduced themselves as Lisa Brock and Perkins Washington. Everyone moved from the pool deck to the living room.

Agents Brock and Washington secured the computer and, once it was safely stored in their car's trunk, they returned to interview Mrs. Joe.

Fay appreciated that both the Sheriff and the Special Agents had thought to include her in their questioning. They did not have to. Mrs. Joe needed her support at the moment.

Around 20:30 hours, the FBI packed up and left. Fay recommended her friend Kramer Shock to Mrs. Joe.

Miss Lyza was grateful and said she would call him first thing in the morning. Fay wanted to be sure Mrs. Joe got decent representation. She feared if left on her own, Lyza might end up retaining a jackleg from the law firm of Cheatum, Gougem, and Howe, as advertised on late-night television.

"Mrs. Joe, could JP and I call on you in the morning?" Fay asked.

"I'd appreciate it."

"We'll be here by 9:00 A.M.," Fay informed her.

Then Fay asked Sheriff Gus, "Would you mind if I talked to the security guard on my way out?"

"No, ma'am." He turned to Deputy Doug. "Why don't y'all follow her on out? See what the guard has to say."

Doug nodded.

When Fay left Mrs. Joe, she was satisfied with the way things were going. The FBI was on the case, and Mrs. Joe would be in expert hands with Kramer Shock.

After parking the red Camaro safely off the road, JP stayed with the car while Fay and Deputy Doug approached the guardhouse.

"Hi, Chief," Fay called. "I see you're working late tonight."

"My relief called in sick. I'm getting a little overtime in," the guard explained.

A light breeze carried the crickets' buzz yet did little to relieve the oppressing humidity. Fay dabbed at the dew forming on her brow with her handkerchief and hoped her underarm deodorant would last the twelve hours the manufacturer had promised.

"Evenin', Commander." The guard nodded toward the deputy sheriff. "Evenin', Deputy."

" Evenin'," the deputy replied.

There was a lot of Navy still left in the man. Fay told him, "Y'all doesn't need to jump every time you see me coming or call me ma'am." She smiled. "Can I ask you a question, Chief?"

"I reckon."

"You keep pretty good track of the comings and goings of the residents, don't you?" Fay wondered.

"I have a computer log recordin' every vehicle in and out," the guard proudly stated.

She knew he did. "Would you check the log and see if Mr. Joe might have left within the past three days?" she requested.

"Don't have to, Commander."

"How's that? And please call me Fay." She extended her hand and introduced herself to him.

He shook her hand firmly. "Lenny Crane. A pleasure to meetcha. The Admiral and I served on the same ship, although at different times. As a result, we have a lot in common. Admiral Joe always stops at the guardhouse to chat with me when he leaves. He's a great guy…brings me iced tea or an occasional cigar."

"The last time you saw him was when?" Fay asked.

"Three days ago. Admiral Joe was comin', not goin'."

"Two days ago, Mrs. Joe left, didn't she?" Fay wanted to know.

Lenny turned away from her and focused his attention on his computer console. He typed in a few commands, nodded his head, and turned back toward her. "Mrs. Joe left at nineteen-thirty-six," he said.

"7:36 P.M. Does it say when she returned?"

"About thirty minutes later." He referred again to

the computer monitor. "Twenty-ten hours."

"Did you speak to her when she passed through?" Fay asked.

"I did. Matter-a-fact, Mrs. Joe asked if I was needin' anythin' from the store."

"Did you?" Fay wanted to know.

"I asked her if she might would fetch me a cola and a pack a-smokes."

"Chief Crane, did you notice if Mrs. Joe seemed nervous or anxious?" Fay questioned.

"No. Mrs. Joe's the same. She always is… happy… full of life."

"Were her dogs with her?"

"Both dogs was in the car. I know 'cause they's always yappin' at me… always yappin'… real arrogant little shits." Lenny's expression was sheepish. "Excuse my French, ma'am."

Fay smiled. "They're called Shih Tzus, Chief."

"That's what I said." He looked both ways and then said, in a low voice, "She should leave them little mutts to home." He wiggled his eyebrows up and down. "If ya know what I mean."

Fay chuckled. He was thinking the same thing she was. The dogs would make excellent watchdogs, so why take them to the store?

"Chief, how many cars came and went say… two hours prior and two hours after Mrs. Joe left and returned?" Fay asked him.

"I'd say near to fifty." Lenny patted his shirt pocket as if he was searching for his cigarettes. "There 'bouts." He spotted the cigarettes resting near the computer keyboard and picked them up.

"Were any cars unfamiliar to you?" Fay swatted at

an errant moth as it batted around her face.

"A few. But if I don't recognize the car or its driver, I stop it… find out what their business is… you know, who they's here to see." Lenny tapped on the top end of the cigarette pack, exposing several cigarettes, and offered one to Fay.

Fay shook her head. "No thanks, Chief."

Lenny raised the pack toward his lips, snatched the cigarette with his lips, and dropped the box into his shirt pocket. "I put in a call to the resident and find out if it's okay to allow the car in," he went on.

"What do you do if they do not answer their phone?" Fay asked.

"I refuse admittance." Lenny ignited a wooden match by flicking the match's tip with his thumbnail, lit the cigarette, and waved the match out. He drew in a lung full of smoke, allowing the smoke to curl back out through his nostrils. "Them's the rules, ma'am."

"Thanks, Chief. The Joes haven't had visitors, have they?" Fay queried.

He removed his ball cap to scratch his head before answering, "Just Sheriff Gus, his deputy, the FBI… and you ladies."

Fay thanked him again and gave him her card. "Will you get in touch with me if anything unusual occurs?"

"Will do, ma'am," the guard replied with a nod.

During their return trip to Pensacola, Fay and Pearce talked about the day.

"Admiral Joe vanished, no mistake about it," Fay stated.

"I refuse to believe Mrs. Joe has anythin' to do with her husband's disappearance," Pearce said as she slowed the car to allow for a squirrel to dart across the street.

"However, if the man left on his own free will, why did he leave in nothin' but his swim trunks?"

"He took nothing with him…not his wallet or car keys, and his towel and robe were still draped over the deck chair, where he had most likely left them before his swim," Fay remarked.

"Thought at present, like dog chasing own tail, getting no place," Pearce commented.

Fay asked her sister, "Chan?"

"Yes. If Admiral Joe had been abducted, why hasn't Mrs. Joe received a phone call askin' for ransom money?"

Chapter 3

The next morning, Fay and JP arrived at Mrs. Joe's home at 09:00. The pleasant morning beckoned. The two sisters stood by the pool once more. A fresh wind, scented with newly cut grass, blew from the river's direction, indicating a day that was promising to be a barn burner. The refreshing interlude was beautiful, and golfers were out en masse.

As Fay sat beside the swimming pool with JP and Miss Lyza, she watched a golfer tee-off and reflected back to when she had enjoyed the game. "I used to play golf," she lamented.

"You no longer play?" Lyza asked.

"I don't do golf, Miss Lyza, unless I have to," Fay explained. "I played often. The more I played, the more competitive I became. In the end, I found myself competing with myself; I could never win. One ugly day, as I recall, it was raining like there was no tomorrow. The wind was blowing, my nose was running like they had opened the flood gates over at the Grand Coulee dam, and I froze my rear end off."

"You have a good point there," Pearce chimed in, accompanied by an all-knowing nod.

"I never use profanity, Miss Lyza, but that day, I do believe I repeatedly unleashed every four-letter word known to womankind." Fay glanced skyward. "For that, Lord, I am truly sorry."

"Miss Lyza," Fay went on, as she watched a golfer slice a ball into the Sawsashaw. "Is your husband a golfer?"

"Alvin and I were avid golfers," Lyza responded. "About a year ago, arthritis began to develop in his ankles. Walking became increasingly difficult for him. So, he gave it up. When he did, I did as well. He swims now."

"Do the golfers enter the community through the main gate?" Fay asked.

"All traffic, in and out of the community, passes through the main gate," Lyza told her.

"Does your husband have any enemies?" Pearce asked.

Mrs. Joe chuckled. "None." She glanced toward her kitchen. "I've made tea. Would you girls like tea and marmalade?"

"Please," Fay said.

"You girls sit tight. I'll be right back."

"Miss Lyza," JP asked. "Where's Callie?"

"I gave her a few days off. She protested, but I insisted." Lyza stood, clutched her chest, gasped, and sat. "Mercy!"

"Miss Lyza," Fay asked. "Are you alright?"

"Why, yes, darlin'. A bit faint. That's all." Lyza took a quick breath. "Yes, I'm fine."

"Why don't I get the tea, Miss Lyza?" Pearce volunteered. Not waiting for a reply, she stood and headed for the kitchen.

Fay watched her helpful sister walk away. *Hey, sis, get rat poison while you're at it and make sure the dogs are fed.* She turned back toward Mrs. Joe, who was sitting between herself and the river. Fay watched a large bird swoop down to the surface, skillfully snatch a fish in its talons, and fly on. Its motion was smooth, decisive, and deadly.

"Does your husband swim in the river often?" Fay asked.

"Alvin keeps telling me he wants to swim to the other side and back," Lyza replied.

"About eighty yards from bank to bank, I'd say," Fay observed. One hundred- and sixty-yards round trip. The distance was short, but the swim could be a challenge when one considered the current. "Did he ever try?"

"No. Alvin only talked about it."

Fay next asked, "Was Callie here on the night Alvin disappeared?"

"Heavens no," Lyza said with a gasp. "Callie usually works from eight to about three."

"How long has she worked for you?"

Lyza thought for a moment. "Mercy, it's been so long, I've lost track."

"A number of years?"

"Oh… I'd say Callie has been with us for at least ten years," Lyza speculated.

Pearce returned with hot tea, marmalade, toast, and something odd. Placing the tray on the table, she poured three cups. Then, JP sat down. Next, she took a dill pickle from the serving tray and placed it on the saucer next to her tea. She smiled at Fay, noticing she was eyeing the dill pickle.

Pearce picked it up, showing it to Fay. "It's a dill."

"Dill pickles," Fay said. "Pearce loves them. When she was small, she often referred to them as baby gator tails."

"Because they're small, green, and bumpy," Pearce added.

Fay smiled again and turned her attention back to Mrs. Joe. They chatted for a bit.

But when Fay turned to ask her sister a question, Pearce was gone – disappeared - like when she was a kid. Fay would take her eyes off her younger sister for an instant, and Pearce would have high-tailed it off to who knew where. Thirty minutes and an army of Secret Service people later, Fay would find her hiding or playing. Fay had found it aggravating, to say the least. Now, like then, JP had disappeared. Did she go back into the house for another pickle? One look at the little dogs, who were sleeping near the patio door, told Fay she had not gone into the house.

"Did you notice where Pearce went?" Fay asked Lyza.

Lyza shook her head, she as stumped as Fay.

Fay rose from her chair and looked in the only other direction Pearce could have gone, across the fairway, in the direction of the Sawsashaw. She spotted her standing on the riverbank. It appeared Pearce was talking on her cell phone. Fay supposed JP might be talking to her boyfriend, Navy Captain Egan Fletcher. She would have gone out of earshot to get and give them all privacy.

Curiosity got the better of Fay. She excused herself and walked across the fairway to the river. Pearce had finished her call when Fay arrived at her side.

"I was callin' the game warden," Pearce explained.

"First dill pickles, and now game wardens? How come?" Fay wanted to know.

"The game warden records alligator sightings."

"What are you talking about?" Fay was confused.

"Well, as I was sittin' there chompin' on the pickle, I got to thinkin' about alligators. Because you said 'baby gator tails.' Alligators are protected by law, you know," Pearce told her sister.

Fay was aware they were. "I know." She decided to be patient and let this play itself out.

"Anyhow, I called the Law Enforcement Division of the Florida Fish and Wildlife Commission. Sure enough, they been trackin' a gator in the Sawsashaw… near here."

Fay, recalling Pearce's abduction theory, said, "Your theory is Admiral Joe got abducted by an alligator. And your chomping on a dill pickle led you to your conclusion?"

"Yeah, that's right," Pearce confirmed.

"Of course. That would explain it. You are brilliant at times, JP."

Pearce acknowledged the compliment with a solemn nod. "I know."

"You thinking what I'm thinking?" Fay asked.

"Yeah. Shot in dark sometimes find eye of bull."

"Chan?"

"That's right. I was fixin' to call Choctaw Bay Dive Shop." JP swatted at a fly. "Want me to call them and reserve a boat and dive gear?"

"You got it." *Mercy, I hope JP is wrong on this one*, Fay thought.

"Y'all thinkin' Alvin's disappearance has to do with his work on the BASS program?" Pearce wondered.

"I've considered it," Fay answered. "The technology involved in the development and deployment of the Bismarck Anti-ship System would be valuable to many foreign countries, especially to China, Iran, and

North Korea."

"Al-Qaeda, too," Pearce added. "You don't think the engineerin' programs he stored on his computer hard drive had anythin' to do with his disappearance?"

Fay replied, "I don't. Otherwise, the data or the computer would be missing as well, JP."

"He wouldn't have been able to download the data either. Which rules out him sellin' the data."

Fay withdrew her sunglasses from her purse, while saying, "True. The FBI, Navy, and the prime defense contractor, Bowman-California Aerospace, would have planted viruses in the engineering program. Software designed to instantaneously destroy the data if an attempt were made to download it. Bowman and the Navy would have developed a way to bypass the viruses without activating them."

Pearce observed, "Alvin Joe disappeared. He took nothin' with him...not his towel...nor his shoes...no cash or credit cards. And his car is in the garage. He didn't leave a suicide note. Nor did Mrs. Joe receive a ransom request."

Fay stood with her back to the Joes' home. She heard the dogs erupt into a concerto of yapping. Mrs. Joe evidently had company; Fay knew it would either be Sheriff Gus, the FBI agents, or Fay's lawyer friend, Kramer Shock.

As Fay turned to retreat across the fairway, a golfer yelled, "FORE!"

Fay knew to duck when she heard that particular four-letter word. No sooner had she covered her head with her hands and arms, emitting the requisite scream, she heard a "CRACK!" An errant golf ball ricocheted off a nearby tree and plopped to the ground at her feet.

"Mercy—that was close!" Pearce exclaimed.

"Some goofball tried to peg me with a golf ball. I am CLEARLY OUT OF BOUNDS FOR CHRIST SAKES!" Fay shouted.

She looked toward the tee and saw a jackass yelling at her and waving a three-iron. She could not hear what he said, although the word "bitch" did manage to carry the distance.

As usual, her sister was laughing at her.

"The jerk is calling me a 'bitch' when he is the lousy golfer?" Fay commented to her sister. She wanted to let this duffer know she was all right and safe and everything, so she flipped him the bird. With her luck, she was probably giving the finger to a full-bird colonel. *Come to think of it, why are they called full-bird colonels?*

Fay stomped across the fairway, back to Mrs. Joe's house. She would not go so far as to say she was angry. She would, however, admit she was damn pissed off.

When she arrived at the Joes' house, her mood changed abruptly for the better. Fay was happy to see her friend Kramer Shock standing with Mrs. Joe near the pool. He, too, was laughing at her.

"Man alive, I'm almost killed by a golfer, and everyone thinks it's funny!" Fay proclaimed.

But then, she regained her composure and hugged Kramer. Almost five years had passed since she had last seen him. He had gained a few pounds, but he looked fit. "You're lookin' good, Kramer. May I speak to you before we talk to Miss Lyza?" Fay asked him.

"Sure, let's find a private spot," her friend replied.

"I want to get you up to speed. Pearce can keep Miss Lyza and the dogs entertained. Let's go around to the front," Fay told him. In light of what had just happened to her, she reasoned it would be safer there.

Fay and Pearce had agreed not to mention anything to Mrs. Joe about Pearce's alligator theory. And when she told Kramer the story, Fay asked him not to say as well. He agreed.

"Pearce and I are headed for Choctaw Bay Diving Shop," Fay stated. "If you need me, call me on my cell."

Mrs. Joe would be in good hands with Kramer.

Sheriff Gus arrived while Fay and Kramer were talking. She introduced the two men, and they all walked back to where Pearce and Mrs. Joe were seated, near the pool.

The sisters left and drove to the dive shop. On the way, both realized they had failed to bring anything to swim in, so they stopped at a nearby mall.

It was about thirty minutes past eleven when the women rolled to a stop in front of Sparky's Choctaw Bay Dive Shop, which was next door to Choctaw Bay Marina. They were driving their father's ex-cop car, so they looked pretty official that morning. Fay observed a short and scrawny gentleman dressed in a white tank top, tan shorts, sandals, and a red ball cap, sitting near the front door of the small, cluttered dive shop. He stood as they exited the car.

"Mornin'," Fay said.

The man, whom Fay presumed to be Sparky, first eyed the car and then eyed them. "Mornin' officas, can I help ya this mornin'?" But then, his eyes widened, and a vast smile parted his lips. He threw open his arms and cried, "Sista! Long time no see ya, girl!"

To Fay's surprise, Pearce knew this man. She seemed to know everyone, for that matter.

By this time, Pearce had approached and embraced him. "Sparky, I want y'all to meet my sister, Faydra."

Sparky released Pearce from his arms, gave Fay the same large smile, and gave her a great big bear hug. "Welcome! Welcome!" he greeted her. He released Fay from his grasp. "The name's Sparky. Come in. We get you ladies set up."

Sparky's shop was well equipped. Fay, an avid diver, found herself lusting over the latest tanks, masks, and fins. The rental stuff Sparky presented was not as lovely as the new stuff, but it was in good repair. She gave Sparky her credit card as security for the boat and gear.

"Sparky help ya pack yah gear down to the boat now, and show ya how she goes," the man offered.

Sparky's speech was not unlike that of anyone who had migrated to Florida from the Caribbean. Fay loved hearing people speak with a Jamaican accent.

The rental boat was moored at the marina. A passing boat sent small rollers from its wake toward the pontoon finger piers comprising the marina at Choctaw Bay.

While the trio walked along the bobbing and creaking floating dock, Fay asked Sparky, "Is the *Mountain Mama* moored here as well?"

"She be over on the next dock," he confirmed, pointing at a sexy two-tone teal colored cigarette boat.

As a child, Fay had admired the longboats designed for the single purpose of going fast. "Go fast boats," as they were often called, were equipped with high horsepower engines able to push them to speeds over one hundred miles per hour. According to the Cigarette Racing Team, Inc., which manufactured the cigarette boat, the long narrow boats reminded people of cigarettes, hence their name.

Fay admired *Mountain Mama* as it gracefully rode out the series of small swells, tugging gently at her moorings. It was like an impatient thoroughbred racehorse pulling at her tether, anxious to run its next race. She estimated the boat's length to be around thirty feet.

"The Sheriff is doing well for himself," Fay said to no one in particular.

Besides going fast, Fay knew the deep-water craft was impractical for any other use, including fishing. For this reason, it tended to be popular with smugglers and dope dealers. What kind of fishing had Sheriff Gus been doing when she had called him the day prior? She supposed he had picked the beauty up for a federal drug auction song.

They arrived at their rental boat, a clean eighteen-foot Boston Whaler. Fay was surprised at the boat's good condition.

Sparky shooed a giant pelican from its roost on the bow. With a squawk, the great bird lurched into the air, flew several yards, and settled on the bow of another boat.

Sparky laughed and shook his head. "Life ain't so bad now, Old Pete," he called after the pelican.

After he stowed their dive gear, he stood at the helm. "She be like a Southe'n lady—a little fussy at times. She floods easy," Sparky told them.

He flicked the ignition key. The motor fired immediately. A small bluish smoke drifted from the stern as the idling engine's exhaust pipe burbled and spat seawater.

"Sometime she floods an' sometime she doesn't. If

she floods, you wait five minutes now. She be fine," Sparky advised. "If you ladies get into a mess, call Sparky on the CB." He pointed to the CB radio located at the helm. "Sparky listen for ya back at the shop. You be shure now. You call, and old' Sparky come. You pack a lunch, Sista?"

The two women first looked at one another and then at Sparky. "No," they said in unison.

He pointed toward the marina. "Go on to the coffee shop now. You go an' you tell 'em Sparky send ya by for some good sandwiches."

It sounded like a great idea. The sisters traipsed back along the bobbing float dock to get their lunch. The Choctaw Bay Marina coffee shop was busy, but the sandwiches were already made. They each purchased a sandwich, along with four bottles of cola and two moon pies. They paid and were, once again, on their way.

Fay noticed a man standing near the bow as they neared the boat. By the uniform he wore, she could tell he was associated with the Florida Fish and Wildlife Commission.

"Mornin' y'all." The man greeted them with a smile. "Nice day for a dive."

Fay smiled. "Mornin'. And yes, it is a wonderful day for a dive."

"You ladies divin' in the bay this mornin', or are y'all headin' up the Saw?"

"Around the mouth." Fay read his name badge: J. CROW. *It must be a Navy thing?* She guessed, based on Mr. Crow's olive skin and black hair, that he had a significant amount of Seminole or Choctaw Indian in his blood.

"The name's Jerry." The man extended his hand.

Pearce and Fay each took a turn shaking his hand.

"I don't mean to be nosy," Jerry continued, "but if y'all's headin' up the Saw, I should warn ya a large gator's been spotted in the river. I wanted to let y'all know to be careful."

"Thanks, Jerry," Fay said. "We'll keep an eye out for the gator." As insane as it seemed, she wanted to find the gator, not avoid it.

"If ya should spot it, maybe y'all might could think to gimme a call? It's becomin' a nuisance. Comin' onto people's land and snatchin' their pets and livestock." He handed Fay his card. "My cell number's on the card."

"You got it," Fay assured him. *Did Jerry say snatching pets? Hmm. Perhaps, maybe, we all might could shoo the gator back towards the Joes' residence?* Fay mused to herself.

"By the way," Jerry advised, "the tide will be turnin' soon." He looked at his wristwatch. "In about two hours. I mention it because we get an occasional bull shark in the bay on the flood tide. They like to feed on the fish schooling around the mouth."

Mercy. Hungry sharks and pugnacious gators all in one place at one time. "Jerry, I would imagine you know the Sawsashawneetah well," Fay said.

Jerry smiled and nodded. "I know the Saw like the back of my paw." He chuckled. "I grew up in Boggy Bayou."

"No kiddin'!?" Pearce responded. "I went to school with a guy from Boggy Bayou…a good friend, but I lost track of him over the years. Last I heard, he was makin' big money over in Saint Pete. Had to do with retirement funds and snowbirds? Anyway, his name is Calvin Tate. Y'all know him by chance?"

Jerry chuckled. "I know who he is. He recently got out of the pokey."

"Prison?" A sheepish grin formed on her lips. "Oh... well, I guess I didn't know him all too well," Pearce said softly.

"Jerry," Fay said. "I was wondering if there might be a spot where things drifting downriver might tend to collect."

"There's a lagoon local fishermen call the Fish Market. Everythin' comin' down the Saw tends to collect there, includin' an abundance of fish." He added, "The bulls are in, y'all might could find one or two there."

The last thing Fay wished to do was find a bull shark. If Admiral Joe had drowned in the Sawsashaw, she reasoned the Fish Market was where they would find his body. "Where's the Fish Market?" she asked.

"Y'all can almost see it from here." Jerry pointed toward the river's mouth. "Yonder. See the old cannery 'bout a mile' cross the bay?"

Fay squinted her eyes, followed his extended finger out across the bay, and nodded. "Yes."

"Head for the old cannery. Then head upriver two hundred yards and drop anchor. That'll put y'all right smack dab in the middle of the Fish Market," Jerry directed.

"How deep will the water be, Jerry?" Pearce asked.

"Not more than twenty-five feet," he replied. "The depth ain't no problem but watch your tide chart. The current will get a might strong in the lagoon on the slack. We're comin' upon a flood tide, so y'all be fine. Just watch the currents, that's all."

Fay looked at Pearce. "I don't think we'll need tanks. Do you?"

"Nope. Four fathoms? Heck, we can free dive. It'll be a whole lot easier," Pearce answered.

"What time y'all plannin' on returnin'?"

"I don't know, Jerry," Fay said. "Three hours… maybe?"

"Tell ya what. If y'all's not back by, say, 3:00 P.M., I'll come out and check on ya," he offered.

Fay appreciated his concern and told him so.

Sparky wished the two women well and helped them cast off.

The boat ran great; they skipped across the shimmering turquoise bay smoother than a Purple Gallinule scampering across a backwater swamp full of lily pads.

The boat even had a name. "SPARKY" was printed in large block letters across her stern. A boat's homeport often would be included below its name. "Montego Bay, Jamaica" was painted on this one.

It was not long before the women began referring to the small craft as U.S.S. *Sparky*.

As the small craft skimmed Choctaw Bay with Pearce at the helm, Fay hoped they would not find what they were searching for.

Chapter 4

Fay remembered watching a film as a teenager that she now wished she had not. *Lake Placid* was the title. *Lake Placid* had featured an enormous alligator, similar to the movie *Jaws* with its abnormally large shark. She had laughed at the story at the time, but she remembered how giant the alligator had been. The film star, Miss Bridget Fonda, had repeatedly fallen into the drink. Although Fay had spent most her life around the water and often thought of herself as clumsy, she seldom fell into the water. Hell, Miss Bridget Fonda had landed in the lake three times in the film's first sixty minutes! Each time Miss Fonda had splashed down, the big gator had accosted her, but the hero had come to her rescue. It was the classic and predictable damsel-in-distress plot, where the heroine was repeatedly rescued by her movie superman love interest.

Fay likened the film to the alligator they were seeking. Game Warden Jerry had not mentioned how large this creature from the deep was. She should have asked, "How large is a fully grown gator?"

Pearce had an answer ready, telling her, "They caught one over to Seminole County... Lake Monroe, I think... fourteen feet, some odd inches long. There's another over in Lake Orange weighin' over a thousand pounds. It was almost the same length. Why, y'all been thinkin' about the Bridget Fonda movie or *The Creature from the Black Lagoon?"*

"Yeah. All that and megalodon," Fay replied.

"Don't worry," Pearce said, pushing her sunglasses back onto the bridge of her nose with her right index finger. "Gators' what they call opportunistic feeders. They eat fish, turtles, snakes, small mammals, and such. Not people."

Hearing her say they did not eat people helped quell the acid raging in Fay's stomach.

Pearce turned her head toward Fay and frowned. "As far as I know, they don't eat people. Maybe they do? Ya got me on that one, Spider." She turned her attention back to her boat driving.

Fay scanned the distant lagoon. Visions of woman-eating sharks, ferocious alligators, and dead men crowded her anxious mind.

Pearce again turned her head toward Fay and lowered her chin slightly. Peering at her sister over the top of her sunglasses, she asked, "You wanna know what the biggest bull shark they ever caught near here was?"

"Man alive!" Fay exclaimed. "I swear. If we were in an *Airbus 380* full of people, spiraling toward the ground, you'd be the one to announce, 'Stay calm, everyone. Odds have it a few of you will survive this crash.'"

Was it possible they could encounter the most giant alligator and the largest bull shark known to womankind, all in the same day? Fay silently wondered.

"Anyways, it's common knowledge pigs kill more people every year than sharks do. Y'all know how many people bring pigs right into their homes. Speakin' of fish and bacon," Pearce chirped. Without breaking stride, she pointed toward their lunch sacks. "How 'bout flippin' me one of them sandwiches?"

Pigs? Do pigs swim? Fay thought to herself before saying aloud, "I don't suppose there's any chance a pig could swim out here and make this any more dangerous than it is already?"

"No. Pigs aren't excellent swimmers." Smiling, Pearce added, "In fact, they sink right to the bottom. They's too fat. Quit worryin', Spider. Your chances of gettin' struck by lightnin' are better than gettin' attacked by a pig. Or a gator, or a shark. All three combined."

Fay glanced skyward. She could see a lone cloud to the West. Lightning. Good grief. "Hey, you want a cola and a moon pie with the sandwich?" she asked her sister.

"Nope. I'll save it for later. We'll be thirsty after all the swimmin'," Pearce decided.

Fay handed her sister a sandwich. "Didn't Mom tell us not to eat before we went in the water?" she remembered.

"Yeah, but I'm hungry," Pearce stated. "Anyway, Mom told us many things about food that didn't pan out. Like we were to cut the crust off our tomato sandwiches." Pearce wrinkled her brow. "I never did know why. But I eat before I go swimmin' all the time, and I've never died yet. Besides, this one here's tuna fish," and she bit into her sandwich.

Fay had no idea why eating tuna rather than ham would make any difference. "I don't think that's the point," she told her sister. "I think it has to do with you getting cramps in your legs. They cramp, and you can't swim, like the pigs, and you sink to the bottom. *Comprendere?*"

"Nonsense." JP took another hearty bite. She chewed, swallowed, and glanced at her sister.

"Remember your dolphin buddies?"

"Juliet and Romeo? I sure do," Fay asserted. "They saved my life. I would have drowned while I was on the op last year if not for them. The dolphins were so sweet; too bad they are not here. We sure could use their help about now."

"Yeah," Pearce reflected. "You gonna eat? Get your strength up." In her best rendition, Pearce quoted a line spoken in *Gone with the Wind,* said by Scarlett O'Hara, "'I will never be hungry again.'"

Pearce had convinced her. Fay grabbed a sandwich.

"Mom was also the one who told us getting our first hairspray was more important than getting our first bra," Fay commented. "But that's when big hair was the style, so I don't know now. You know, I tend to agree with y'all on the sandwich."

"I do recall Mom tellin' me about the hairspray," Pearce said. "But I was ten when she died, and my first bra was still a few months away."

"You got your first bra when you were eleven? I think I would have remembered. Where was I?" Fay asked.

JP swerved the boat to avoid a log. "You was in college at the time…or married to that no-load jackass Navy lawyer, who I never liked…old what's-his-face…what was his name?"

"Oh, yeah… David…whom…you never liked," Fay stated.

"That's what I said."

"In David's defense, he was the one who led me out of my wild days," Fay told her.

"That's right! BYU almost kicked you out, as I recall."

Fay sighed. "It got so bad, I ended up having to beg them not to expel me. Dad would have killed me. And the media would have had a field day with the story. Mercy." Fay shook her head. "Thanks for reminding me. Up 'til now, I'd done a good job forgetting about my mad existence."

They arrived at their destination. While Pearce slowed the boat, Fay eased her way to the bow and chucked the anchor into the water. The depth gauge on the dashboard registered twenty-five feet of the waterline. Game Warden Jerry had told them it would be twenty-five feet deep. The water was crystal clear. The women reasoned they could cover more area if they swam on the surface. Should they spot something interesting, they could dive down to take a look-see.

They jumped into the water after slipping on their dive fins and facemasks with the attached snorkel. Fay was happy to discover the water was warm, which was great because they were not wearing wetsuits. Pearce carried one of the spear guns that they had rented for protection against treacherous sea creatures. They decided to leave the second gun in the boat.

Fay soon lost track of time; perhaps thirty minutes had passed, but she wasn't sure. Logs and branches covered the lagoon's sandy bottom, not to mention the numerous cans and bottles dropped by uncaring fishermen. It was sad to see how the fishermen had abused this beautiful spot.

Fay watched as Pearce gracefully dove from the surface. Her sister had spotted something. The sun highlighted her tea-brown skin against the lagoon's white sand as she headed for what appeared to be a log. Pearce swam with the loaded spear gun ahead in her outstretched right arm. The log moved.

Fay swallowed a mouthful of water. *Oh crap.* Pearce had found an enormous gator napping on the bottom. Fay did not know why her sister needed to get a closer look at this monster. But onward Pearce swam.

Fay was aware that Pearce had been, at one time, a Florida State kickboxing champion. Most recently, she was also a Tae Kwon Do student. This was all well and fine, but the gator did not know this.

Mercy, JP, why go out of your way to harass an alligator clearly twice as long as you are? Fay asked herself.

Fay held her breath when Pearce prodded the gator with the gun's spear. The gator startled and swam off. Fay understood that alligators were pretty docile when confronted underwater. To face one on land, especially a female near her nest, was a whole new basketful of crawdads. Pearce kept paddling toward the spot where she had rousted the gator. She stopped, pulled up, released air from her lungs as if she had gasped, and shot for the surface. Fay surfaced, righted herself, and slid the dive mask from her face to her head.

When Pearce surfaced, she spat water between her teeth and coughed. "I found Admiral Joe," she hollered and pointed downward with the index figure on her right hand. "Did y'all see that big assed ol' gator down there?" She was grinning like this was a good thing to find. "I'm goin' back down." She flipped her feet into the air and dove below the surface.

Fay slipped her mask back over her face and peered into the water. Her gaze followed Pearce as she swam back to where the gator had been, which was where Fay feared poor Admiral Joe's body would be. Fay hoped his body would be intact rather than half-eaten. What would happen if a person were to barf underwater? She was sure, when she considered the physics involved, one would drown. She now knew why her mother had warned her children not to eat before they went swimming.

Fay had no desire to look at Admiral Joe's alligator-mangled body. Pearce could locate and mark his remains. Instead, Fay knew they would need the boat, so she swam back to *Sparky*.

She had not taken more than ten strokes when she noted the gator drifting about twenty-five yards away on her port side. He seemed to be eyeballing her. She recalled seeing the animated cartoon *Peter Pan* several times, so she knew what it meant to get "the evil eye" from a sea-croc, and she was getting it from this old boy. She picked up her pace—*stroke, baby, stroke*.

By observing the seals and the penguins at a large aquatic theme park in Florida, she knew all a trainer had to do was wiggle a mackerel at them. They would fly from the water and land on the deck. That was precisely what Fay did when she reached the boat; she flew right from the water and landed in the boat in a wet and trembling heap.

Considering the gator, she knew she needed to get her sister to safety as fast as possible. Fay gathered herself together, lunged for the ignition key, and fired off the engine. In the movies, in desperate times such as these, the boat, naturally, would not start. This predictable maneuver was how films created big-screen drama, tension, and suspense. True to form, the engine revved, coughed once, and died. *Jeez, Louise*.

Fay flicked the key again. Nothing. Gas fumes filled the air, and she noticed a rainbow-colored sheen forming around the hull. She flooded the engine.

Sparky had said, "Wait for' five minutes, and she be fine."

Fay did not think she had five minutes to spare. In five minutes, her sister would be gator chow. She looked back to the spot where she had last seen Pearce. Her sister was swimming for all she was worth, with the gator hot on her heels. Pearce was a good swimmer.

As Fay watched her sister make a valiant attempt to stay ahead of the gator, she recalled an observation Charles Darwin, the evolutionist, had once made: "He who hesitates is… lunch."

Fay grabbed the remaining speargun and prepared to swim to her sister's aid. Just as she was about to leap from the boat, she spotted a shark. A giant bull shark hovered about three feet back and about five feet below the boat's stern. Pearce was heading directly away from the gator's jaws into those of the waiting bull shark.

Were these two creatures working this area together? The gator herded Pearce toward Jaws Junior, and fish and reptile would split the profits? Out of the frying pan and into the fire, as they said – or in this case, out of the fire and into the inferno.

Fay needed to think fast. She pointed the speargun at the shark. After shoving the gun into the water, she fired. She must have hit the fish, as the speargun ripped from her hands and disappeared into the water. This was not a good move on her part. Now there was an angry alligator, a wounded bull shark, and a blood trail in the water. Blood would attract more sharks.

Fay lunged for her dive knife and prepared to leap

from the boat into the water. But then, she noticed a large boat bearing down on her location. It was *Mountain Mama*. Game Warden Jerry sat on the bow with what appeared to be a high-powered rifle strapped across his back and a road flare in his right hand. No, not a road flare; it was dynamite.

From nowhere, her two new supermen, Warden Jerry and Sheriff Virgil, arrived on the scene to save the day and rescue the damsels in distress. When *Mountain Mama* roared past her, Fay saw Sheriff Gus at the helm. He smiled and waved as he headed toward Pearce and the alligator.

Jerry lit the dynamite and prepared to throw it at the alligator. It might have been a firecracker? She did know it was illegal to shoot an alligator, whatever it was. Perhaps blowing one up would be okay? Jerry would know the law. She supposed the explosion would scare the gator away. If all it took was throwing a noisy object at an alligator, Fay knew two little dogs who would serve the same purpose.

Pearce seemed to tire. She abruptly stopped swimming and turned to confront the oncoming gator. As she lifted her dive knife above her head to strike at the approaching gator, *Mountain Mama* coasted up beside her. Sheriff Gus grabbed Pearce's outstretched arm and plucked her from the water. Almost one hundred and fifty pounds of tea brown woman, dead weight! It was most impressive. Fay did not believe Pearce even knew why she was suddenly flying from the water and landing in Virgil's boat. But there she was, safe and sound.

There was an explosion, and the excitement was over. This, of course, meant the engine would now start.

Fay twisted the key and... bingo! The engine fired. She scurried to the bow, pulled anchor, returned to the helm, mashed down on the throttle, and headed for *Mountain Mama*, which now drifted about one hundred yards away. As she pulled alongside, Deputy Doug reached out and grabbed *Sparky*'s deck rail. After securing *Sparky*, he helped her aboard.

Fay was relieved to see Pearce standing next to Virgil at the stern... relieved because she was standing. This meant her sister's legs and feet were still intact. All the two women could think to do was to embrace one another. They were both shivering uncontrollably. Fay did not know if it was because they were cold or because they were frightened.

"I've got warm blankets below for y'all," Sheriff Gus said to the women. "And there's coffee makin's, a pot, and a cooktop in the galley."

They thanked the Sheriff and went below. After wrapping themselves in every blanket they could find, Fay put on the coffee.

The uncontrollable shivering, the teeth chattering, and the goosebumps eventually subsided.

Pearce said, "I told Sheriff Gus where to find Admiral Joe's body. He called the Coast Guard."

"The gator almost got you!" Fay exclaimed.

"What! No way! He could catch me if he'd a mind to. He was just bein' curious... tryin' to figure out if I was a buddy," Pearce insisted.

Fay gazed at her sister with a wary eye. "How is it you know so much about wildlife?"

Pearce smiled. "Remember when Daddy would take us on his famous survival trainin' adventures?"

"Much to Mom's chagrin," Fay recalled.

"Well, that's true. Mom did invest a fair amount makin' sure we gals sparkled," Pearce sighed. "When he and I was out livin' off the fat-of-the-land, he taught me all about plants and animals. When he took y'all out into the wilderness, didn't he teach you about what plants and animals to eat or avoid?"

"I must have missed those lessons. I was too busy complaining about the spiders and snakes and the fact I couldn't take a hot shower."

"Too bad," Pearce quipped. "All I know is, Daddy kept tellin' me knowin' how to survive in the wilderness could save my life one day."

"I remember, but a Girl Scout I am not." Fay gave her sister a once over and sighed. "I bet we look like hell."

Whatever makeup they had applied to their faces earlier in the day had long since washed away. Their hair was straight, stringy, and all plastered around their heads, and their lips had a bluish-purple shade to them. Fay's nose was running like a worn faucet in a cheap motel.

"This is not a good look for us," Pearce commented, accompanied by a solemn nod.

Fay nodded in agreement. "At least you have a great tan."

"It's them Injun' skin pigments going nuts when the sun comes along. You should see me when I take off my bikini. Why I look like one of those chocolate cookies with the white cream filling!"

"Ah…go ahead and rub it in, Sacajawea. All I do is burn." Fay was about to say, "I wonder what's keeping the Coast Guard," when she heard the approaching helicopter's thumping rotors.

The sisters scurried topside to watch the action.

A massive red and white Coast Guard chopper approached from the West. Fay saw two divers drop from the open door and disappear into the water as it hovered twenty feet over the water.

Before long, a relatively decent-sized crowd of dayboaters and fishermen had assembled. Fay knew how quickly the news crews would find out about this story from the CB chatter. Reporters and their chopper crews seemed to have a knack for finding a breaking story quicker than a blowfly finding carrion. She had difficulty seeing the difference between blowflies and the media.

Premature news coverage of Admiral Joe's apparent drowning deeply concerned her. She did not want Mrs. Joe to learn about her husband's death by viewing it on television. Fay expressed her concern to Sheriff Gus and Deputy Doug.

Sheriff Gus listened, nodded, and turned to his deputy and pointed. He did not say a word. He pointed, and Deputy Doug headed for the radio to order the area sealed from the TV news crews.

Fay loved it when Sheriff Gus pointed, and people began scurrying around.

They had found poor Alvin Joe. The only thing remaining for her to do was break the sad news to Mrs. Joe. She would not wish that detail on her worst enemy.

Fay recalled that her duties as a Navy lawyer included counseling sailors and marines regarding wills, life insurance, divorce, and such. Occasionally, she would draw what they in the JAG office called "Death Detail." When a serviceman died, a sailor from her office, and usually the base Chaplain, were assigned to break the news to the next of kin.

No one in the JAG office had wanted to pull the Death Detail, so they had all drawn straws. The short straw had won or lost, depending on how one looked at it. Fay had won/lost the Death Detail about ninety percent of the time. More precisely, the only time she had not drawn the detail was when she was not in the office. In her group, she had made up the straws. She had gotten used to being the bearer of sad news, and she had acquired an awful nickname as a result. In the office, she was referred to as "Josephine Black."

Now, in Alvin Joe's case, Fay had managed to draw the short straw once again. This time, there was one straw, and she was present, so she was likewise in charge of straws that day.

Death Takes a Vacation and *Meet Joe Black* were two films based on the same plot. The latter, which starred Mr. Brad Pitt, was a remake. Death, or the Grim Reaper, decided in each film he wanted to see what it's like to be a human. He took on a human appearance and fell in love with the daughter of the man whose soul he had come to claim. He claimed a few more souls along the way, discovered he liked peanut butter—and that was the plot.

Faydra preferred to wear her white dress uniform whenever she performed this detail. Most people appreciated her visit on behalf of the U.S. Navy or the Marine Corps. They appreciated her concern for the family. She got to know the families well and, as a result, would often get invited to funerals. This was a great honor for her, and she made it a point to attend all funerals if they were held in the Puget Sound area.

There was nothing good about any of this, and occasionally, she had had people take one look at her, determine what she was up to, and slam the door in her face. She supposed people reasoned that if she did not tell them, death did not happen. She was not the Grim Reaper; she was but his messenger. How would it look on her resume?

Company: Death, Inc.
Job Title: Messenger.
Duties: Deliver death notices for COO (Chief Operating Officer).
Immediate Supervisor: Mr. Joe Black.

Fay called her brother, Will, on her cell and asked him to grab her whites and a black scarf and to meet her at the guardhouse at the Citrus Tree Retirement Community entrance. He said he would be there in ninety minutes.

Fay watched as Admiral Joe's body was lifted from the water, via a med-evac sled, to the Coast Guard chopper. The chopper continued to hover until the two divers were safely aboard. It headed off toward Choctaw Bay Marina. Sheriff Gus told her the Medical Examiner had been contacted and would meet the chopper at the marina to claim the body.

Later, Fay forgot about the short ride back to the marina aboard *Mountain Mama*. Her mind was as numb as her butt. Below deck, she sat mesmerized, rocking back in forth in cadence with the wave action against the boat's hull, her mind blank as she stared at the bulkhead.

Chapter 5

As *Mountain Mama* neared the floating dock at the marina, Fay leaped from the deck and onto the pier. Her internal afterburners kicked in as she sprinted, barefoot, the length of the groaning, squeaking dock. She felt compelled to reach the Cartman County Medical Examiner before the media did. The ME would speak to the reporters regarding any death, even if the ME had little information on the deceased. In this instance, she did not want to risk even the slightest information being passed between the ME and the press.

When Fay arrived at the dock's shore end, she halted; she had gotten a splinter in her left food. She was distracted when the Guard chopper lifted skyward from the marina parking lot. She watched as the red and white bird thundered over her head, heading toward Choctaw Bay. Admiral Joe's body had been delivered. Standing where the ramp connected the dock to land, she spotted what she presumed to be the ME's car and sprinted across the sun-heated asphalt in his direction.

When Fay reached the coroner's car, she was breathless. The car's engine was running. Through the dark tinted windows, she could see the ME seated behind the steering wheel, writing on a clipboard. A light rap on the window was all it took to get his attention. When he lowered the window, Fay saw that he was actually a she.

"Excuse me," Fay gasped and extended her right

hand through the open window. "Commander…Fay," she swallowed, "Green. NCIS. Whew. Out of shape and out of breath. Running in this hot Florida sun is not…healthy. I tried to call you…"

The ME firmly grasped Fay's hand. "Hello. Sue Nguyen." She shut the car's engine off and opened the door.

The ME's black waist-length hair was tied back with a black bow. It trailed behind her like a bridal veil as she slipped out of the car. The petite woman conveyed a professional image in her white blouse, dark blazer, and matching knee-length skirt and pumps.

"You related to the deceased?" Dr. Nguyen did not offer a reason as to why she had not answered her phone. Had she done so, Fay would have been breathing much easier.

"No. A family friend," Fay puffed. "Excuse me. I…ran from the dock. Whew."

"I noticed you were limping when you crossed the parking lot. Did you injure your leg?" the other woman asked.

"What?" Fay panted.

Dr. Nguyen pointed behind Fay. "You were limping when you ran across the parking lot."

"I suppose I did," Fay muttered as she lifted her left foot into her hands. Hopping on one leg, she attempted to balance herself and examine her foot all at the same time. The sole of her foot was black… and wet with blood. "Yeah, I cut it all right. Looks like a nasty slice," she reported.

"Hop up on the hood. But hold on—"

As Sue spoke, Fay jumped onto the hood, knowing what Sue was going to say. "Nice to meet you,

Sue...yikes!" Fay exclaimed as she sprang from the hood. "Damn, the hood is hotter than a black iron skillet at a Sunday morning pancake feed." She'd been in touch with the hood for a second, but it was apparent she'd stir-fried her backside.

Sue Nguyen completed her sentence, "—for a minute. The hood will be hot. I'll get a blanket for you to sit on and my first aid kit. Be back in a second."

Now she tells me. Fay leaned against the driver-side car door. She rubbed her burned butt while simultaneously holding her left foot like a wounded pup with a sore paw... and watched blood drip and form into a small pool on the asphalt. *Crap. What else could happen?*

Sue returned. After tossing the blanket onto the hood, she pointed at her impromptu operating table and directed, "Hop up."

Fay obliged.

Sue grasped Fay's left ankle. Her dark olive eyes surveyed the sole. She pursed her lips with a "Hmm," and then she went to work attending to the injury.

Sue washed Fay's feet with mineral water and patted them dry with a towel. "You have a small laceration, and a big sliver jammed into your foot. Probably a splinter from the dock," Dr. Nguyen informed her, examining the injury again. "This is gonna sting a little. I'm gonna pour alcohol on this before I patch you up."

"Patch me up?" Fay did not like the sound of it. "OH...GOD!" she shrieked when Sue applied the alcohol, yet the stinging soon subsided.

"Okay? You're okay now. Get ready. I'll do it once more," Sue warned.

"Go for it." Fay clenched her teeth, closed her eyes,

held her breath, and prepared for the pain.

Sue applied another dose.

"Ahhhh…God! Mercy. Sweet Lord, that hurt!" Fay yelped.

"You're a courageous lady, Fay. Now I'm gonna remove a nasty sliver. The laceration won't require stitches."

"That bad, huh?" Fay gasped.

"Yeah. Pretty bad. But my bad luck. No amputation today. I think you'll live." Sue looked at her with lively eyes. "You want me to do it?"

"Right here? Right now, Sue?"

"Yep," Sue stated, as if this was a routine medical procedure for her.

Fay did not think she should be concerned. The woman was a doctor and a medical examiner. Sue was probably more proficient at patching and sewing than Mrs. Joe's entire family of Filipino seamstresses combined.

Not wanting to sound like a giant baby, still Fay had to ask, "Is it gonna hurt, Doc?"

"No, not at all. I'll numb it with my special cream. You won't feel a thing. Save you a trip to the hospital. Look," Sue said, with mock impatience evident in her voice, "I'm a busy girl—busy, busy. You want me to patch you up, or not? I have a sale going on right now. My rates are cheap cheap, so come on," she snapped her fingers twice, "let's go."

What a little saleswoman! "Let's do it!" Fay exclaimed.

Sue smiled. "I won't need you to sign a waiver for this service call? In case I screw it up?"

Fay laughed. "No, not at all. Go for it, Doc." *When*

you are in the swamp up to your ass battling alligators, you tend forget your original intention was to drain the swamp. Fay had had an actual purpose for tracking down the ME. Having Sue attend to her foot while she sat on the hood of a coroner's car, parked in the middle of a parking lot, with a dead man lying in the back, seemed odd to Fay.

On the other hand, it seemed like Hong Kong's Night Market. Merchants in the city hawked their wares after business hours in a typical open-air market setting. This included many dentists who worked on patients on the street. The market offered the finest bargains in the world for a savvy shopper.

"Have you ever visited the Hong Kong Night Market, Sue?" Fay asked.

Sue giggled. "When I was a small girl, my family lived in Kowloon. I visited the Night Market on occasion. Why, do you think this seems like the Night Market?"

"I do." Fay could see her sister and Sheriff Gus approaching. "Hey!" she called out and waved.

"Is handsome Sheriff Gus coming?" Sue giggled again.

"I won't argue with you there," Fay replied.

As her smart-ass sister drew near, JP noted Fay's foot. "You got time for a pedicure, Spider?" she teased.

"Very funny. No, I brought a piece of the dock over here embedded in my foot," Fay told her.

Virgil removed his sunglasses. He dropped them into his shirt pocket, before commenting, "We kinda figured it; we followed the blood trail."

Fay introduced Pearce to Sue.

The ME finished her handiwork by applying cream

to the wound and wrapping a gauze bandage around Fay's foot. "There we go. Your foot is gonna be sore after the cream wears off." Sue smiled. "Try to stay off it for a few days, take two aspirin, and call me in the morning."

Everyone is a comedian these days. Fay laughed anyway. She admired people who could find a moment to be humorous, even in stressful times. When timed correctly, humor could be a good tension reliever.

"I'm glad you're here, Sheriff," Sue said. "I need your John Hancock on a document."

Fay chatted with her sister while Sheriff Gus and Sue attended to business.

When they returned, Sue said, "Handsome Sheriff said you can provide me with information regarding Mr. Joe's next of kin."

"Yes, I can," Fay confirmed.

"Where's your car?" the ME asked.

Fay pointed, saying, "We parked near Sparky's shop."

"Okay, get in, and I'll give you a ride. I don't think you tracked me down so I could remove a sliver from your foot. You talk and I'll drive," Sue proposed.

Fay was faced with the daunting task of figuring out how best to jump from the hood without further injuring her foot. What happened next would become the highlight of her day.

JP's jaw dropped when Sheriff Gus stepped forward to sweep Fay into his arms.

Fay was easily gathered up by the Sheriff and carried to the passenger side of the car. He held her in his muscular arms until Sue opened the car door for Milady. He gently placed her in the passenger seat, stood, and closed the door, as if he were holding a valuable item.

He turned and walked away without even waiting for a "thank you very much." It was awesome. In the film *Gone with the Wind*, he would be Rhett Butler, and Fay would be Miss Scarlet O'Hara. For a brief moment, on that day, Fay declared, the South had risen again.

Sue returned to the driver's side, opened the door, and hopped in. "Okay," she said as she started the car. "I assumed you were a goddamn reporter when I saw you racing across the parking lot," she grumbled. "Maybe I should wear my glasses more often. What can I do for you?"

Her comment about the reporter gave Fay the answer that she'd risked life and limb for. Nothing was going to be said to the press. Fay had not seen a single news varmint in the vicinity, but rest assured, they would be there.

"I was going to ask if you would not speak to the press until I had time to tell Mrs. Joe about her husband's death," Fay told Sue.

"Reporters know when I'm not in the mood for their nonsense. When I see them coming, I give them my 'ask me a question, and you will die' look, and they immediately turn around and go bother someone else," Sue asserted.

Fay laughed. "Will you share your autopsy report with me once you have finished it? And could you, please, teach me that look?"

Sue grinned. "Of course. You looking for anything in particular?"

"Not at all," Fay answered. "It appears the man drowned. I suppose I would be curious to know if he had a heart attack, was hit by a boat, or whatever."

"My husband works tonight. I think I'll prepare for the autopsy when I get back to the morgue. I'll call you in the morning, okay?"

"I appreciate you, Sue. But you don't have to go out of your way. I can call you," Fay said.

"I'll call you. Besides, it's good for me to follow up on my patients."

Fay was not being completely open with Sue. She had several problems with Admiral Joe's apparent drowning. Why would a former seaman risk being hit by a boat by swimming in the Sawsashaw after dark? And why would he leave his towels and robe at the pool, as opposed to taking them with him to the river?

When they arrived at the retired cop car, Fay thanked Sue. "You did a great job on my foot."

"One thing, Fay. Before you go, will you identify the deceased?" Sue requested.

Fay nodded and limped behind Sue to the rear of the car. After identifying Alvin Joe, Fay extended her hand toward Dr. Sue Nguyen and wished her well.

"Try to keep off your foot for a few days. No golf or tennis tomorrow," Sue advised, laughing while handing Fay the numbing cream.

Fay examined the handwritten label affixed to the tube. "EBLA?" she read quizzically.

"*Eutectic Blend of Local Anesthetic...* my own special, fast-acting blend," Sue explained.

"Thank you," Fay stated. "I've got one free day left in Florida, and I'm off to D.C. for mass meetings, I'm gonna rest and enjoying my family."

By the time Fay and Sue had finished talking, Pearce and Sheriff Gus had caught up with them.

Fay agreed to meet her brother at the Citrus Tree

Retirement Community guardhouse. The sisters drove from the marina to the guardhouse in a few minutes. Fay needed to shower and put on makeup, and her hair looked like she had styled it in a broken toaster oven. Fay still had not figured out how she would remove her wet swimsuit and get into her uniform.

A call from her brother confirmed he was waiting near the guardhouse. Shortly, Fay arrived. She noticed that a black Chevrolet SUV with dark tinted windows was parked nearby. Experience told her those black beauties were Secret Service vehicles. This meant her father had decided to come along with Will.

Fay and JP stopped next to the Secret Service Sports Utility Vehicle. The SUV's doors opened at the same time. Will, her father, and Louie, his Secret Service person, got out. Pride filled her soul. Her dad had known it would be hard for her to tell Mrs. Joe about her husband's death and so he would be there in support. It seemed appropriate for Bill Green, a Navy aviator prior to serving one term in the U.S. Senate followed by two terms in office as President, to join her. She was more than sure Mrs. Joe would appreciate having him there.

Lenny Crane was on duty. And while there was a motel near the marina, it would be much faster if Fay showered and dressed in the women's locker room at the golf course clubhouse. Lenny placed a call to make the necessary arrangements.

While Pearce and Fay changed their clothes, Bill Green, Will, and the Secret Service agent waited. Having her sister assist her with dressing was a godsend for Fay. Her foot was becoming sorer as Dr. Nguyen's numbing cream wore off. While Pearce tended to the laceration, Fay sat on a bench.

Pearce administered the numbing lotion to Fay's foot before wrapping it in a new bandage. Fay was able to return to the former cop car using her sister as a crutch. She had one more task to complete, and she vowed that once it was over, she would go to the nearest bar and get hammered.

Chapter 6

Fay spent the afternoon and evening with Mrs. Joe. She described to Lyza how and where she and Pearce had found her husband's body. As Fay told the story, Mrs. Joe became increasingly alarmed. Then, Mrs. Joe fainted. At around 20:30, Mrs. Joe's sister, Teresa, and her husband, Bernard, arrived from St. Pete.

By then, Lyza had recovered, and Fay had finished telling Mrs. Joe about her husband. Fay and her father agreed this would be a good time to leave. But before leaving, Fay took Teresa aside to express her concern for Lyza's health. Teresa appreciated Fay's concern and assured Fay she would monitor Lyza for the next few days.

JP drove herself and Fay back to Pensacola. Fay dozed off. JP must have carried her from the car to her bed because Fay awoke there at twenty minutes past midnight. She got up, shed her uniform, slipped into her pajamas, and limped to the bathroom to brush her teeth.

Before retiring to bed, Fay placed a call to Frank Farmer in Seattle. Frank, a thirty-year Seattle police detective, had been assigned to investigate the homicide of a Navy SEAL. He had worked the case from the SPD side, while she had worked it from the Navy side. They had become friends and, when it came to sleuthing, she considered Frank her mentor.

Fay admired Frank's experience. He had forgotten

more about investigating than she would ever know, as they say. Paul Theroux, the guy who wrote *The Mosquito Coast*, once said, regarding experience, "Remember this. Experience isn't an accident. It's a reward that's given to people who pursue it. That's a deliberate act, and it's hard work."

It would be three hours earlier in Seattle, so Fay reasoned Frank would still be up when she placed the call to him. Sure enough, Frank was watching television, according to Mrs. Farmer. The two women had a friendly chat, and then Mrs. Farmer called Frank to the phone.

"Whatcha watchin', Frankie!?" Fay asked when he answered the phone.

He chuckled. "A TV series rerun called *Line of Duty,* Fay. They actually do a pretty good job, for a TV program anyway, at showing forensic procedures and crime scene investigation."

"Y'all learnin' anything?" Fay teased.

Frank chuckled again. "Yeah. I'm learnin' I should've been an actor instead of a cop!"

It was Fay's turn to laugh. Then, Pearce poked her head around the edge of Fay's bedroom door.

"Hold on, Frank," Fay told him, placing her hand over the phone. "Hi, honey."

"I was bringin' y'all an aspirin and to see how ya was doin'. Sorry to bother y'all. But I heard talkin' in here," Pearce commented.

Fay motioned for her sister to enter the room. "I'm talking to Frankie," she told JP.

Pearce proceeded into the room and softly closed the door behind her.

"It's my sissy, Frankie. I'm going to put you on speaker. Hold on. You there, Frank?" Fay asked.

"I'm still here," he confirmed.

"Hi, Frankie, this is JP! How's you and Mrs. F?" Pearce said in greeting.

"Hi, sweetheart, we're fine, and Mrs. F sends her love to you guys. You kids staying out of trouble?"

"Who, us? No, sir," JP responded.

They could hear him laughing.

"I have a question for you, Frank," Fay said.

"Are you working? I thought you were on leave?"

"I am on leave, until tomorrow," Fay replied. "Then we're off to D.C. for meetings, meetings, and more meetings. I have a friend whose husband died recently."

"Oh, I'm sorry to hear it. Accidental, or natural?" he wondered.

"He drowned," Fay told her mentor. "But there's something about his death that's bugging me. I thought I'd run it by you. Okay, Frank?"

"You know it's okay, Fay. Hold on while I get a notepad." There was a brief pause, before Frank returned, saying, "Okay, lay it out for me."

Fay and Pearce spent the next forty-five minutes recapping the story of Admiral Joe's death, including their encounter with the alligator.

Fay finished by asking Frank, "So what do you think?"

"I'm amazed you two found the body. Good work," he congratulated the sisters.

"Thanks, Frank," Fay replied.

"Your instincts are good," he continued. "Do you remember what I told you about lingering questions?"

"You said I'd know my investigation was done when I had an answer to all my questions," Fay recalled.

"That's right. But you still have unanswered

questions, don't you?" Frank asked.

"Yes, I do," Fay confirmed.

"Okay. Let me feed your question back to you. See how it sounds."

"Okay," Fay told him.

"Why did Mr. Joe go swimming in the river, after dark, when he knew he ran the risk of getting hit by a boater?" Frank asked her.

"I can't answer that one."

"Let's play it out by exploring your second question. If Mr. Joe did go for a swim in the river…, what did you call that river again?"

"The Sawsasha," Fay informed him.

"That's easy for you to say. Let's call it the Saw for short," Frank decided. "So, Mr. Joe goes swimming in the Saw. But he leaves his towel and robe at the pool. Doesn't make sense, does it?"

"I'd wear my robe to the river, Frank. And I'd take my towel to dry off with after my swim," Fay stated.

"I would too. You've made an assumption here. Remember what I told both you kids happens when you assume?" Frank asked them.

Pearce volunteered the answer this time. "The minute we assume, we may realize we made an 'ass out of you and me?'"

"That's right, JP. Faydra, what did you assume?"

"I assumed the alligator grabbed Admiral Joe in the river and drowned him," Fay replied.

"The alligator may have grabbed Mr. Joe, but it may have happened somewhere other than the river," Frank speculated.

"His swimming pool? The gator could have been in his pool before he entered. The gator would have held him under until he drowned and dragged him to the river," Fay guessed.

"Is that possible?" Frank asked her.

"Yes, it is. Folks here are forever finding gators in their swimming pools, Frank. I'll have the ME analyze the water in Admiral Joe's lungs," Fay decided. "If he drowned in his pool, there would be chlorine mixed with the water in his lungs."

"Play it out. An answered question usually generates another question which, in turn, demands another answer."

Fay thought for a moment. "How did the gator get into the swimming pool, and why didn't Admiral Joe see it?" she wondered.

"What if the gator was never in the pool?" Frank surmised.

"Alligators are opportunity feeders," Fay said, remembering. "If the gator found Admiral Joe in the river but he drowned in his pool… oh…" She caught herself. "An assailant might have drowned Admiral Joe in his pool and chucked him into the Sawsashaw to make it look like an accident. God, Frank, poor Alvin Joe may have been murdered!"

"What does your gut tell you?"

"I'm floored," was all Fay could say.

"Who would your suspect be, Fay? Mrs. Joe is your current suspect," Frank said.

"Mrs. Joe is a small woman. Much smaller than me. JP or I would have had difficulty lifting a dead Alvin Joe straight up and out of the water," Fay replied. "His body would have to have been carried or dragged from the pool to the river."

"What is the distance, in feet, from to the river from

the pool?" Frank wanted to know.

"What would you say, JP? I'd guess about three hundred feet?" Fay asked her sister.

Pearce nodded.

"It would be physically impossible for Mrs. Joe to have moved her husband from the pool to the river," Fay concluded.

"Unless?" Frank prompted.

"Unless she had help."

"Does that make sense to you?"

It did not make sense to Fay. "Murder is often a crime of passion," she stated.

"Is there a pool boy in the picture?" Frank asked.

Fay laughed. "No!"

"You have to have motive and opportunity before you can have a suspect. But I'd say go with your gut feeling. I always do," Frank advised. "It sounds to me like your sheriff…Virgil Gus?"

"Sheriff Gus. Yes," Fay confirmed.

"It sounds like Gus is a good man. When you get your water test results from the ME, lay it out for him," Frank recommended. "Let Gus and the FBI take it from there, and you two will have done your good job."

"Thanks, Frank," Fay replied, stifling a yawn.

"You kids have had a tough day. Time for bed. But call me and let me know how you're doing. Okay?" Frank said, before signing off.

Later in the morning, Fay spoke with the ME. Sue Nguyen's autopsy confirmed that Admiral Joe had drowned. There was no evidence of violence or trauma, other than that caused by the alligator.

Fay asked Sue to analyze the water in Joe's lungs. Sue agreed to run the tests and to call her later. Fay decided to wait for the test results before she called Sheriff Gus with her theory.

Fay's Saturday was spent sailing with her family. If she were ever granted one day when she could make time stop, this would be the day. Because of the lengthy time commitment required by her op, Fay knew this would be the last day they would spend together, as a family, for a long time.

Sue Nguyen called Saturday evening. The water in Joe's lungs had tested positive for chlorine. Admiral Joe had drowned in his pool. Sue said she would note the water test results in her autopsy report. Fay told her she would contact Sheriff Gus.

Fay asked Dr. Nguyen if she had found drugs or alcohol in Admiral Joe's system. If he had been inebriated, he could have wandered too close to the pool and fallen in. Curiously, Dr. Nguyen's tests had revealed a large dosage of the drug *gamma-hydroxybutyrate* present in his bloodstream. This concerned Sue.

When Fay called Sheriff Gus, he was surprised when she told him about the chlorine in Admiral Joe's lungs.

"I'll put my best detective on the case," Gus assured her.

Fay would have given anything to be there, in person, when the Sheriff delivered the order. She could imagine it, though. Gus would point, with not a word said, and his detectives would upset their coffee and donuts as they sprang from their chairs and cleared the room in their haste to fulfill Sheriff Gus's silent order. *Make it so*.

Sheriff Gus wished her goodbye and good luck. She wished him the same and asked if he would keep her posted on the investigation. He promised he would.

This last day at home was a mixed bag for Fay. She was happy to be with her family, yet she was sad that she had to leave her father and brother and her newfound friends, Miss Lyza, Sheriff Gus, and Doctor Sue. She was satisfied that, with Frank Farmer's patient coaching, she was giving direction to Admiral Joe's death investigation, which now rested in Sheriff Gus's capable hands.

Physically exhausted from her bout with the alligator, the injury to her foot, and having to deal with telling Mrs. Joe her husband had died had left Fay emotionally spent. Still, she was anxious to begin the upcoming meetings in Washington, D.C.

Anxiety might be a mild word to describe how Fay felt about the upcoming meetings. She and her associate and friend, Gifford Champion, had been asked to lead a task force comprised of lawyers from the Justice Department's Anti-Trust Division, special agents from the FBI's White Collar Crime Division, and the Underworld Crime Division, as well as agents from the Naval Criminal Investigative Service and investigators from the Defense Criminal Investigative Service. Fay wanted a roster card like a professional baseball team manager so that she could keep track of them all because there were many different players from the many agencies.

Fay also understood she was in charge for a limited time. But once this op came down, these people would fragment. This meant each department would compete to be the center of attention and demand credit for the operation's success.

Fay was not bothered by it. Instead, she would set it

up and disappear into the background and let another take credit. The Galaxy Friendship Association was the big fish they were after. She still had a strategy to present. She would persuade the task force to support her proposal, and then limp off to Chicago to meet with a man she referred to as "Hell's Henchman." Her success hinged on her ability to persuade this man, whose business it was to operate outside the law, to assist her.

Chapter 7

Fay knew military flights were not as comfortable as commercial flights. But they afforded her the one thing she could not get on commercial flights: peace and quiet. It seemed whenever Fay traveled, she was heading to a meeting or a conference. As a result, she had many preparations to attend to. On commercial flights, people sitting next to her would often strike up a conversation. She reasoned that being the daughter of a former President of the United States had cursed her with a certain celebrity status but had also bestowed upon her a responsibility to be accommodating - especially if the person was a Republican.

So, in such situations, Fay would put aside her project and indulge them, which meant she would not get done whatever she had to do. By the time she would arrive at her destination, she would be behind in her preparations. This would mean she would be up all night putting the finishing touches on what she could have done on the plane. With her sleep time cut short, the day would drag from lack of rest. She tended to get a tad bitchy when she did not get enough rest.

Due to heightened security at the civilian airports, resulting from community unrest, the airport transit time was reduced by flying military air. There were few passengers on military flights, especially cargo flights, which meant she could do her thing without interruption.

The military sandwiched a couple rows of seats between the cockpit and the cargo.

Other than the obvious, both travel methods were via airplane, but the similarities between the two ended there. Military cargo flights did not have flight attendants; hence, there was no one to serve food and drinks.

When aboard a military cargo flight, a pilot would point out where the food and, more importantly, where the coffee was. It seemed like most military pilots were male, and they seemed to think Fay would know how to make coffee since she was female. Chauvinistic as it seemed, she understood she was a passenger on their airplane. Since the pilots were going to all the trouble to fly the damn thing, the least she could do was make the coffee. Hell, she usually ended up serving the sandwiches to them in the cockpit too. All in all, it was a small price to pay for free travel and a little peace and quiet.

Yes, there was one other difference between commercial and military air travel: flying on military meant self-service. Fay loaded and unloaded her own luggage. She always had a lot of stuff to carry, including a suitcase, a laptop, a briefcase, and a pocketbook, so she tended to run out of hands. In times such as these, Fay had learned to feign helplessness. The male pilots were always ready and willing to help. On the other hand, female pilots would not give her the time of day… no matter how much help she needed.

Seating on a military plane was configured differently from commercial aircraft because the seats faced in the opposite direction. Fay was used to riding backward. Actually, it was much safer should the plane come to a sudden halt…at, say, three hundred miles per hour. Babies riding in car seats and commuter rail passengers riding backward were safe from injury in a head-on collision for the same reason.

Some military planes did not even have windows or properly working heating systems. Blankets and flashlights were handy to have on such flights. And the propeller-driven aircraft were noisier than the jets. The prop jobs had a tendency to vibrate more than the jets did. So, earplugs were also handy.

Once airborne, things tended to mellow out. Except perhaps air turbulence, which seemed more unsettling than on a commercial flight. The plane would begin to creak, rattle, and groan. Did anyone say peace and quiet? Well, at least she did not have to entertain the creaks, rattles, and groans. Next, the cargo would join in, and before long, Fay would begin to think the whole damn mess would vibrate apart and fall to the ground. Crash and burn, as they say. But it never happened. All things considered, she would choose flying military rather than commercial.

Fay had chosen this particular military flight because it left Eglin Air Force base at 07:00 on Sunday. This meant she was forced to give up her cherished morning at her favorite Pensacola church. The prior Sunday, she had sung "Jesus the Same" with the choir. Other than her sister, Fay had been the only white person in the entire church. No one had seemed to notice.

The flight was non-stop to Andrews Air Force Base, located southeast of D.C., and too good an opportunity to pass up. Since the Beltway, which circled D.C., ran past Andrews, it would be easy for her to transfer from there to the NCIS HQ in Quantico.

So, there she sat, the engine parts and her. Since Pearce was a licensed commercial pilot, she was often allowed to ride in the cockpit, leaving Fay alone to complete her preparations for the next day's meetings. Today was no exception.

The flight arrived at Andrews in the early afternoon. A Navy staff car was waiting for the two women, which surprised Fay. Usually, the Navy got their arrival time screwed up, and she had to wind up taking a cab.

Fay knew she could not conduct the op without Gifford Champion. He had worked for the CIA. His many years of intel experience and his vital Capitol Hill connections would prove invaluable.

****

Following his morning meeting with FBI agents Lisa Brock and Perkins Washington at Jacksonville's FBI field office, Cartman County Sheriff Virgil Gus returned to the Cartman County Public Safety Building. He glanced at his wristwatch, noting the time, as he walked along the hall toward his second-floor office.

The FBI had searched Admiral Joe's computer hard drive, revealing that he had been working on a design for a Navy top-secret anti-ship missile system: the BASS project Fay Green had told him about. Two companies, Young-David Defense Systems, located in Atlanta, and AmeriCon, an abbreviation of American Aerospace Consolidated, situated in Phoenix, were the project's co-prime contractors.

Virgil Gus arrived at his office and, after checking for messages, headed for the morgue. Because the BASS data had remained intact on Admiral Joe's computer hard drive, both Gus and the FBI believed that whatever secrets the data contained had not been compromised. If Alvin Joe had died for reasons other than natural causes, the motive would not have been related to his computer's secrets.

The question remained: was Alvin Joe's death an accident, as the evidence suggested, or had he been murdered? A visit to the ME would hopefully help Virgil fill in the blanks.

Gus approached the Cartman County morgue and forensic laboratory. Dr. Nguyen, sitting at a stainless-steel table, was hunched over a microscope.

"Excuse me, Dr. Nguyen," Gus said as he pushed through the double swinging lab door.

"That you, Virgil?" Sue looked up. "Be with you in a minute!"

Sheriff Gus quietly surveyed the lab. It had been several weeks since he had last visited the morgue. The Cartman County detective who had been assigned to a death investigation was always required to attend the autopsy.

Dr. Nguyen looked up from her microscope. Flipping her long black hair away from her face with a toss of her head, she greeted him. "Hi, Sheriff. What brings you to the boneyard?"

"Hey, Sue! I came to visit your guest."

"Oh…I don't know if I have time right now, Sheriff. I'm a busy girl…busy, busy," Sue Nguyen teased. "Just kidding. Alvin Joe, I presume?"

Nodding toward the door Virgil knew led into the morgue, Sue continued, "He's on ice. You want to view the body?"

"That, and I want to talk to you about your autopsy report," Gus informed her.

"Hold on." Sue slipped on her reading glasses,

jumped down from her perch on the tall lab stool, and walked to her desk. Lifting a file from her desk, she instructed him, "Come on. Let's go see what Alvin is up to."

Virgil followed Sue through the double doors leading into the morgue. Sue dropped the file she was carrying onto a small table and proceeded to a stainless-steel wall of drawers.

"Let's see," she mused, her gaze scanning a wall chart listing the names and corresponding locations of the current morgue population. "Joe…Joe. Where did they put you, Mr. Joe?" Her searching finger came to a stop partway down the list. "Ah," she reached for the drawer.

Virgil moved closer as Sue pulled the drawer to its entire length.

"Here he is," Sue said at last.

Virgil had seen many corpses…young, old, maimed and mangled beyond recognition, others not. Even though he had grown accustomed to the sight, he was uneasy viewing one who had been snatched from the jaws of an alligator. He braced himself as Sue Nguyen drew open the cadaver pouch that shrouded Alvin Joe's body. To Virgil's surprise, Alvin looked perfectly normal for a corpse. No mangling. No nasty gashes or torn flesh.

"Where did the gator grab him?" he asked the ME.

"Here." Sue pointed at Alvin's left leg.

Virgil leaned closer to better see Alvin's leg. "It appears the gator dragged him. There's no sign he struggled to free himself from the gator's grasp," he observed.

"That's what I thought," Sue confirmed. "No

defensive wounds suggest Mr. Joe did not struggle with the alligator." Sue pointed at a large wound on the victim's left leg. "A ten-centimeter laceration on the upper thigh, deep into the quadriceps muscle, so that the gator's lower jaw severed the femoral artery."

"Did he bleed to death?" Virgil asked.

"He would have, had he been alive. But he was already dead before this happened," Sue explained.

"Looks like the leg has been gnawed on," Virgil pointed out.

"The alligator ripped the kneecap, exposing the knee joint." Sue straightened up, saying, "His hip was also dislocated."

Virgil winced. "The gator could have dislocated his hip by draggin' him."

"One might think that. The victim's left leg shows the trauma. It's his right hip that's dislocated." Sue shifted her gaze from the corpse to Virgil, before asking, "You have lunch yet, Sheriff?"

Virgil stood and lightly patted his stomach. "Not yet."

"You are done looking?" Sue asked him.

"Yeah, thanks. I guess."

"Night, Alvin," Sue said to the corpse and slid the drawer shut.

Virgil turned toward the small table where Sue had placed the autopsy report. "I'd like to take a look at your report, if y'all don't mind," he requested.

"You feel like taking me for a boat ride, Virgil?" she replied.

"Sure. When?" he asked.

The urgent look in Sue's eyes answered his question.

"Give me a few minutes to round up Deputy Doug and my lunch," he told her. "Meet you in the parkin' lot?"

"Okay, handsome, I'll put you on my social calendar," Sue confirmed. "Mind if we call the Game Warden? He's an alligator expert."

"We goin' up the Sawsashaw?" He smiled. "Take the gator's route to Alvin Joe's pool?"

Sue smiled. "Kind of like that."

Sheriff Gus called Deputy Doug, instructing him, "Doug, get Jerry Crow and meet me and Dr. Nguyen in the parking lot. We're going for a boat ride."

Forty-five minutes later, the foursome was racing across tranquil Choctawhatchee Bay aboard the *Mountain Mama*, heading for the Sawsashaw River. Deputy Doug piloted the boat, while Virgil and Sue reviewed the autopsy report. Doug slowed *Mountain Mama* as the bay narrowed into the river, knowing that the wake caused by the high-powered cigarette boat would erode the riverbank. On spotting the Joes' home, Deputy Doug throttled back on the power, bringing the boat to a fast drift. He skillfully nosed the bow gently into the soft riverbank adjacent to the Joes' home.

Virgil thought Sue was being mysterious about this unusual expedition. "You have an idea how Alvin Joe died?" he asked her.

"My job is to tell why he died. Your job is to tell how he died," was all the ME said in reply. Sue rose from boat's padded leather seat, made her way to the bow, and hopped onto the grass bordering the golf course, waiting for the three men to join her.

Doug and Jerry secured the *Mountain Mama* as Sue and Virgil crossed the fairway toward the Joes' home.

"You normally don't take a personal interest in accidental death investigations," Sue said as they walked.

"That's right," Virgil confirmed.

"Maybe you're more interested in Miss Faydra Green than you are in Alvin Joe," Sue remarked.

Virgil kept walking in non-committal silence.

"Oh, I don't know," Sue continued, "but I think Miss Faydra Green's interested in Sheriff Gus."

"Why would you think that?" Virgil asked her.

"I saw the way she looked at you when you snatched her from off the car hood. I saw her heart," Sue said, bringing her right hand to her chest, "through her eyes. Women know these things."

Virgil Gus remained silent as they walked on.

A beat later, Sue resumed talking. "I found something in Alvin Joe's bloodstream you might find interesting."

"I read your report," Virgil acknowledged. "Alvin Joe drowned in his pool, evidenced by the chlorine in the water that had filled his lungs."

"True, Sheriff," replied the ME. "That's why Alvin died. You want to know how he died?"

"Of course. A moment ago, you asked me why I've taken a personal interest in this death," Virgil reminded her. "I am wondering the same about you. You don't usually leave your lab to conduct a field trip."

"The FBI came by my office this morning," Sue stated. "It's unusual for the FBI to concern themselves about a man who drowned accidentally."

"Admiral Joe was workin' on a top-secret Navy program," Virgil offered.

Sue nodded. "I thought so."

They reached the low fence bordering the Joes' yard and swimming pool. Sue stood at the gate, looking at the house. She turned and looked back across the fairway at *Mountain Mama*.

Lyza Joe opened and stepped through the patio door onto the pool deck. She smiled at the visitors as she motioned to them to enter her property.

"Afternoon, Miss Lyza," Virgil called as he passed through the knee-high gate and into the yard.

Immediately, two yapping dogs rushed from the house and skidded to a stop at Lyza Joe's feet.

Sue and Virgil continued to skirt the pool as they moved toward Lyza.

"Miss Lyza, this is Doctor Sue Nguyen," Virgil said as they neared the spot where Lyza stood. "Sue is the Cartman County coroner."

Lyza smiled and offered her hand to Sue. "I met Dr. Nguyen when I came in to identify my Alvin's remains, Sheriff." She offered her guests a seat. "Would y'all like iced tea?"

"Please," Sue replied.

"Thank you, Miss Lyza," Virgil responded. "If it wouldn't be no trouble."

Lyza smiled, "No trouble," and retreated to her kitchen, with the two huffing and snorting mop-dogs at her heels.

Virgil watched until she had disappeared through the doorway leading to the kitchen, before turning to Sue and asking, "What do you think?"

"Miss Lyza's a nice lady." Sue frowned. "Too bad the alligator didn't eat the little dogs." Her gaze surveyed the pool and the Japanese garden beyond. "Very nice. This garden makes me think about my home." She turned toward Sheriff Gus. "I suppose the FBI and your CSI Unit conducted a thorough investigation back here?"

"They even tore apart the pond filter and pump system," Virgil confirmed.

"Here we are," Lyza said in a melodious voice, returning with iced tea and deviled eggs. After setting the refreshments on a nearby table, she handed Virgil and Sue the iced tea. She sat next to Sue, before asking her guests, "What brings you two here today?"

"Miss Lyza," Sue began, "I have a question for you regarding your husband's medicines. Were you aware he was taking a prescription drug called *sodium oxybate*?"

"I don't know. It doesn't ring a bell." Lyza thought again. "I look at all Alvin's various medicines to be sure I know what he is taking and why. No, I don't recall anything called *sodium oxybate,* Doctor Nguyen."

"*Sodium oxybate* is another name for a drug known as *GHB*, or *gamma-hydroxybutyrate.*"

Lyza shook her head from side to side. "No… I don't recall." She shifted her gaze from Sue to Virgil, informing them, "The FBI conducted a comprehensive search. They made no mention of, nor did they ask me about *sodium oxybate.*"

"My CSIs didn't mention it either, Sue," Virgil said.

"Miss Lyza, did your husband have trouble sleeping at night?" Sue asked.

"Not at all. Alvin slept like a baby." Lyza hesitated, then asked, "What is *sodium oxybate*, Doctor?"

"The drug is used to treat sleeping disorders," Sue explained. "It's used in treating the rare but dangerous complications of the sleep disorder narcolepsy."

"Mercy, no!" Lyza exclaimed as she brought her right hand to her chest. "As I said before," she went on in a calmer voice, "Alvin slept like a baby."

"Thank you," Sue said and sipped her iced tea. "Prior to his swim, had your husband been working with any chemicals, such as an engine degreaser, floor stripper, or drain cleaner?"

Mrs. Joe shook her head no.

Virgil's gaze drifted from Lyza Joe and settled on the fence that ran between the Joes' yard and the fairway. "Miss Lyza, is the gate, as a rule, open, or is it left closed?" he asked the widow.

Lyza looked toward the gate. "We never open the gate," she responded. "Otherwise, the dogs get out onto the fairway and bother the golfers. In fact, Alvin and I seldom use the gate. Why, despite his arthritis, Alvin thinks himself still spry. I think it's painful for him, but he always jumps over the gate."

"Do you jump over the gate as well?" the Sheriff asked.

"Why, heavens no," Lyza exclaimed as she lightly grasped Sue's left arm. "I no longer go out onto the golf course."

Sue and Virgil visited with Lyza for a while longer and left.

As the two walked back toward *Mountain Mama*, Sue said to Virgil, "I have a question for Warden Crow."

"What are you thinkin'?" he asked.

She stopped walking, turned back to face the Joes' home, then turned back around and continued walking. "See that gate in the fence?" the ME asked.

Without looking back, he replied, "Yeah."

"Something about the gate bother you, Virgil?"

"I've been wrestlin' with it," the Sheriff said. "The gator crawls from the river, crosses this fairway, and stops at the gate. The gate is never open, so he opens it, crawls into the pool, and takes a nap."

Sue picked up where he had left off. "No one sees the gator crawl across a busy fairway and open a gate. Alvin Joe comes along and jumps into the swimming pool. Gator grabs Alvin... holds him under the water until he drowns. The gator drags Mr. Joe from the pool, through the gate, stops to close the gate... drags him across the fairway and into the river. No one sees the gator."

"Pretty ridiculous," Virgil decided.

"I think the gator is one smart reptile, Virgil, unless he has a monkey for a companion to open and close the gate for him."

Virgil concluded, "Alvin Joe was assassinated."

"I agree with you, Sheriff," Sue replied. "I knew that Faydra Green was thinking his death was more than an accident when she asked me to test the water in Alvin's lungs for chlorine."

"How?" Virgil wondered.

"Call it woman's intuition. I told you I found *GHB* in his blood. Faydra Green asked me to be sure to point you in the right direction. That's why we are here," Sue explained.

"Sue, murder requires motive," Virgil told her. "Granted, the FBI established he was workin' on a top-secret Navy project, but the data was intact. Therefore, the motive wouldn't be based on his top-secret project's theft. I've got no motive."

"Sheriff, I point, you find." Sue slipped her right hand into the crook of Virgil's left arm as they walked. "I'm the coroner, and I'm here to tell you how he died. You're the cop, you tell me why he died."

As they neared *Mountain Mama*, Sue called out to Jerry Crow, "Warden Jerry, I have a question."

He stopped his conversation with Deputy Doug and looked in her direction. "Sure."

Sue stopped near the boat, turned, and pointed back at the Joes' home. "How long would it take for the alligator to crawl from here to the swimming pool?" she asked.

Jerry stroked his chin. "Dependin' on the time… if it were 'fore dark and the sun was hot, a gator would most likely haul up onto the bank first so's he could sun his self. If—"

Sue interrupted Jerry, "If he stopped to sun himself, as you suggest, golfers would have spotted him, and either reported him or shooed him back into the river."

"That's right, Sue," Jerry confirmed.

"It would be unlikely the alligator could cover the distance from the river to the house, across a wide-open area such as the fairway, and not be spotted," Sue stated.

Jerry agreed, "Not likely."

"What about nighttime, Jerry?" Virgil asked.

"Night's a different story. If the gator had a purpose, he'd be movin' fast to his objective. He wouldn't be spotted after dark," came the Warden's reply.

"Considering' the obstacles, includin' the fence and gate, it would be unlikely the alligator would have attempted to crawl from the river to the house and back again," Virgil said.

"Not even on his best day, Sheriff. Besides," Jerry reminded them, "that's why the fence and gate are there to begin with. To keep the river critters out of the swimmin' pool."

Virgil looked from Jerry to Sue and said, "Got it."

He shifted his gaze to Deputy Doug. "Would y'all go on up to the house and ask Miss Lyza if she wouldn't mind takin' an inventory of her glassware? If one's missin', bring one like it on back. We'll wait for y'all here."

Doug nodded and walked off toward the house.

"What are you thinking, Sheriff?" Sue asked.

"I'm back to the *GHB*. The drug you found in Alvin Joe's blood. A large enough dose would cause him to lose consciousness. If he had taken a drink out with him to the pond, a drink laced with *GHB* perhaps, he would have collapsed into the pool and drowned." Virgil sighed. "Unless we find evidence to the contrary, Mrs. Joe is my suspect. She had an opportunity. But I still need a motive."

"I can buy that theory. But how did the deceased get from the pool to the river? The alligator didn't bring him there," Sue pointed out.

"You told me his right hip was dislocated. Once the victim had died, someone could have dragged him from the pool to the river by his feet. Could the pullin' have dislocated his hip?" Virgil wanted to know.

"Easy to do," Sue told him.

Deputy Doug returned with a crystal tumbler in his hand. He handed the tumbler to the Sheriff without saying a word and stood waiting for further instructions.

"Thanks, Doug." Sheriff Gus accepted the glass tumbler from Doug. He shifted his gaze downward, scanning the ground surrounding his feet. He spotted what he was looking for and stooped to pick up a rock. After hefting the stone in one hand and the tumbler in the other, as if he were weighing the two items for balance, he called, "Yo, Doug! Heads up!"

Deputy Doug focused his attention on the Sheriff as

he turned to face the river. With the rock in his right hand, he wound up like a baseball pitcher and chucked it into the river. When the stone struck the surface, Virgil pointed at the expanding circle of ripples.

"I want divers. Have them search from there, in a radius, back to shore. I want the match," the Sheriff pointed to the tumbler he held in his left hand, "to this."

Chapter 8

Gifford Champion had arrived at his Falls Church hotel at midnight. He and Fay met for breakfast and an organizational meeting at 06:00 hours Monday morning. The task force meeting began at 08:00 hours in the NCIS Quantico headquarters conference auditorium.

Although she was wrapped up in the process at hand, Fay remained concerned about Mrs. Joe's well-being. She made a mental note to phone Sheriff Gus as soon as she could.

Whether caused by stress, or a virus she may have picked up from her swim with the gator and the shark, or perhaps a combination of the two, Fay had lost her voice. She was talking when her voice stopped in mid-sentence. Her mouth was doing its job, but the rest of what made her angelic voice happen was not. She sat and Gifford took over.

It was exasperating not being able to talk. Fay became adept at scribbling out signs and posting them on the projection screen. She would accompany the verbiage with an appropriate emoji, or hand gesture, or finger gesture, as it were.

Her foot was sore but feeling better by the day. She could not talk, nor could she walk without limping. Fay recalled the adage, "Talk the talk and walk the walk." For the time being, she could do neither.

In regard to her foot, Fay had lacerated it while in

Florida. It was difficult for her to walk in high or low heels, and when she tried to walk in flats, she could only walk flat-footed. She was walking slower than a nursing-home queen with a bent walker. Finally, Gifford had acquired crutches from somewhere. And while Fay detested having to use the crutches, they were much faster, her foot would heal quicker, and she did not mind the sympathy she was receiving.

A JAG lawyer - a Marine Colonel - entered the meeting room late Wednesday afternoon, pausing near the stage side door. She caught Fay's attention, signaling she wanted her to come to the entrance by wiggling her index finger. Fay excused herself and met the colonel. It proved to be a good time, as the conference room was too warm for her, and she had been about to fall asleep anyway.

"Sorry to interrupt, ma'am. There's a gentleman on the phone. He said it was urgent," the Marine told her.

Fay still had no voice. Displaying an index finger to the colonel, in the "wait a minute signal," Fay reentered the room, caught Pearce's attention, and motioned for JP to join her.

Pearce rose from her chair and came to Fay at the door. Fay pointed at the Marine colonel, indicating she should tell Pearce what she had told Fay.

"Commander Green has lost her voice, ma'am," JP explained.

"There's an urgent call for Commander Green. Please follow me," the Marine told the sisters.

They followed the Marine to a nearby office.

"You can use my phone." The Marine pointed to a phone with three blinking lights. "Mr. Kramer Shock on six." She smiled and left the office, closing the door behind her.

Pearce snatched the phone from its cradle, punched the line six-button, and said, "Petty Officer Pearce, speakin'. How can I help you?" Pearce listened for a bit, before replying, "Faydra has lost her voice, but she can still hear. Y'all tell her yourself. Hold on, Mr. Shock."

Oh, God. Fay knew what this was all about. *Bad news.* Kramer Shock would only interrupt her in a meeting if it were a matter of life and death. He was calling to tell her Mrs. Joe had been arrested for the murder of her husband. This would be the worst thing he could say to her. She hoped she was wrong.

Holding the phone to her ear, Fay managed to croak, "Hey there, Kramer. Go ahead, I'm sitting."

"Faydra, I'm sorry to interrupt. I got a call this morning from Lyza Joe's sister, Teresa. Take a breath."

She did.

"Miss Lyza died this morning."

Fay had not spoken much since she had lost her voice. "NO!" Her voice was back. "Damn!" she croaked. "Kramer…I…I don't know what to say. How?"

Hopefully, he would not tell her Mrs. Joe had committed suicide. However, it could be a genuine possibility.

Covering the phone, Fay told Pearce, "Miss Lyza is dead." She looked for the speakerphone button and clicked it. "You're on speaker, Kramer."

"No problem," he replied, before going on. "According to Teresa, Miss Lyza is an early riser. She rises around 6:00 A.M. When Teresa had not seen her by 7:00 A.M., she grew concerned. After knocking on her bedroom door, she went in."

"She was dead?" Fay asked.

"She had taken the time to lay out Admiral Joe's white dress Navy uniform on the bed next to her. As if he was lying beside her. She died of natural causes."

Fay's eyes flooded with tears. Her throat tightened, and she was back to squeaking. "Natural causes, Kramer?" was all she could manage.

"She must have known she was going to die. She was wearing the red dress you made such a fuss over," Kramer told her.

"I did not know how much she loved Alvin," Fay whispered. "She died from a broken heart."

"That's what we think. I contacted Sheriff Gus. He and the ME just left here. I'm going to stay with her sister and help her get things in order."

"You're a good man, Kramer. Is there anything I can do?" Fay wanted to know.

"Admiral Joe's funeral has been scheduled for Saturday at Arlington National," he informed her.

Fay said, "Near us, here in D.C."

"I'm going to try to get Mrs. Joe's funeral arranged for the same time," Kramer said. "I'll take care of getting her remains to D.C."

"I have a meeting scheduled in Chicago on Saturday. I'll reschedule to attend the funerals," Fay replied. "Please assure Teresa and her husband JP and I will attend."

"Will do," Kramer answered. "Oh, before I forget, Teresa said Lyza had mentioned to her that if something happened to her, she wanted to be sure her beloved Shih Tzus had a good home."

Mercy. Fay knew what was coming next.

"She wanted you to have her dogs. She told Teresa she knew you loved her dogs, and she knew you would give them a good home," Kramer relayed.

I am…speechless, Fay thought. "Me. A dog mama?" she asked, in her normal speaking voice. *Two Shih Tzus?* "Kramer, I—"

"Before you say anything," he interrupted, "I told Teresa you wanted me to have the dogs."

"Kramer. I… yes. Okay! Yes. Please, by all means. The dogs are yours. But you owe me!" He did not know she hated the little mutts. *Carpe Diem. Seize the day. Praise the Lord.* Realizing an opportunity to get favor mileage out of this, Fay gave him the dogs.

"Thank you. My daughters will love the dogs. And we will be forever grateful for your generosity," Kramer told her.

"Think nothing of it. Just promise me I can come to visit my little pups. Okay?" Fay asked. She did need to get to Tallahassee to visit with Kramer's two beautiful baby twin girls. She was their godmother, after all.

Fay finished the call by saying, "If there is anything I can do…anything at all…let me know."

Mrs. Joe, dead. Fay could not believe it.

****

Sheriff Virgil Gus and Sheriff's Deputy Doug stood squinting through hand-shaded eyes into the late afternoon sun, searching the surface of the Old Saw. They watched for the three U. S. Coast Guard divers who were combing the murky river bottom, searching for a crystal tumbler.

"Too bad about Miss Lyza," Deputy Doug said.

Virgil nodded but remained silent.

"Like tryin' to find a field mouse in a vat of coffee," Doug commented. He removed his cowboy hat with one hand and patted the perspiration from his forehead with a white handkerchief with the other.

"It's a long shot, at best." Virgil glanced at his wristwatch. "Six-ten." Shifting his gaze to the waning ginger sun, he said, "I'll give them another forty-five minutes before we pack it in." He licked his lips. "You thirsty, Doug?"

"My throat's a might dry. I'll run fetch us a co-cola from the cooler."

"Naw, Doug," Virgil told his deputy. "Y'all stay put. I'll fetch the co-colas."

****

Fay had a nagging feeling Gail Foster, Assistant Attorney General from the Justice Department Antitrust Division, had not bought into this operation. Gail's lack of enthusiasm and the JD's Antitrust Division's track record for winning the Sherman antitrust cases were less than stellar. Even the infamous Enron anti-trust cases, while successful, had been hit-and-miss prosecutions from the get-go.

Gail had been fidgety all week, with frequent pencil tapping, knee-jigging, and foot kicking, indicating she was full of pent-up frustration. Fay knew she needed to confront Gail, but she did not want to put Gail on the defensive.

Fay said to Special Agent Andy Moss, from the FBI Organized Crime Unit, "Andy, are your people in the Chicago office ready?"

Andy stood to address the group, beginning by saying, "The Chicago office is ready. They have been advised you will be meeting with Mr. Stumpanato. The Chicago office knows he is considered untouchable regarding his business operations. Agent Valdez and I will fly to Chicago tomorrow; we will monitor your progress. If you need us, call." He smiled and sat.

"Thank you, Mr. Moss. I'm counting on you," Fay stated. She turned to Special Agent Karen Yoo from the FBI's White Collar Crime Unit. "Karen, are your people in Phoenix ready?"

Karen stood, replying, "Commander Green, I was advised by our people in Phoenix we now have a federal judge on board. We've been cleared for phone taps, and the judge has made himself available on an around-the-clock basis to issue search warrants, as needed. Special Agent Cross and I are flying to Phoenix on Monday."

"Thank you, Karen," Fay responded, before addressing the group. "Ladies and gentlemen, it goes without saying we are all tremendously exposed. Several of you are placing your lives on the line." In truth, Fay and Pearce would be the ones putting their lives on the line. She asked, "Gail, the prosecution will be handled by your office… any words of advice for the operation team members?"

Assistant Attorney General Gail Foster stood to speak to the group. "Commander Green… team members." She forced a smile. "You are aware the successful prosecution of the Association Galaxy Friendship and its corporate membership hinges on your individual abilities to perform your tasks within legal guidelines. Suppose I'm to deliver a winning package to the Attorney General and, ultimately, the District Court. and expect them to hand down indictments. In that case, I need to know you people have done your jobs. That means supplying me with accurate and legal documentation…in other words, by-the-book issued and served warrants. Give me willing and credible informants. Assure them the Justice Department's

Antitrust Division will grant them a complete pass on prosecution under our Amnesty Program. I want legal wiretaps and legal surveillance, people. Remember, the people and the corporations we have targeted can afford better lawyers than we can. Be sure you've double-dotted your 'i's' and double-crossed your 't's'. Any error you make will prove fatal should this end at trial."

Gail took a sip of water and continued, "Federal law requires that when your UCN, in other words, informant, is wired and recording, you must have an interception order signed by a judge. Or you must have consent from one of the parties involved."

As Fay listened, she grew convinced Gail was ready to go to war.

Fay conveyed a warm and gracious smile to her, saying, "Thank you, Gail. As you know, all operations have a name. Our operation, as yet, is nameless."

After asking around the room for suggestions and getting a few good ones, Fay asked Gail Foster last. She was hoping if she could attach Gail's label to it, Gail might feel more endeared to the operation. "Gail, I was hoping you had an idea for a name."

Gail had been writing fast and furiously as the others in the group had presented their names, so Fay knew she was working on a name.

"How about…" Gail hesitated. "Ah…hell, I don't know. I've never been asked to name anything before. Except for my kids and my dog."

"Come on, Gail," Fay encouraged. "You heard these suggestions. They suck."

"How about *Operation Jackleg*?" Gail's face flushed red.

It was customary for an operation's name to be

associated with the operation type. Fay recalled *Operation Foul Ball*, an FBI sting that had investigated and netted several sports memorabilia dealers who had been selling forged autographs of famous sports personalities, primarily via an Internet auction house. She liked Gail's name but what might the connection be? Fay recalled that "jackleg" was a slang term for a thief. The GFA was stealing tax dollars.

Fay looked at Gifford. Gifford nodded in approval.

"*Operation Jackleg* will be the name of our operation," Fay announced. The satisfied look she saw on Gail's face told her she had brought Gail into the fold.

****

A startled Sheriff Gus spilled half a bottle of cola on the floor of his boat when a U.S. Coast Guard diver surfaced near him at the stern of *Mountain Mama*. "Damn-nation!" he shouted at the grinning diver. "Y'all 'bout scared the piss right outta me."

"Y'all thinkin' I's a gator, Sheriff?" the diver quipped.

"Something' like that." Virgil chuckled. "Damn, man, you gotta try to warn me better next time." He surveyed the area around his feet. "Now look what y'all went and done. I lost a good bottle of co-cola."

The diver laughed again. "We found your tumbler, Sheriff," he informed him, lifting the water-filled crystal tumbler from beneath the water's surface.

"Hang on," an excited and pleased Virgil said. "Let me get my fishnet."

After retrieving a landing net, Virgil extended it toward the diver, who dropped the tumbler into the net. "Much obliged."

"No problem, Sheriff." The diver waved. "We're

outta here." He turned and slipped under the surface of the Sawsashaw River.

****

The two funerals were moving. Fay was also surprised to find that her father had agreed to attend. Her father's willingness to participate instilled apprehension in her.

Fay was about to go undercover. When former President William Green showed up for any function, the news media was, as a rule, attracted. The last thing she needed was to have her face on camera. Fay solved the problem by distancing herself from her father and wearing oversized sunglasses. She made like a recluse spider. No one even knew she was there.

Several generals, admirals, senators and congressmen were in attendance. There were officers and enlisted people who had served with Admiral Joe over the years. Fay also spotted Vern in the crowd but made no effort to interact with him. He would understand why. Alvin Joe's immediate family and Mrs. Joe's family were there as well.

Fay's father had flown to the funeral with Florida governor Kenneth Brix. Fay was proud when her dad was asked to give the eulogies. And he was spectacular, bearing in mind the request had been spontaneous and he had not even known the Admiral. Her father's speeches reminded Fay that he was a great and amazing man.

The flowers were as plentiful as they were beautiful. The standard twenty-one-gun salute was accompanied by a bagpiper's rendition of "Amazing Grace," as Navy jets flew overhead in the Missing Man formation. Fay kept her own, until a singer sang "Hallelujah." As the stirring and haunting song drifted through her heart, she thought about how much the Joes had loved each other. The melody must have discovered her hidden secret chord, because Fay lost it at that point. Her oversized shades were the single thing that masked her sorrow.

Chapter 9

Sheriff Virgil Gus sat in his office, sipping colas with Deputy Doug and Detective Boyd. He was perplexed as to why a mechanic would have killed Alvin Joe before failing to steal his military secrets. A top-secret Navy operation had not caused Admiral Joe's death.

"Doug, what did we hear from the guy at Choctaw Bay Marina regardin' the stolen boat?" Virgil asked.

"The marina manager said a fisherman rented the skiff on the same day Alvin Joe died," the Deputy reported.

"Alright," Virgil said, "we need a description of the boat: hull number, color, make of the outboard motor, and whatever else you can think of. Get the information on over to Ron Harmon at Choctaw Bay Sun and have him run a story describin' the boat. If anyone has seen it, we want to know about it."

Doug smiled. "Already done."

Sheriff Gus lifted his drink, signaling a toast. "You make me right proud, lad. Oh… and add a five-hundred-dollar reward for any information. We want that boat ASAP!"

"I'll send an artist to the marina," Lonny Boyd said. "We'll have them work up a sketch of the fisherman and circulate it to the communities around the bay. Maybe someone saw something."

"Get right on it," Virgil ordered, taking a pencil from his desk. After inserting the pencil into the crystal tumbler's mouth, Virgil inverted it. Balancing the glass on the pencil and being careful not to touch it with his fingers, he raised it to eye level. As he studied the tumbler, he said, "Gentlemen, we need a motive. Why would anyone want to kill Alvin Joe?"

****

"Miss Green, Mr. Champion, Miss Pearce. Welcome to my home," Mob boss Joey Stumpanato greeted them from behind a massive dark cherry wood desk. "What can a humble businessman do for the United States Navy?" He glanced at Gifford Champion. "And the CIA?"

Fay raised her eyebrows. "You are well informed, Mr. Stumpanato."

"The successful operation of my business enterprise depends on my gettin' timely and accurate information." Stumpanato smiled as he rocked forward in his leather executive chair. Folding his hands and resting them on his desk, he continued, "Now, what can I do for you, Commander Green?"

"Mr. Stumpanato—" Fay started.

Joey waved a dismissing right hand. "Please, please, my friends, call me Joey," he urged.

She smiled. "Joey. And, please, I'm Fay." She cleared her throat and proceeded. "Joey," Fay went on, turning to acknowledge Gifford and Miss Pearce, "we would like to ask a favor, on behalf of your government."

"My government?" His black olive eyes brightened as Joey chuckled. "You're speakin' of the same government that's been bustin' my balls for as long as I can remember?"

Those were the ball busters she was speaking of. "Yes, sir," Fay confirmed. She sat forward. "Look, I'll get right to it. We need your help."

Joey's eyes widened; a smile formed on his lips. "Direct and to the point. I like that, Fay. You got my attention."

Fay had never said she was not direct and to the point. Direct and to the point was the only thing guys like Joey "The Guppy" Stumpanato understood. And if she, the understander, were, say, to accompany her point with a piece - a gun - aimed in the direction of he, the understandee, then the concept of understanding would take on an even higher degree of clarity. But it was inappropriate to produce her gun at this juncture.

Still, Fay did say, "As lead NCIS investigator, I am conducting an investigation, in conjunction with the FBI and the Justice Department, into an organization known as the Galaxy Friendship Association."

Joey turned toward Vincent Astoria, his attorney, who sat to his right. "Vinny, whadda, we know about this Galaxy Friendship Association?" he asked.

"The GFA membership comprises twenty of the country's largest defense contractors," Astoria responded.

"They are subcontractors," Fay clarified. Even though Vincent was a thug lawyer, she liked him. He was medium height, tanned, with silver hair and the most intense steel-gray eyes she had ever seen.

"I stand corrected. Sub-contractors," Vinny noted. "Major government defense contracts are solicited, via the bid process, to the defense contractors. A large portion of the work is subcontracted out, again via the bid process. The subs are GFA members. I believe the

GFA meets and then a member company is chosen, along with an agreed-on bid price. The remaining GFA companies submit bids higher than the chosen company's bid. The bid is fixed at the GFA price, and the contract is awarded to the supposed low bidder. The work is divided by the winning bidder with other GFA member companies." Vincent paused, before glancing at Fay and asking, "Correct?"

The thug lawyer knew his stuff. "You're on target, Mr. Astoria," Fay said. Perhaps the phrase "on target" was not the right word to use around these people?

"Bid riggin'." Joey frowned. "Sounds illegal." The frown disappeared from his face; his eyes brightened. "Sounds lucrative. Are we doin' business with these GFA grease-balls?" he asked Vincent.

"Not to my knowledge," Vincent denied. "Although the Brotherhood of Aerospace Workers represents a number of the members' employees."

Joey chuckled. "We may be missin' an opportunity, Vinny."

Vincent smiled and nodded his head. "The GFA is run by Roman Justine," he went on.

The constant smile Joey had been sporting drained from his face. "Continue," he said in a chilly voice.

The mention of Roman Justine's name seemed to displease Joey. Fay knew that he and Justine had a difference of opinion.

It was better not to ask, but Fay did anyway. "The GFA's illegal operations have cost the taxpayers billions of dollars in excessive defense spending. We, your government, want to shut them down," she told Joey

"You talkin' about a marriage here, Faydra?" Joey asked.

Perhaps this would be a shotgun wedding? Fay wanted to say that but nodded instead. "We have an idea. But we need to get inside the GFA," she explained.

"A mole?"

Fay nodded again. "Correct, Joey. A mole with a wire," she confirmed.

"And you would be this mole?" Joey suggested.

"We've identified a GFA member," Fay stated. "Our candidate, our pigeon, is a man named Don Valley, CEO of AmeriCon, a Phoenix-based defense subcontractor."

Joey watched with evident fascination as Fay continued to speak. "I would like your permission to represent myself as your attorney," she requested.

"For what purpose?" Joey inquired.

"We need to get Don Valley's attention in a grand way," Fay detailed. "You hold sway over many labor unions associated with aerospace manufacturing. Including union workers employed by AmeriCon, which is now manufacturing missile parts for a Navy ship-to-ship program known by the acronym BASS. The contract with the Brotherhood of Aerospace Workers, AmeriCon's largest labor union, expired last month. Our plan would be to have you, with me acting as your mouthpiece, initiate a work slow-down at AmeriCon."

Joey frowned. "Slow down AmeriCon's production lines at a time they can least afford it?" he asked skeptically.

"Exactly," Fay replied, observing that Joey was quick on the uptake. "And as the BAW legal counsel, which brings Valley right to me. We're hoping we can get through Valley to GFA's president and benefactor, Roman Justine."

oman Justine," Joey said with contempt. "I don't honor that *gavone* with my most foul words."

Fay had reviewed the extensive FBI files on both Roman Justine and Joey Stumpanato. She was well aware of the former business relationship between the two men. Still, she had to make it look like "she didn't know nothin,'" in Joey's vernacular.

"Justine and I go back," Joey began explaining. He rocked back in his chair and loosened his burgundy silk necktie. "We was both young Turks at the time. We come up through the ranks together. My father, may he rest in peace, hired Roman Justine fresh outta law school. Even though he was my father's lawyer, Justine and I was close. He was my *compare,* my buddy. And we was doin' pretty well too. But Justine went south. You know, began stealin' from the Family. That pissed people off, includin' my father. And it hurt me personally. I'd vouched for the guy early on, it made me look like shit." Joey paused. "Excuse my foul mouth, ladies," he said, grinning.

Fay excused him with a smile. Joey seemed like a living cliché, a man with many mannerisms that were similar to his TV and movie-wise guy counterparts.

"Not a problem," Fay told him. "Miss Pearce and I have heard that word used once. Profanity has become ingrained in our Navy culture."

Her sister was completely fluent in profanity.

Joey continued, "As I said, a few people was pissed. There was talk they wanted to set him up for a piece of work. Ice him, in other words." He looked stern. "You know what they do when a sick puke like Justine steals from the Family?" he asked.

Fay shook her head and swallowed. "No, sir."

"Roman Justine," Joey said with contempt. "I don't honor that *gavone* with my most foul words."

Fay had reviewed the extensive FBI files on both Roman Justine and Joey Stumpanato. She was well aware of the former business relationship between the two men. Still, she had to make it look like "she didn't know nothin,'" in Joey's vernacular.

"Justine and I go back," Joey began explaining. He rocked back in his chair and loosened his burgundy silk necktie. "We was both young Turks at the time. We come up through the ranks together. My father, may he rest in peace, hired Roman Justine fresh outta law school. Even though he was my father's lawyer, Justine and I was close. He was my *compare,* my buddy. And we was doin' pretty well too. But Justine went south. You know, began stealin' from the Family. That pissed people off, includin' my father. And it hurt me personally. I'd vouched for the guy early on, it made me look like shit." Joey paused. "Excuse my foul mouth, ladies," he said, grinning.

Fay excused him with a smile. Joey seemed like a living cliché, a man with many mannerisms that were similar to his TV and movie-wise guy counterparts.

"Not a problem," Fay told him. "Miss Pearce and I have heard that word used once. Profanity has become ingrained in our Navy culture."

Her sister was completely fluent in profanity.

Joey continued, "As I said, a few people was pissed. There was talk they wanted to set him up for a piece of work. Ice him, in other words." He looked stern. "You know what they do when a sick puke like Justine steals from the Family?" he asked.

Fay shook her head and swallowed. "No, sir."

"Like I said, they ice him," Joey repeated. "He goes into a trunk of a car. Later, if they find him, he's got twenty-dollar bills stuffed in his mouth and up his ass. A sign he stole from the Family." Joey paused as if to let what he had just said sink in.

"I had no idea," Fay said.

"It ain't a pretty picture… so I am told. I was sorry for the puke, so I asked that Justine be given a pass instead. As it turned out, he was chased from the Family. He shoulda been grateful— me savin' his life and all. But he wasn't. The wanker disrespected me. To this day, we don't see eye-to-eye. From what I hear, that *Babbo* still has a hard-on for me." He shrugged his shoulders. "But whaddya gonna do?"

Fay smiled. She had no clue what the man had said to her. But she surmised Justine had gotten caught stealing from Joey's father. It seemed that was a significant wrongdoing punishable by death. The high-minded Joey had convinced his father and his business associates to banish Justine from the Family, rather than kill him. The Family had approved. Or perhaps they had been short of twenty-dollar bills at the moment. The unappreciative Justine had still seen fit to disrespect Joey in a way which remained unclear to her, and so the two men had been arch enemies ever since. Fay did not grasp his reference to Justine's "hard-on." Still, she reasoned the remark had little to do with Mr. Justine's sexual interest in Mr. Stumpanato.

"You knew this?" Joey asked her.

Fay had not known any of this, but still, she replied, "I do my homework."

He seemed impressed. "I'd love to see the Feds break Justine's balls, Faydra." Joey reached for the humidor on his desk and opened it. He removed a large cigar. The expression on his face suggested a man who had just caught a world record rainbow trout. The concept of either the cigar or the federal government busting his old nemesis seemed to bring great pleasure to him. Mob boss Joey Stumpanato continued to smile as he poked a small hole in one end of the cigar.

He eased back in his chair, with lighter in hand. As he was about to light his cigar, which looked to Fay to be Cuban, Joey caught himself and sat upright. "Where's my manners, Vinny?" he exclaimed. "Broads don't like cigar smoke. Excuse me. I mean, *ladies* don't like cigar smoke." He flipped the unlit, illegal, and expensive cigar into a nearby waste basket. "There's gotta be more in this for me than me knowin' that Roman Justine got his balls busted by the Feds for bilkin' them out of a few million measly C notes," he went on, directing this comment at Fay.

Fay had known this was coming. "I knew you'd think that, Joey. What's in it for you, right?" she asked him.

"Enlighten me," the mob boss prompted.

"Hypothetically speaking?"

Joey grinned. "Of course. Hypothetically speakin'."

So, Fay hypothetically laid it out for him. "Let's say it became known, by an enterprising businessman, such as yourself, that the U.S. Navy was about to wage an all-out drug war," she proposed. "The war on terror is over, and the world is at peace, for the moment. There's not a whole lot going on right now to keep the Navy busy, so they join forces with the U.S. Coast Guard by patrolling our nation's coastlines and airways. Ever seen a *Zumwalt* class destroyer or an F-Fifteen up close, Joey?"

He shook his head, responding, "No."

"Awesome weapons. Those slow-moving drug-laden tramp steamers, speedy little cigarette boats, and twin-engine airplanes don't stand a chance against something like that," Fay told him.

Joey nodded his head. "Not a snowball's chance in hell."

Fay detected an uneasiness in his voice, but she went on. "The lost revenue, not to mention the tremendous loss of equipment and their replacement costs…"

Joey's eyes shifted back and forth, indicating his uneasiness. "Somethin' such as this would put a big dent in our enterprisin' businessman's bank account," he finished for her.

"A multimillion-dollar dent," Fay said, with a twinkle in her eye.

"As I said before, you got my undivided attention."

Fay knew she had. "What if the Navy, as they were going about their business sinking ships and blowing little airplanes out of the sky, were told not to bother certain ships and certain airplanes? As they went about their smuggling, say, marijuana?" she suggested. "Call them free passes, if you like."

"What about the Colombian cocaine and the *babania*?" Joey wanted to know.

"Heroin? Nasty stuff," Fay said. "I think any businessman who was forewarned on those products but allowed to pass free on the third would still have a tremendous advantage over his competition. I'm not a bean counter, but I'd predict the juice from the G-bud alone would make a nice nut for any smart businessman."

The mob boss appeared to consider what she had

said. "You're a smart one. You're quick on the up take. I like that." He glanced at Vincent. "Some guys have all the luck, huh, Vinny? We always seem to be in the wrong business at the wrong time."

Joey turned back to Fay, telling her, "I ain't sayin' I should have any interest in the comin's and the goin's of the Columbians. Or the four-twenty trade, but if anyone was to ask me about you or your employment status, I'd refer them to Vinny here. He will confirm, to anyone who asks, that you are indeed an attorney for the Stumpanato family. Will that do?"

Fay knew that "G-bud" and "four-twenty" were crime boss speak for marijuana. She smiled. "More than fair," she told him. "You'll be seeing media coverage on this, but rest assured we will not compromise you, your business, or your family, in any way."

It sounded funny to Fay to hear the word "attorney." She had not seen a courtroom in almost a year, as she had spent her time, of late, playing detective, or commando, for the Navy. Was she a private eye or an attorney? But since she worked for the government, she guessed perhaps she would be considered a public eye rather than a private eye.

"I understand," Joey said. "The Feds, the FBI, and the CIA," he nodded in Gifford's direction, "have done business in the past with the Family. Castro, Hoffa, Kennedy…even Lucky Luciano."

"I'm aware Mr. Luciano had an agreement with the Navy during World War Two to provide spies on the docks of Italy," Fay stated.

"That's what I understand. Which brings me to my next point," the mob boss went on.

Here it comes. Fay had again anticipated what Joey

was about to request.

"You recall the arrangement between the Navy and Luciano?" Without letting her respond, Joey continued. "Luciano was in the joint at the time. The Navy offered him a get-outta-the-joint-free card in return for his cooperation in allowin' the Navy to place spies on the waterfront in Italy."

It seemed to Fay that Joey and she both understood. "Yes, the Navy did agree," Fay confirmed.

"My son, little Joey, is servin' ten years in Joliet for drug traffickin'. His mother cries every night. It's a sad thing for the entire Stumpanato family." Joey's expression took on a morose, almost little boyish look. "You understand."

Fay could never understand his way of life, but she assured him, "I can imagine." *Serves the little Babbo right.*

"I would give my left nu…" Joey caught himself, "give my own life to see that boy free—and for his mother to be happy again. Not to mention, all that cryin' and wailin' is drivin' me nuts."

Fay was well aware of Little Joey's living arrangements. And she was sure Big Joey would give his left gonad to gain his son's release from the Graybar Hotel. "You want a deal for your son similar to what the Navy worked out with Luciano?" she asked him.

Joey nodded. "I could give a rats ass about the G-bud. You get my son outta the joint, and we got a deal," he insisted.

"I can't promise you anything," Fay warned. "My associate, Mr. Champion, would need to speak with the U.S. Attorney on the matter."

Fay could have handled the negotiations with the

U.S. attorney. But Gifford knew Gail Foster as well as she did. Anyway, Champion needed a project, and when push came to shove, he did have more push with the various government agencies, so he got elected to do the shoving. Fay shot a quick smile in Gifford Champion's direction.

Champion responded with a half-hearted smile that seemed to say, "Gee, thanks."

"You can promise me Mr. Champion," Joey asked, nodding in Gifford's direction, "will speak with the U.S. Attorney on this matter?"

"You have my word that I will encourage Mr. Champion to speak with the U.S. Attorney on this matter," Fay promised.

Joey seemed satisfied. "My fate, or should I say, my son's fate, is in your hands, Faydra. Vinny and his people are at your disposal." He glanced at Vincent. "Vinny, tomorrow mornin', take Faydra around. Let it be known you're announcin' your retirement and Faydra here," he pointed toward Fay, "is bein' groomed to replace you as the Family attorney. Let it be known you are goin' to let her cut her teeth by sendin' her to Phoenix to deal with the BAW people. Call Jake Lanetti, the BAW union boss. Tell him Faydra is our new hired gun. She gets what she wants."

Vincent nodded in agreement.

"Good! Now, I have a concern," Joey told Fay.

Joey had been accommodating, so Fay asked, "What would your concern be?"

His evaluating dark eyes darted back and forth between Pearce and Fay. "If you're gonna play the part, you're gonna have to be the part," he told her.

She was not sure what he had in mind.

Joey continued, "I can tell by the look on your faces I need to explain myself."

Fay acknowledged this with an unsure nod.

"It goes without sayin' Roman Justine is an astute man," Joey explained. "It's gonna take great actin' on your part to fool the man."

"Our people employ the best makeup artists in the world. He won't recognize me, if that's what you're driving at," Fay assured him.

"I'm sure they do. Remember when those makeup artists are done -- if you can recognize yourself in the mirror, your disguise ain't good enough," Joey cautioned.

Fay said, "The FBI warned me about that."

"The deception begins with a good disguise. Justine employs the best P.I. in the country. Don't think for a minute he won't investigate you. Those people will be into your business often and always. Expect your phone and your home to be bugged. You'll need to be in character every second every day," Joey urged.

"I'm prepared for that," Fay confirmed. "You have advice for me?"

"Justine will see through you in a heartbeat. Unless you're what you pretend to be. You need to get dirty," Joey advised. "Walk the walk; talk the talk, as they say." His eyes darted back and forth from Pearce to her and back to Pearce again. "Ya both look like Girl Scouts."

"Get ourselves dirty," Fay confirmed.

"What I'm talkin' about is a look. A way of talkin'. A presence," Joey clarified, before offering an analogy. "If you came into my garage, dressed like an auto mechanic, socket wrench in hand, lookin' for work, I should wanna hire you?"

"Maybe," Fay said.

"Maybe no. I wanna see grease on your hands, under your nails, on your face, in your hair. I need to believe I see an auto mechanic. I wanna smell an auto mechanic. I wanna hear an auto mechanic," Joey insisted.

"I see. I need to have a little larceny in my heart. Right?" Fay asked.

"A little larceny in your heart," Joey repeated. "You gotta look like ya done somethin' wrong. Like you got somethin' goin' on, Faydra, that ya don't want nobody knowin' about."

"A tall order," Fay concluded. "I need to sample the fruit of a forbidden tree, so to speak."

Joey nodded his head. "Yeah. You gotta be like Eve and take a bite from the forbidden apple."

He stood, tightened the knot on his necktie, and walked to a small oil painting on the far wall. He pulled at one edge of the picture frame, exposing a small safe. Joey twisted the combination lock. He opened the door, and his right arm disappeared deep into the safe. Joey withdrew a stack of U.S. currency. He hefted the bills as if weighing them.

He walked over to Vincent and handed the pile to him. "Twenty large," Joey assessed.

Vincent counted the stacks. "Nineteen large," he clarified.

Joey shook his head and smiled. "I gotta be slippin'."

He returned to the safe, withdrew one more banded stack of one-hundred-dollar bills, and tossed it to Vincent.

"Twenty large, boss," Vinny told him this time. Then, the lawyer stood, walked the several paces to where Fay sat, and handed the cash to her.

Oh, I get it. One thousand dollars equaled one large. Quick math told Fay twenty large equaled twenty thousand dollars.

Fay asked, "Twenty thousand dollars. Joey, what am I…?"

Joey returned to his desk and sat. "Call it a retainer," he told her, looking stern. "This is the end of the innocence, *consigliere*."

Fay swallowed hard. The cash, now resting illegally in her lap, represented five violated federal laws to her, plus at least three violated Navy regulations. She had to admit that she had managed to get herself dirty in one fell swoop. She glanced at Gifford Champion. His stoic presence served to reassure her that, maybe, she would be all right with this.

"You not only look like a Girl Scout, but ya talk like a Girl Scout. We gotta work on that," Joey decided. "Rule number one; don't ask questions. You acknowledge, 'Twenty large.' That way, I know you know what I expect to get back from you, when I ask you for it. *Capisce?*"

Don't ask questions? How could she not do that? She was a lawyer…a detective…a woman! She may as well be bound and gagged. "*Capisco*," Fay confirmed. *Talk the talk.*

"Then you say, 'would there be anythin' else,' not a question, a request," Joey instructed.

"Would there be anythin' else," Fay parroted. *Rule one: request, never question.*

"Yeah, I'm glad ya asked, Fay," Joey replied. "I want ya to take a trip to Vegas before a week from Friday. There's a little sportsbook down the street from the Mandalay Bay casino. It's called Willy's."

"Willy's," Fay noted.

"Yeah. Ask for Sally. He's a guy. Tell Sally ya wanna place a wager on the Monday night football game. You bet the Rams to cover the spread and bet the over too," Joey told her.

"A two-teamer."

"Yeah," Joey confirmed with a smile. "Now you're talkin'."

"I bet twenty large. What if I lose?" Fay wanted to know.

Joey's eyebrows arched. "There ya go again with the questions," he warned.

"Sorry. I meant to say, would there be anythin' else?" Fay corrected herself.

He smiled. "There ya go."

"Hmm," Fay said.

"When ya meet with Vinny tomorrow, he'll lay it all out for you. Fair enough?" Joey asked.

"Yeah," Fay replied, smiling at the Guppy.

Pearce had not said one word since the meeting had begun, but now, she opened her mouth to speak. "I have a question."

Joey turned toward her and raised his eyebrows, a signal he had acknowledged her request to speak.

Pearce asked him, "How'd ya get the nickname 'Guppy?'"

Fay knew this could not be good. Pearce had asked the one question she should not have asked. The made men, the soldiers, the *goombahs*, the wise guys—all were hardened men. As hardened and as dangerous as they were, no one had ever had the nerve, or the balls, as Joey would say, to ask that question. She could only hold her breath and hope the killing would be quick and merciful.

Joey sat back in his chair and ran his diamond ring-laden fingers through his long black hair. He placed his fingers on the bridge of his nose and frowned. Fay counted the tense moments as they passed before he finally rocked forward, clasped his hands together, and rested them on his desk.

"You know, Miss Pearce," Joey said, "all my life, I'm surrounded by tough guys. *Goombahs*, think they got brass balls. But I tell you, no one ever asked me about my nickname." He smiled. "'Guppy.' I'm touched. It shows ya care, so I'm gonna tell ya somethin' nobody else knows about me."

Pearce smiled. Fay relaxed.

"My father's name was Jonah Joseph Stumpanato," Joey divulged. "My father honored me by givin' me his name. I became Jonah Joseph Stumpanato Jr. My father's associates knew him as 'Jonah the Whale' Stumpanato. Accordin' to my mother, my father refused to let anyone call me 'junior.' It was a natural tendency for people to do so. But my pop thought it made me sound like a queer, faggot, or somethin'. Anyway, it seemed gay to him, and I had to have a name, so they began callin' me Guppy. You know, my pop was 'the Whale,' a big fish. When it comes to fish, what's smaller than a whale? A guppy, right?"

Pearce snickered and smiled.

It was far beyond Fay to point out to him that a whale was not a fish at all. Marine biology lessons aside, a whale was indeed a big fish this day.

"Nice story," Pearce replied.

As he pointed toward Pearce, Joey turned to

Vincent, "This one's honest. If we hadda few more like her in our ranks, I'd sleep better at night." He turned to Pearce and spoke, "Tomorrow, me and you are goin' around. I'm gonna personally show ya my city. Show ya the museum. They got a German U-boat there you'd like to see. Afterward, we'll go to the Mile and do shoppin'."

Pearce nodded. How could she refuse? Shopping…the magic word. How could any girl refuse an offer to shop?

Although a doubt must have shown on Pearce's face, because Joey said, "Oh, don't worry. I'll be sure everyone knows you're not my *comare*. Tell her, Vinny."

"He means mistress, Miss Pearce."

"Yeah," Joey chuckled. "Nothin' funny or I got your sister here to answer to. Right, Faydra?"

You got that right, bubba. "Sure as shit," Fay said matter-of-factly, hoping there was no jest in her voice. She detested profanity, but you had to swear around these guys. Otherwise, they wouldn't respect you.

Joey looked uncomfortable for an instant but then smiled. "Ok, it's settled," he confirmed. "Miss Pearce and me do the town, and Fay, you hang around with Vinny for a few days. He'll get ya acclimated. Miss Pearce, you have a first name, don't you?"

Oh…oh. Years ago, and in no uncertain terms, Pearce had let it be known she was never to be addressed by her first name. This could get ugly.

"I go by JP, mostly," she told him.

But Joey would not let it rest. "Tit for tat. And the name is…?"

"Jansche," Pearce revealed.

His face showed surprise. "And you don't like this

name?"

Pearce frowned. "I like the name well enough. My mother was an American Indian. Tribal lore told of a woman with great strength and wit. They called her Jansche." She spelled out the name.

"Your mother is not living?" Joey asked.

"She died when I was two years old," Pearce explained, at which Joey frowned. "President Green and his wife adopted me. President Green is my biological father." Pearce smiled. "Anyway, my name isn't pronounced like it's spelled. The J has an H sound, it's pronounced, 'Hanshee.' When I was a kid, the other kids would tease me, as kids tend to do. I'd hear names like Banshee and…well, other not so nice names. Finally, I got fed up with everyone mispronouncin' my name or teasin' me, so I gave up on it. Now you know."

Joey seemed to consider her reasoning and then nodded. "We do have somethin' in common regardin' our names." He smiled. "For what it's worth, I think Jansche is a beautiful name," he said.

Would her nosy sister be safe with Joey? Fay wondered. What if her beloved sister and best friend were to get caught in friendly mob gunplay?

Vinny would later assure her the chance of gunplay, while remote, would result only in the killing and maiming of those actually doing the playing. According to Vincent, lawyers never got shot. There was a code these wise guys had that forbade it. Since anyone would assume Pearce was a lawyer, at least in theory, she would be safe.

Oh my God. What have I gotten us into? Fay thought to herself.

And that was how they ended it. Fay became a mob

lawyer—a thug, like her new pal and mentor, Vincent Astoria.

Chapter 10

While her sister and Joey shopped, Fay, using her alias Faye King, spent her day in the courtroom with her pal Vinny. His client was a young man. Okay, let's call it what it was; the kid was a punk. Anthony Antonelli was Joey's cousin. *Aren't these people all cousins?* Anthony had been arrested for armed robbery.

Fay reviewed Mr. Antonelli's deposition. However, this was not her case; she was observing - killing time - bonding with her buddy, Vinny, the thug lawyer, learning the ropes. It was late in the afternoon. She was minding her own business, yawning, filing her nails, and thinking about what shoes would look great with the red silk dress she had received from dear sweet Mrs. Joe. Fay had her eye on sexy red shoes, but she kept recalling her mother's words: "Only whores and children wear red shoes." Therefore, she was seriously conflicted about the color of the shoes, for the time being.

The victim, Salvador Verona, was on the stand when Fay picked up on something he said that did not sound right to her.

The prosecuting attorney, a green lawyer, "still wet behind the ears," as they said, was prosecuting a slam-dunk. They had videotapes showing Anthony's accomplices robbing the store, with a gun no less. Anthony had been driving the get-away car. But what's the difference whether you're holdin' the firearm or you're holdin' the steerin' wheel? The kid was gonna get time, and the prosecutor was so sure she had a lock on this trial she wouldn't even plea bargain.

Fay could have cared less whether the kid got one year or life. He had, without a doubt, committed the crime. The only mystery remained was how many minutes it would take the jury to deliberate. This might be the only trial where she had not heard the words "I object" uttered even once.

It was Vinny's turn to ask his gratuitous question of the star witness so the court could get home in time for their dinners, their kids' soccer games, mariachi band practices, or whatever it was they needed to do. Fay decided she would do what well could be the dumbest thing she had ever done. Premeditated dumbness was not her style, but she could not let this one go by.

So, Fay asked Vinny, "Mind if I cross-examine?" Besides, this would be a good opportunity for her to practice her thug speech patterns…and her new disguise.

"*Essere il Mio ospite*," he whispered in Italian. "Be my guest."

"*Grazie*." Fay smiled at Vinny, stood, straightened her skirt, smiled at the prosecutor, smiled at the jury, smiled at the judge, and approached the witness. "Good afternoon, Mr. Verona. How ya doin'?" she asked.

"I'm fine, and you?" the victim replied.

"Couldn't be betta, Mr. Verona. I'm Faye King; I'm an associate of Mr. Astoria over there," Fay said, pointing in Vincent's direction. "I'd like to ask a few questions. Do ya mind?"

The witness nodded. The judge, who had been nodding off all afternoon, frowned.

"Mr. Verona, would ya consider yourself to be a

good businessman?" Fay asked.

"I think so," came the reply.

Fay followed this up by asking, "How long have ya been a business owner, sir?"

"I've been at the same location for twenty-three years," Verona explained.

"Twenty-three years. Have ya ever been robbed before?" Fay inquired.

And then it came.

"I object, Your Honor," Miss Wet Behind the Ears barked.

What the heck could she be objecting to?

"Miss King," the sleepy judge said as he motioned for the prosecutor to sit. "Is there going to be a point to your line of questioning?"

Fay turned her head toward His Honor and smiled. "Yes, Your Honor," she promised.

"Overruled," the judge barked and returned to his semi-sleeping state.

Fay turned back to the star witness. "Mr. Verona, have ya ever been robbed before?" she repeated.

"Yes," the victim acknowledged. "Once before."

"You had said earlier you're a good businessman. Correct?"

"That's correct," Verona asserted.

"I'm sure ya are," Fay told him. Her foot was beginning to ache. To take the weight from it, she placed her hand on the front rail of the witness stand for balance and lifted her foot. It felt much better. "Do ya keep your own books, sir?"

The witness sat straight up. There seemed to be a look of pride on his face as he responded, "I've kept my own books from the day I opened for business."

"Do ya file your quarterly business taxes on time?" Fay asked next.

"I do," he boasted. "Never missed a deadline."

"Do ya prepare your own taxes at the end of the year?" Fay asked.

"I prepare and file my own taxes," Verona stated.

Fay remarked, "It's safe to say you have a good handle on the amount of money flowing in and out of your business."

"I track it to the penny, Ms. King," the victim asserted.

"Mr. Verona, do ya ring up every sales transaction on your cash register?"

"All sales are accounted for," Verona confirmed.

"You keep excellent track of your money, and you pay your taxes on time," Fay stated.

"I object," the prosecutor barked. "Your Honor, whether Mr. Verona pays his income taxes on time or not is not an issue here."

"Sustained." His Honor frowned at Faye but said, "Continue."

Not a problem. It was always a plus when your opposition restated your question when asking for an objection. In this instance, Fay had not mentioned income taxes. She had been referring to his business taxes.

"How much money did you say was taken by the robbers, Mr. Verona?" Fay asked him.

"Three-thousand-nine-hundred dollars," Verona informed her.

That was what she thought he had said earlier. If what Anthony had claimed in his deposition was the truth (yet why would a punk ever tell the truth?), Mr.

Verona was wrong about the amount taken from him. If so, she had him.

Fay turned her head toward the jury and asked, "Is that the exact amount that was taken from ya, Mr. Verona?"

"Approximately," he confirmed.

She turned back to face the witness. "Within a few dollars," Fay said.

"That's right."

Fay turned to the judge and placed her weight back on her sore foot, wincing. "Ouch! Your Honor, with the court's permission, I'd like to test the accuracy of Mr. Verona's memory that he was robbed of three-thousand-nine-hundred dollars… and change," she requested.

"You may proceed, Ms. King," the judge said, with a quizzical across his face. "How do you propose to test the accuracy of the witness's memory?"

"Your Honor, if it may please the court, exhibit B," Fay stated. "The cash register allegedly recovered from the trunk of Mr. Antonelli's car will have a transaction history for the day's business. The witness states that all sales are rung up on the register."

The judge watched Fay with curiosity as she talked and limped toward the cash register.

Fay went on, "The subtotal function exhibit B will record actual dollar totals from when Mr. Verona opened for business until the time the cash register was removed from his store."

"Go ahead, Ms. King."

"Thank you, Your Honor." Fay had no idea how to operate the mechanical contraption. She needed help. Mr. Verona would know how to run the total, but by now, he was looking a little "hot under the collar." Fay knew he had figured out what she was up to.

"Mr. Verona," Fay asked him, "from where ya sit, will ya explain to me how to run a subtotal on the register?"

"It's electronic," he pointed out.

"We need to plug it in." Fay looked back at the judge. "Can we find an extension cord or help me move the register close to a wall outlet?"

While a husky bailiff muscled the cash register near a wall outlet, Fay studied the jury. They did not know what she was up to, but she could tell she had aroused their curiosity.

When the bailiff had finished moving and plugging in the cash register, Fay turned to the witness. "Mr. Verona, please instruct me how to run a subtotal on your machine," Fay requested. She did not want to ask him if, in his opinion, the machine was in good working order or if he knew if it had been damaged in the robbery. She hoped this thought had not occurred to the prosecutor.

"Turn the key to the right, to the 'subtotal' position," Verona instructed her. "Next, press the key marked 'total.'"

The prosecutor jumped to her feet and was at Fay's side quicker than a woman on her way to a Neiman-Marcus sale.

Fay followed Mr. Verona's instructions, and lo and behold, a number flashed on the cash register's digital display screen.

Fay feigned poor eyesight by drawing her face closer to the display. Who was she kidding? She did have poor vision.

As she squinted, Fay asked the prosecutor, "What's that say, Ms. Scanlan?"

"Two-thousand-nine-hundred dollars and thirty-nine cents," Prosecuting Attorney Scanlan replied.

"Two-thousand-nine-hundred dollars and thirty-nine cents," Fay repeated to the jury. She turned and limped back toward the now pale witness. "I believe you stated 'approximately' three-thousand-nine-hundred, Mr. Verona," she recalled. "Based on what Ms. Scanlan noted, that's a stretch, sir."

Fay turned to the judge. "I've no other questions, Your Honor," she told him, then limped back to her chair next to Vinny and sat. Her foot was about to fall off. She pawed through her purse, searching for a painkiller.

Earlier, Fay had heard Sal Verona state that he had been robbed of almost four thousand dollars. She reasoned he had sensed an opportunity to profit from his misfortune by overstating the loss to his insurance carrier. Not thinking anyone would believe a thug over him regarding his loss, he could make a few extra bucks off his insurance company. The guy was as big a crook as the crooks who had robbed him.

Fay poured water from the decanter provided by the court. Popping a painkiller into her mouth, she washed it down and then said to Vinny, in her best thug lawyer English, "You can close. I gotta get over to that Miracle Mile, or Magnificent Mile, or whatever the hell they call that shoppin' place, and get me some shoes. Wanna meet later for dinner?"

"Yeah. And you can tell me what happened here," Vinny replied. "You almost had the star witness impeach himself."

If Fay's hunch was correct, the jury would be so irritated with Sal Verona for attempting to cheat the IRS and his insurance company that they would vote to acquit. It could happen. Juries had been known to do strange things.

"No. You tell me," Fay said as she patted him on the shoulder. "You got a ringside seat for the finale." She leaned over and whispered in his ear, "Wanna bet Anthony walks?"

"Loser buys dinner," he whispered back. "Besides, I need to tell you about Roman Justine before you leave town."

"Okay. Deal. I hope your credit card is paid up, baby-cakes. I eat expensive," Fay told him. "Oh… and, Vinny," she whispered, glancing at his grease-ball of a client, Anthony, "tell that little shit to wipe that smirk off his face."

Fay stood and left the courtroom.

****

Virgil Gus finished packing and closed his backpack. He was about to call it a day when he heard his cell phone chiming. He had placed the phone inside his backpack and cursed under his breath while he fumbled with the pack.

Finally, Virgil found the source of his irritation. He clicked on the phone, stating, "Gus."

The call was from Lonny Boyd. "The missing skiff has been located and secured in the boathouse at Choctaw Bay Marina," Lonny informed him.

"We'll be there in fifteen," Gus told the detective.

Lonny met Sheriff Gus and Deputy Doug in the parking lot at the marina. Together, the three men proceeded to the boathouse. The manager met them at the entrance.

On spotting the skiff, Virgil said to his deputy, "We'll want to get a truck over here to haul the boat back to the county evidence storage compound. And get the crime scene investigators here."

"Right," he acknowledged and reached for his radiophone.

Doug completed his calls to the county motor pool and the CSI unit, reporting that everyone concerned had been dispatched.

The marina manager stood aside as the three cops scanned both the skiff's interior and exterior for any visible evidence. Virgil would leave it to the Crime Scene Investigation Unit to conduct the detailed investigation, exploring the boat for microscopic evidence and latent fingerprints.

****

The shopping district in downtown Chicago was called the Magnificent Mile, not the Miracle Mile. Fay found this out when she told her cab driver that she wanted to go to the Miracle Mile.

He asked her if she was kidding. "Do you want me to take you to Hollywood?" he asked skeptically.

Imagine, the Miracle Mile was in Hollywood! What Fay wanted was located on upper Michigan Avenue and was called the Magnificent Mile, even though it was more than one mile long, due to its large concentration of Chicago landmarks and shops. She believed they called a long mile like that "a country mile."

But Fay did find those shoes she was looking for at Saks "just slap down a week's pay, and you're out the door with the shoes of your dreams" Fifth Avenue.

There were far too many interesting-looking restaurants along the country mile for Fay to pass up. Serious shopping could give one an appetite.

So, she called Vinny. "Get your butt down here,"

Fay told him. "I'm hungry, and my foot is so sore it feels like it's gonna fall off. You got one hour."

Contrary to her mother's remembered advice, Fay bought the red shoes.

Fay and Vinny ate at a place called, NoMi, located in Park Hyatt, Chicago. NoMi served upscale French cuisine. The seventh-floor restaurant boasted a view of Michigan Avenue and the lake. Because the evening was warm, they opted to dine on the terrace. According to Vincent, Tony Chi, whoever he was, had designed the entire restaurant, including the one hundred twenty-seat main dining room.

Chef Sandro Gamba had put together an original menu, including sushi/sashimi flown in daily and *Carnaroli risotto*, Gamba's signature dish, featuring wild mushrooms, prosciutto, and fresh parsley. Fay believed she would do well as a restaurant critic. She loved to dine out, so this was a real treat for her.

Their waitperson told them that for breakfast, Gamba served a monster meal inspired by those prepared by his grandmother in France: authentic hot chocolate, baguette, fruit tart brioche, and apple compote.

Frickin' French. Why aren't they fat like us Americans? Fay wondered.

After dinner, the two thug lawyers planned to meet Joey, Pearce, and Mrs. Stumpanato, thank God, in the adjoining lounge. It featured a wenge wood bar, Bolivian rosewood floors, and backless eel skin stools. Fay did not know what wenge wood was, but she suspected it was not a bar made from mispronounced chinaware. Vincent was kind enough to explain wenge wood was used in African ceremonial masks.

The meal was costly. Fortunately for Fay, the jury

had let the little greaseball walk – had acquitted him. So, Vinny had to spring for dinner.

Fay had gotten a punk off the hook, yet she reasoned the smart-assed little jerk would be back in court within the month, which meant he would be "in the joint" by year's end. Anthony's acquittal had deferred the inevitable, while at the same time, she had ingratiated herself to the mob.

During the dinner, Vinny handed her an envelope. Fay should have been paying attention but was not. She took the envelope from him, opened it, and looked inside. It contained many crisp one-hundred-dollar bills.

She glanced at Vinny. She had learned not to ask questions. "Five large," Fay stated.

Vinny provided the answer to her unasked question by saying, "Mr. Antonelli, Anthony's father, sends you his gratitude."

This was not the time or the place for her to argue the point with him. There were laws - laws she had not yet already broken - forbidding her, a government employee, from accepting cash or a gift for services rendered from anyone, much less a mobster like Mr. Antonelli. Fay smiled as she discreetly slipped the envelope into her purse. *What're another ten years in Leavenworth?* She would have to figure out what to do about it later.

"Joey asked me to warn you about Roman Justine," Vinny said next.

Fay sipped at her wine and then placed the glass back on the table. "One of the nation's ten wealthiest men and one of the top celebrity magazine's ten sexiest males…years two thousand and seventeen and two thousand and eighteen…Yale Law…*Skull and*

Bones membership, with ties to the Trilateral Commission and the Bilderbergers," she reported, relaying all the intel she had gotten on the man. "His middle name is Cassius, after his mother's father. His mother's maiden name was Creston. He broke his arm while skiing, age twelve. He is six feet three inches tall. He weighs two hundred and three pounds… brown eyes, bald, scar on his left hand…Armani suits, gray tones preferred…Gucci shoes. He prefers not to wear cologne." She smiled. "What did I leave out?"

The flame from the flickering table candle twinkled in Vincent's eyes as he quizzically gazed at her but said nothing.

"What?" Fay asked him.

"Oh… nothing. I was waiting for you to yawn after that dissertation," he teased.

Fay laughed. "Come on. I have to know this stuff, so enlighten me. What did I leave out?"

"You left out what Joey wanted me to warn you about," Vinny told her.

"Which was?" Fay prompted.

"That Roman Justine's sexual behavior would make the Marquis de Sade look like a boy scout."

Fay leveled her gaze at Vincent, leaning forward on the table on her folded arms. In a deep voice, she said, *"Marques de Sade? Le dites."*

"You speak French as well?" he asked, surprised.

"Oui. I studied languages when I was younger. I had visions of becoming a diplomat," she explained. "Now, tell me about Justine."

"His sexual interest is varied," Vinny divulged.

"Yeah?" Fay whispered. "How so?"

"Men, women, bondage, porn, kink, sadism,

masochism, rape." Vinny shifted in his chair. "He's been negotiating to acquire the severed heads of mass murderers Jeffery Dahmer and John Wayne Gacy."

"What do you mean? Who cut off their heads? And don't you dare tell me it was the Queen of Hearts," Fay exclaimed.

Vinny chuckled. "The feds. It was reasoned that science could determine what made them tick if they analyzed their brains."

"Oh…yuck, Vincent." Fay glanced at her dinner plate. "I'm still eating. That's totally sick," she protested, spearing her filet minion with her fork. "Roman, the puke, is a headhunter?"

Vinny nodded and watched her saw off a bite-size piece of steak with her steak knife. "I know. The fact remains that Roman Justine is not one to turn your back on. He has an extensive collection of shrunken heads, even a piece of Hitler's skull. He has several slices of Albert Einstein's brain."

Diners sitting at the table to the left of Fay and Vincent craned their necks at the sound of the clank when Fay dropped her knife and fork. Her jaw dropped as she sat back with an incredulous look on her face.

"No…frickin …way!" Fay gasped.

Vinny nodded.

"Where'd he get all this stuff?" Fay asked.

"The little heads came from a tribe in the Amazon. The piece of Hitler's skull came from his Russian oligarch business pals, and the slice of Al's brain came from a doctor in New Jersey who keeps the whole brain in his basement," Vinny explained.

"Justine is a sexual predator as well," Fay concluded.

"Oh, he likes his hos."

Fay snickered. "According to what you say about Justine's sexual preferences, the man has a hard time keeping his hose in his pants."

Vincent smiled. "No. Not his hose. Hos…as in whores and hookers."

Fay's face brightened. "Oh…dem kinda hos. He's got a craving for the ladies of the evening," she said.

Vinny nodded. "He takes *leuprolide* to manage his sex drive. But I think he has learned how to monitor his intake, leaving an edge…bringing him to almost normal."

"I didn't know that," Fay said.

"I know you didn't know. Hence the warning," Vinny replied.

"Tell Joey thanks…I guess?"

Vinny went on. "Roman Justine hates women, he hates Joey Stumpanato, and he will despise you as well." He stated the obvious. "You're a woman, and you work for Joey. Watch out."

Fay's gaze drifted from Vincent's warm gray eyes downward to her dinner. "Looks like I'm going to have to send my dinner back for a reheat," she said.

I'm a thug lawyer now.

Needless to say, Vincent and Joey had been blown away by Fay. Later that evening, she overheard Joey tell Vincent that she had kept the kid out of the joint. Every goombah west of Philly would want her to defend them in court now.

Well, I've got one word for them, Fay thought. *No-friggin'-way.*

Chapter 11

Sheriff Gus reviewed the crime lab's fishing skiff photos. *What would drive anyone to murder Alvin Joe?* he wondered.

Although the murderer had used a sophisticated method, he had not taken great care to hide his tracks. Whoever the murderer was, both the tumbler and the skiff had his fingerprints on them.

Detective Boyd sat across from the Sheriff's desk, watching him shuffle through the photos. "What are you thinking, Virgil?" he asked his boss.

"Have you ever had a case where you had this much evidence and no motive for the crime?" Virgil responded.

"Can't say I have."

"A murder is usually committed for a few reasons," Virgil recounted, "lust, greed, passion, or jealousy."

"Alvin Joe was not having an affair, and he had no known enemies," Lonny said. "That eliminates the lust, jealousy, and passion motives."

"What about greed?" Virgil asked.

"We looked at his bank accounts. Nothing unusual, no large cash deposits or pay-outs…nothing unusual about them at all."

"What about off-shore accounts?"

"We couldn't find any, Virgil," Doug informed him. "Why? You think he might have been selling military secrets to the North Koreans, Iranians, or the Chinese?"

"Could be. But from what I know about Alvin Joe, he didn't seem like the type. But then again, you never know."

****

"Here's my shopping list," Fay said, handing it across their hotel coffee shop's breakfast table to Gifford Champion.

He took the list and scanned it. "Two luxury sport utility vehicles, a suite at the Royal Palms Resort and Spa, dresses, business suits, and jewelry, an American Bank checking account—a two hundred fifty-thousand balance," he read aloud, before emitting a low whistle. "The business jet and the twenty thousand dollars in cash won't be a problem."

Gifford tossed her list on the table, looked at Fay, and grinned. "And what would you like for Christmas, Mrs. Gates?"

A sly grin formed on Fay's lips. "I need to appear prosperous." She lowered her voice. In her best Joey Stumpanado impression, she said, "Besides, what self respectin' mob lawyer would be caught dead lookin' anythin' but well-to-do?"

"Roman Justine's financial equal?" Champion teased.

"Hardly. He's one of the richest men in America," Fay replied. "I have to appear affluent enough to get his attention."

Gifford surveyed the list again. "I'll call the DEA. We can get your toys from their drug seizures inventory. We'll have the vehicles licensed in Arizona and the jet licensed in Canada. Victoria, B.C. probably."

"I'll see if Bart Hay is available, Gifford," Fay said.

"Your Secret Service pilot boyfriend?"

"Yes, sir. None other," she confirmed. "When we locate the jet, we'll have JP hook up with Bart. They can fly the jet to Phoenix."

"I'll get the guys at Langley working on establishing new identities for both you and JP. Law degree and grade transcripts from the University of Virginia Law School for you. Bar association, a few club memberships, Illinois State driver's licenses, a luxury condo in Oakbrook," Gifford listed. "Anything else?"

"No, sir. That should do it," Fay replied. "What time does our flight to Phoenix leave tomorrow?"

"Out of O'Hare at 06:30."

Fay noted the time. "Oh-yawn-thirty it is. Perfect."

****

"Motive and opportunity," Virgil Gus said to no one in particular. "Other than Mrs. Joe, who had the opportunity to spike Alvin Joe's drink with *GHB*?"

Detective Lonny Boyd scratched his head. "Everyone, including Alvin Joe, had an opportunity to spike his punch," he observed.

Virgil arched his eyebrows. "A suicide?"

"Possibly, but not likely," Doug decided. "The area surrounding the pool is wide open. A golfer, boater, neighbor…anyone could gain access to the Joes' swimming pool."

"How'd your interviews with the neighbors go, Lonny?" the Sheriff asked.

"Nothing. No one saw anything, Virgil. No domestic complaints. According to the neighbors, other than the dogs, the Joes were as quiet as quiet could be."

"Your report said Mrs. Joe's prints were not found on any chemical products?" Virgil asked.

"We found the housekeeper's prints on the drain cleaner and the floor stripper," Lonny stated. "The deceased's prints were found on a can of engine degreaser."

"The housekeeper," Virgil asked, "what's her name again?"

"Callie, Virgil."

"Where was she on the night Mr. Joe disappeared?"

"She checks out," Doug said. "She was at the dog races with her sister."

"We're back to the boat." Virgil picked up the photos of the skiff. He rubbed his chin with his right hand and frowned. "Hmm," he rumbled.

"Whatcha thinkin'?" Doug wanted to know.

Virgil eased back in his chair. "How many prints did CSI lift from the skiff, Lonny?"

"Twenty-seven, including one ear print. They also found mud and grass wedged in the bow. It matched with the grass in front of Joe's place. We're running checks on each set," Doug assured his boss. "As you know, we have one set matching those we lifted from the tumbler."

"Let me know the minute you come up with somethin'," Virgil ordered, dropping the photos onto his desk. "It's clear the guy who rented the boat visited the Joes' home. We found both the victim and the tumbler in the river. We are safe in presumin' the guy who rented the skiff is our perp. The boat was discovered how far away from the marina, Lonny?"

"About a hundred yards up-river from the Fish Market."

"On the opposite side of the river from the Citrus Tree Country Club."

"That's right," Doug confirmed.

Virgil leaned forward in his chair. Placing his elbows on his desk, he asked, "Lonny, tell me. How'd our fisherman get to the marina to rent the boat? How'd he get from the boat to wherever it was he was goin' after he ditched the boat?"

"An accomplice drove him to the marina then picked him up at a preplanned location near where he later ditched the boat?" Doug speculated.

"Or?"

There was silence.

Then, Lonny reported, "We found twenty-seven prints on the boat. An accomplice, I think. He delivered it to a preset location between the marina and the Joes' home. Two people traveled to the scene, drugged Alvin Joe, carried him to the river. They tossed both him and the tumbler into the river, hid the boat near the Fish Market, and drove away in a car they had stashed near the place where they left the boat."

"Yep. That's kinda what I was thinkin'," Virgil said. "Did the marina manager take a deposit for the skiff?"

"The guy paid cash."

"Uh-huh." The Sheriff rocked back in his chair. He considered Lonny for a moment, before asking, "Did you get a chance to meet Miss Faydra Green?"

"The President's daughter?" Doug asked.

"Former President's daughter."

"No," Lonny replied. "Dang, Virg. The woman is a looker, I hear. I'm damn right sorry I missed that. Why?"

"No reason," Virgil answered. "I got a phone call from Miss Faydra Green last night. We chatted for a spell. To be honest, it was more personal than business."

Lonny grinned and slapped his knee. "You old dog, you."

Virgil grinned as well. "Yeah, she's a handsome woman, alright. Tell you what, though. She's a smart looker."

"How so?"

"She's quick, Lonny. Quick on the uptake, so to speak. She was about a day ahead of me on figurin' out Alvin Joe was murdered," Virgil marveled. "And she went right to his body."

"That was amazing. You had a chat last night. Anything to offer on the case?"

"Nothin' new. Faydra wanted to see how things were goin'… with the case, that is. But it's what she said about them dogs that's got my wheels to turnin' right now," Virgil admitted.

"Those frickin' dogs." Lonny shook his head. "They ought to come up with a way to shut them damn mutts up."

Virgil shook his head from side to side. He looked at Lonny. "I got me a will and last testament now."

Lonny's eyes brightened. "How so?" he asked.

"Oh, I happened to mention to Miss Faydra I didn't have no family or nothin'. And as a result, I'd not gotten 'round to gettin' up a will. Why, I'm here to tell ya, she'd like to come unglued on me. Next thing I know, I got one emailed to me… first thing this mornin'. Now I got me a will," the Sheriff recounted.

"Who'd you leave your millions to, Virg?"

"Charity."

"She a hooker?" Doug teased.

Virgil laughed. "Yeah. Right. The only hookers I know are the ones you guys arrest and haul in here from down on Benton Street." His voice took on a serious tone. "Miss Faydra is the executor of my estate. I guess

I got me a lawyer too, huh?"

"Yeah. I reckon you got that and more." Lonny Boyd shook his head. "You gotta be careful with women," he warned his boss. "They's sneaky. Why, one day, you think you got yourself a lawyer. The next day, you wake up, and you got a toothbrush in a cup by your sink, feminine products under your sink, and a bra hanging in your shower."

Virgil listened.

"Then," Lonny went on, "'fore you know it, you're givin' her your credit card, and you're wagging your head up and down to everythin' she says. All of a sudden—boom—you wake up one mornin' and find out you're married, and there ain't no hope for you!"

Virgil smiled. "You're married. Is that how it happened?" he quipped.

"Yeah. Kinda."

Virgil chuckled. "Your perspective on matrimony seems twisted to me, lad. Anyway, I'm back to motive, Lonny," he said, steering the conversation back on course. "The motive of greed is still on the table. The one valuable thing Alvin Joe possessed was the top-secret project he stored on his computer. Correct?"

Lonny nodded. "It's worth millions to the right people."

"Exactly, which eliminates the Koreans and the Chinese," Virgil concluded.

Lonny considered for a moment. "Or any competitor who is developing the BASS project."

"In other words," Virgil said, "industrial espionage."

"That possibility exists. Whoever killed Alvin Joe was either unaware of the project or didn't care about it."

"If our perp was unaware the project existed," Virgil surmised, "we are back to no motive. If the perp knew the project existed and knew its potential value but chose not to steal it, the project itself had no value to the killer. Which leaves?"

Lonny exclaimed, "Crap, Virgil!" and sat back in his chair with a satisfied look on his face. "Damn, boy! Looks like we got ourselves a motive!"

Chapter 12

The next day, Phoenix, Arizona
"What is he up to, Gifford?"
"They're talking," Gifford observed through a pair of small binoculars.

Fay and Gifford, seated in an SUV, were in surveillance spy mode.

Under her breath, Fay urged, "Come on, man, get with it."

"Do I detect impatience in your voice, Commander?"

"Yeah." Fay fanned her face with a sports magazine. "Surveillance sucks. And it's hotter than Sharon den Adel in a mini."

"Who?" Gifford asked.

"Do a search on it, bro."

"Thanks. It makes one wonder how the feds do this day in and day out," Gifford observed.

"It's this sitting, this watching, this god-awful sweltering heat that builds those mighty donut bellies." Fay chuckled. "Speaking of donuts, I could use some food. How about you, sir?"

Gifford offered, "How does Chinese sound?"

"Anything will do. I'm famished," Fay replied, continuing to fan her face.

"Mercy, it's hot! About one-ten!" Gifford exclaimed. He tapped at his cell phone. "Sharon den who?"

Fay pointed toward the car's dashboard. "More air," she ordered. "And it's Adel."

Gifford responded by flicking the air conditioner power setting to its highest level. Then, he went back to his cell. "Oh. My! Hello!"

"Sharon den Adel?"

"All of her. And then some," Gifford observed.

As the car's heat was replaced with cooler air, they continued to watch while a man attempted to charm the mini-skirt off one of Phoenix's many rent-a-chicks.

"Don Valley. Devoted husband, AmeriCon CEO, pillar of the community," Fay said, describing the man they were surveilling. "Help me, sir, what have I left out?"

"Womanizer," Gifford added. "What's his bimbo count?"

"This week? I think this is hooker number three in the last four days. So far, we have Valley on three counts of first-degree tackiness. I think we're going to need to have more on him."

"What Mrs. Valley would say if she knew her husband was blowing, excuse the pun, the milk money on hookers?" Gifford asked.

"No question." Fay snapped another photograph. "She'd be pissed. But I don't think us confronting Don Valley with photos and threatening to expose him to his wife will be a compelling enough reason for him to want to cooperate with us."

"Valley appears to be our boy, all right," Gifford corroborated. "But I agree with you; we need more."

Fay sighed and smiled. "Chinese food, huh? Any recommendations?"

"I know a great restaurant, not too far from here. It's called Bo-ling," Gifford suggested.

"Bowling?" Fay asked, amused.

"Sounds like bowling," Gifford acknowledged. "I decided I liked the place when the owners converted a neon sign from an old bowling alley, blacked out the 'w,' and hung the sign over the entrance."

Fay laughed. "No shhh-ah…how quaint!"

"The last time I dined there, the menu boasted 'Sweat and Sour Children.'" Gifford chuckled.

Fay laughed again. "A typo? I know I'm going to like your restaurant." With that, she snapped another photo. "Let's go."

As Fay and Gifford sped away, she kept her gaze on the man conversing with the woman through the window of the white Cadillac. Don Valley was apparently trying to determine if his latest conquest might not be a cop. "Ima Hooker" was likely evaluating how many minutes of downtime Don John Valley would cost her.

"Tacky bastard," Fay muttered.

Fay closed her eyes and rested her head on the passenger seatback. When next she reopened them, they had arrived at Bo-ling.

Her cell phone chirped.

Fay answered her phone with a "Hey!" She knew who was calling: JP, from the airport.

Their conversation was brief.

When the call was over, Fay informed Gifford, "Our eagles have landed." She watched the flickering Bo-ling sign. "Dad came with them."

Gifford did not respond.

"I know he wants to help, and I'm sure he will be accommodating. I don't want him to draw attention to me or our operation," Fay continued.

"Go easy on your dad, Faydra," Gifford suggested. "He managed to run the most powerful nation on earth for eight successful years, without screwing anything up. He is trusted with national secrets no one will ever know but he and a select few. I think he will be able to pull strings for us that we might have had a difficult time with."

"You're right. Maybe I am being too protective," Fay acknowledged. "Thank you." She reached across the seat to pat Gifford's forearm. "His health is failing," she went on, sighing. "I'm looking forward to seeing him, and yet I wish it were under different circumstances. This whole GFA thing has been a strain on us all."

"The Galaxy Friendship Association is a major reason we have the excessive defense spending and cost over-runs the taxpayers have been suffering over these past five years. For America's sake, we need to put Roman Justine and the GFA out of business," Gifford declared.

Fay glanced again at the flickering red neon Bo-ling sign. The whole idea behind the sign brought a smile to her face.

"We can sit here all night worrying about cost overruns and wasted tax dollars, or we can go inside and worry about calorie overruns and expanding waistlines," Fay stated. "Your call."

Gifford open the car's door. "I've never thought of Chinese food as fattening."

****

As he spoke on his cell phone to Virgil, Deputy Doug sounded excited. "Sheriff. Y'all'd better get on down to the morgue. We have our fisherman!" he exclaimed.

"You there now, Doug?" Virgil asked.

"Me and Lonny's here," the Deputy confirmed. "Come on down. We're on to somethin'."

Three minutes later, Sheriff Gus was pushing through the double doors leading into the county morgue. Doug, Lonny, and Sue Nguyen stood next to a stainless-steel gurney. On the gurney lay a body.

"This is the guy who rented the skiff?" Virgil asked them.

"We found our fisherman, Virgil," Lonny Boyd confirmed, pointing to the corpse.

"No kiddin'?"

"Yup." Lonny nodded. "Same guy. He matches the composite sketch. The marina manager is on his way over to give us a positive, but his prints match a set we lifted from the skiff."

"What about the tumbler?" Virgil asked, moving closer to the gurney.

"Same thing."

Virgil surveyed the corpse from head to toe. His gaze settled on Dr. Sue Nguyen. "Who, why, when, and where?" he asked the ME.

Sue's solemn face brightened. "That's what I like about you, Sheriff. You're direct and to the point." She took several steps away from the corpse, retrieved a clipboard from a nearby table, and returned. After studying a report, she looked up at Virgil and asked, "You want the condensed version?"

He nodded. "Always."

"Ronald Reagan Stanton…age forty-five…drowned 10:00 P.M. on the same night Alvin Joe died, give or take an hour," Sue reported. "Found by two fishermen in the

Sawsashaw River about two hundred yards from where Alvin Joe's body was found."

"Thanks, Sue." Virgil shifted his attention to Lonny Boyd. "Fill in the blanks."

"Other than his jingoistic name, Stanton was a transient," the Deputy explained. "One prior. Nothing more than car prowling." He offered Virgil a large evidence envelope that he had been holding in his left hand. "Here's his personal effects."

Virgil accepted the envelope as his searching gaze darted around the room.

"Here," Sue said, offering him latex gloves.

After slipping his large hands into the gloves, Virgil opened the envelope and peered at the contents inside. He glanced back at Lonny. "That's it?" he asked, surprised.

Lonny nodded. "Just the wallet, Sheriff." He hesitated. "It's what's inside the wallet that will pop your cork."

****

The evening dinner crowd at Bo-ling Chinese Restaurant was small. Five tables were occupied by what appeared to Fay to be Phoenix's affluent youth. She and Gifford were shown to a table situated adjacent to a sizeable tropical fish aquarium. Fay sat facing the aquarium and was soon mesmerized by its tranquil ambiance.

They sat in silence until the waitperson arrived seeking their drink orders.

"Do you have iced tea?" Fay asked, shifting her gaze from the antics of a small bright orange and white stripe clownfish to the waiter.

"No. I'm sorry," the waiter apologized. "We do have

cola. Would that be okay?"

"How about a whiskey and cola?" Fay asked.

The waitperson smiled and noted her order on a small order pad. Then she turned to Gifford Champion. "And for you, sir?"

"Same for me."

The waitperson smiled, bowed, and left the table.

"Where are you?" Gifford asked, looking at Fay. "You seem to be a thousand miles away."

"I'm sorry, Gifford. I was thinking about when we first met."

"Seoul, Korea. You were angry at me when you discovered I was writing a story about you and not about the sinking of the U.S.S. *Jonathan Carr*, as I had led you to believe," he reminisced.

"I thought you'd betrayed me. I was mad…and hurt," Fay admitted.

Gifford's gaze shifted from Fay's eyes to her lips and then back to her eyes. "The image of you, standing there, your white dress uniform amplifying the crimson shade of your face…your lower lip was quivering, and all the time, you were trying so hard not to cry. Or throw something at me. That single image will forever be etched in my memory. I felt like an ass. I was ready to trash the entire story in exchange for a smile and your friendship," he divulged.

Fay smiled. "I'm glad we're friends, Gifford. And thank you for volunteering for this op."

"No. Thank you, Commander," he asserted. "At the time, I knew I had the right partner for the job, and I still do."

"Speaking of Korea," Fay said, "from time to time, I think about our dear friends Colonel Jangho Kim and

President Lee Ka Eun."

"You may have heard the annual APEC is going to be held in Aspen, Colorado next month? President Lee Ka Eun will be attending, as will all the twenty-one-member nation heads of state," Gifford offered.

"I would imagine her attaché Jangho would accompany her?" Fay guessed.

"Do you think Kim could be useful to us?"

"At the moment, no," Fay replied. "But I do have him on my mind."

The waitperson returned to their table with their drinks, ready for the dinner orders.

Fay had not yet looked at the menu, so she told Gifford, "Order for me. This desert heat seems to have warped my brain."

Gifford looked through the menu before placing his order in Mandarin. The waitress was delighted to hear her native tongue spoken by an American, and she scribbled down Clifford's order. She bowed once more and walked into the kitchen through the double swinging doors.

"How many languages do you speak again?" Fay asked him.

"Seven."

"Doesn't surprise me." Gifford Champion was a whiz kid, in Fay's opinion.

"I'm a creation of years of CIA-sponsored language schools, I'm afraid," Gifford said.

"Mandarin clearly being one of them," Fay replied.

"Plus two Chinese dialects, Korean, Japanese, and Russian," Gifford revealed.

Fay whispered, "I'd imagine those are useful for a spook to have at his command."

"Very helpful," he whispered back.

"Et vous parlez Français aussi bien," Fay replied. *("And you speak French as well.")*

Gifford smiled. "*Oui*. Oh, you speak French too!"

"*Oui*," Fay confirmed, before holding up her glass for a toast. "Voici à vous mon ami." *("Here's to you, my friend.")*

"And to you." Gifford clicked his glass against hers, completing the toast.

Soon their food arrived, delivered by the waitperson and a matronly woman. More bowing, smiling, and Mandarin-speaking ensued.

In English, Gifford said to Fay, "Faydra, this is Mrs. Mu-Wong, Bo-ling's owner."

Then, Gifford spoke to Mrs. Mu-Wong in Mandarin.

In English, Mrs. Mu-Wong said to Fay, "I am honored to meet you, Fay Green, honorable daughter of the great man, William Green." Mrs. Mu-Wong bowed again.

Fay smiled, drew her hands into the Anjali Mudra position near her face, and returned the bow. As a president's daughter, she knew diplomacy and protocol well. "The honor is mine, Mrs. Mu-Wong," she replied. "You have an exquisite restaurant. I am looking forward to your hospitality."

Mrs. Mu-Wong answered, "The dinner is my pleasure for my honored guests to enjoy this evening." She smiled, bowed, and slipped away from the table.

Gifford must have read the concerned look on Fay's face. "Don't worry," he assured her. "We'll leave our waitperson a tip equivalent to the dinner."

"And we will send Mrs. Mu-Wong roses first thing in the morning." Fay flashed him a smile. "Great choice.

I needed this."

Concern came to Gifford's face. "How's your foot?" he asked.

Fay considered her foot. "It feels fine. I hardly notice it anymore. Thanks for asking."

He studied her for a moment, and then asked, "What's bothering you?"

Fay offered him a weak smile. She sighed. "A lot is bothering me," she divulged. "But I'm back to thinking about our pal Sussy Baka."

"Sussy Baka?" Gifford repeated, confused. "Yeah, yeah, yeah, I know, do a search on it."

"It's from a videogame," Fay explained. "The term 'sussy' describes a shifty or suspicious character."

"Oh! That Baka! Okay. now I've caught up with you!" Gifford exclaimed. "You mean regarding his insatiable appetite for the hos?"

"Yeah. I have a hunch there is more to this than meets the eye," Fay relayed. She sighed again. "Oh well, that is his business, I guess."

She sat back with her drink in her hand and took a long sip. She allowed herself to relax and unwind. But the brief interlude did not last long.

Her eyes widened. "Ho!" Fay gasped. "The ho!"

"Ho ho what, Santa?" Gifford quipped.

"No. The hos. The hookers," Fay clarified. "Vinny Astoria told me Justine has a voracious appetite for prostitutes." She sat up. "Valley's pimpin' for Justine!"

"Why would the CEO of one of the largest defense contractors in the nation pimp for one of the wealthiest men in the country?" Gifford asked skeptically.

"Recall what Joey Stumpanato told us," Fay instructed him. "Justine has gotten Valley dirty by having him commit a felony. Made him taste fruit of the forbidden tree, so to speak. He will hold this over Valley's head, like the Sword of Damocles."

"He's got Valley by the short hairs," Gifford observed, sipping his drink while considering what she had said.

Fay smiled and nodded. "Exactly."

"When Justine asks Valley for more, Valley will discover he's already committed several felonies," Gifford guessed. "To put it another way, it's a clever blackmail."

"Justine has a razor-sharp mind," Fay realized.

"Does that surprise you, Fay?" Gifford asked drily. "He *was* an attorney."

Chapter 13

Monday morning, GFA conference room, Phoenix, Arizona

The surveillance photos showing mob lawyer Faye King appeared on the projection screen in the Galaxy Friendship Association's Phoenix, Arizona conference room, as Roman Justine watched with curiosity. Don Valley, PI Lou Grossman, and Carmen Gray, GFA attorney, were in the audience.

Grossman remarked, "She's a good-looking whore. What would she bring in the Russian market?" He pressed a button on the projector's remote control.

"Freeze it there," Roman Justine said.

Grossman stopped the projection on Faye King emerging from Joey Stumpanato's Chicago office's entry doors.

"Now, give me a zoom on her face," Justine commanded.

An image of Faye King's face filled the screen. Justine studied her face.

"Anybody recognize her?" he asked.

All in the room remained silent.

"Huh," Justine grunted. "I agree. Joey's bitch is a good-looking woman. Mousy brown hair…brown eyes…she could stand to wear a little make-up though." He nodded toward Grossman. "Continue."

The picture on the screen changed as Grossman continued speaking. "We dug into King's past but found several dead ends."

"What do you mean?" Justine asked.

"King graduated from University of Virginia Law School, the bottom of her class," Grossman explained. "Grade transcripts check out. Born Makenna Faye Kingman in Montreal."

"Her age?"

"Thirty-eight, Mr. Justine," Grossman answered.

Justine smiled. "Go on."

"Ms. Kingman migrated to Seattle when she was twenty years old and worked as a flight attendant for Aero Pacific Airlines for three years. She was fired for decking a male passenger."

"No shit!" Justine exclaimed. "How'd that happen?"

"He allegedly grabbed one of her boobs, and she clocked him. According to our sources, the man was carried off the plane on a stretcher. The man filed a lawsuit against Aero Pacific, the parties reached an out-of-court settlement, and the airline fired her," Grossman stated. "Kingman went to college after changing her name from Kingman to King. She went on to law school after that."

"You said she graduated at the bottom of her class?" Justine clarified.

Lou Grossman glanced at his notes. "That's right. Dead last. She was on academic probation several times." He leafed through his notes, before then reporting, "Her IQ is one-thirty-seven."

"It would be as daunting to graduate last in your law class as it would be to graduate first," Justine lamented. "She is a smart lady. A woman who would go out of her way to keep a low profile, unless she sandbagged on her IQ tests as well. The Guppy would not have allied himself with her otherwise," he concluded. "Did you learn anything else about Joey's gunslinger?"

"Her first and only job as a lawyer, before going to work for Joey Stumpanato, was with the law firm Barrymore, Rothschild, and Gain, in Falls Church, Virginia," Grossman relayed.

"I know the firm. They are primarily government litigates."

Lou Grossman said, "Like law school, King kept a low profile at Barrymore. Until she was assigned to the legal team representing the government in the *U.S. Navy v. Bowman-California Aerospace* antitrust case."

"Bowman-California lost the case," Justine recollected. "A fifty million dollar fine, restitution, and one year all expenses paid at Club Fed for its chief executive. I recall the case; the decision had financial ramifications for our GFA members as well. When the ruling came down, Bowman-California's stock dropped twenty-two percent. I lost a ton of money."

"Turns out the guy who got her fired from Aero Pacific was a guy named Grady Adcock," Grossman said, with a smirk.

"Who is Grady Adcock?"

"Adcock was Bowman-California's CEO," Grossman replied. "He is now deceased, so the trail ended there."

Justine leached forward in his chair. With an incredulous look on his face, he exclaimed, "Adcock! Bowman's CEO? Jesus H. Christ! The whore set the asshole up." Justine shook his head. "Impressive. Fricking brilliant. Were you able to find out what part she played in the Bowman antitrust case?"

"King was the lead attorney," Grossman answered.

Roman Justine rubbed his forehead with his right hand. "Gerald Cozell was the lead attorney. If my memory serves me."

Lou Grossman referred to his notes. "Cozell's name is here. Says Cozell conferred with King throughout the case. She's pulling strings from behind the scenes?" he wagered.

Justine clenched his jaw and said, under his breath, "That god-damned whore cost me ten mil. Again, like law school, Miss King keeps a low profile."

"So it would seem, Mr. Justine." Lou Grossman checked his notes. "Following the trial, Barrymore, Rothschild, and Gain deposited one million dollars into Faye King's bank account for three consecutive years."

"A bonus, I presume?" Justine asked.

"Three of five annual payments."

"What's her annual?" Justine wanted to know.

"High six figures. We could not confirm the exact amount."

Roman Justine chuckled and turned to Carmen Gray, his legal counsel. "I think you're in the wrong business, Mr. Gray," he said.

"Her income would place her in the top one hundred lawyers in the nation, Roman," Gray replied.

"That is extraordinary for a student who graduated last in her class," Justine assessed. "How does Joey Stumpanato afford a highly priced lawyer? And why has he set her on the BAW?"

Carmen Gray answered. "We don't believe her entire income is coming from the Stumpanado family. There could be retainers from other mob families involved. But we have not be able to determine where all her money comes from. We verified two hundred fifty thousand in her bank account. We have no idea if there are offshore accounts."

"Naturally there would be," Justine commented.

"She hired on with Joey," Gray went on. "The next day, she defended a sleaze-ball mob kid accused of armed robbery. A slam dunk conviction. Yet she got him acquitted!"

Justine smiled. "What happened to Vinny?"

"Mr. Astoria has retired, Mr. Justine," Gray informed him.

"Ah, too bad. I like Vinny."

"She's a hired gun, as you alluded to, Roman," Gray said. "Joey has decided to go after you through one or more of the GFA member companies."

"It would seem Mr. Guppy has a vendetta," Justine said.

"So it would seem," Gray replied. He turned to Grossman and asked, "You mentioned earlier King changed her name before entering law school?"

"As I said before, we found a few inconsistencies in her past," Grossman confirmed. "Although we did discover her law school tuition was paid in full by an anonymous trust fund."

"Anonymous?"

"That's right, Roman," Grossman confirmed.

"Did you run a check on her credit history?" Don Valley asked.

"Please, Mr. Valley," Grossman responded, "have a little faith in us. We're the most prestigious private investigative firm in the country. We're the best at what we do."

"In your opinion," Roman Justine said, "why would King's history show any inconsistencies at all?"

"I'd say the mob has done a good job of erasing, altering, or confusing her past. But I'm confident we cut through the smoke and mirrors," Grossman boasted. "I think we have a pretty accurate past history on her."

A photo of Pearce flashed on the screen. "Corazon Garza," Grossman announced. "King's confidant, bodyguard, and pilot. Her address is listed as the same as Faye King's."

Justine turned toward Lou Grossman. "Are they lesbians?" he asked.

"We believe so. King is most likely genderqueer."

Justine's lips formed a wide grin, and he lightly clapped his hands together. "How delightful it is. It's intriguing. Corazon Garza would be an alias?"

"Definitely an alias, Mr. Justine."

As the photos of Corazon Garza played across the screen, Justine studied them. "Lou, is Garza a sand-monkey?" he asked.

"We think she's Arab," Lou Grossman responded. "Although an Arab with white hair and blue eyes is uncommon."

"She's a woman," Justine said with a chuckle. "What woman do you know, Lou, who knows what her natural hair color is?" Justine leered at the photo of Corazon Garza. "That is a fine-looking bitch, gentlemen. I'm curious, Lou. Does the carpet match the drapes?"

"Aaah… I'm not sure, Mr. Justine. Garza has worn the headscarf since we began the photo surveillance. We didn't get any nudes," Grossman responded.

Justine smiled. "There's an extra fifty K in it for you, if you can confirm that for me." He eased back in his chair, continuing to consider the photo of Corazon Garza.

"Tell me, Mr. Grossman," Justine resumed, "other than other women, what are King's passions? I don't think two dozen roses would turn her head."

"She has a passion for sushi and Milwaukee's Finest beer."

"Milwaukee's Finest!" Justine laughed. "That's the cheapest crap there is! She can afford Dom Perignon at three large a pop and she's drinking liquid shit at less than a dollar a can?"

"Odd as hell, Mr. Justine," Grossman replied.

"Our land-shark eats raw fish." Justine tapped his chin with his pen. "Carmen, what do you suppose a bluefin tuna sells for these days?"

"Last I heard," Gray replied, "starting at two hundred per pound but can go as high as five thousand dollars per pound on the Japanese market."

"Get in touch with our people in Japan," Justine commanded. "Have them ship a slab to King for us. Arrange for it to be delivered along with the two-dozen roses, by tomorrow, to King's suite. My compliments. Oh, and send along a six pack of Milwaukee's Finest."

Roman Justine's gaze shifted, refocusing beyond the men seated at the table to a man who was sitting alone in the shadows at the back of the room.

"I'll see to Faye King," Justine said, with a slight nod of his head.

The man in the shadows rose from his chair, unnoticed by the others. With an emotionless expression on his face and with nothing more than a confirming nod, he slipped out of the room.

A sinister smile formed on Roman Justine's lips as

the man he called "Doctor" closed the door behind him. Justine's gaze returned to his men.

"Faye King is an irritant, gentlemen," Justine proclaimed. "We have other, more serious business to attend to." He nodded toward Carmen Gray.

"Our sources in Washington, D.C. have informed us that the Justice Department is mounting an investigation into the GFA," Carmen Gray announced.

"We don't want another antitrust investigation on our members' hands like the one Bowman-California suffered," Justine said. "We'll direct the association membership to be cognizant of the government's activities. Our next GFA meeting will be held offshore. There is no discussion between association members regarding member activities on anything but secured phone and computer tie-lines from this point forward. Is that clear?"

All the men nodded affirmatively.

****

The following afternoon, in Roman Justine's office

"Mr. Justine, a Ms. King is calling for you." Justine's personal assistant relayed the message over his desk intercom. "Will you take the call?"

"Thank you, Jason," Justine responded. "I'll take the call." He smiled as he activated the phone intercom. "Good afternoon, Ms. King," he said in greeting. "What can I do for you?"

"Mr. Justine, I wanna thank ya for the bluefin," Fay said. "Why am I the lucky girl?"

"Union business. Specifically, the BAW. And a welcome to Phoenix," Justine explained.

"Oh? Nothin' more romantic than union business?"

"I have the feeling, Ms. King, should I decide to

romance you, my intentions would have to be more pronounced than a few pounds of fish, cans of brew, and a handful of flowers," Justine said. The smile on his face broadened. "You represent the union."

"Yeah. But what does that have to do with you, Mr. Justine?" Fay asked.

"I was hoping you would meet with me to discuss that in person…say tomorrow, for lunch?" he suggested.

"I'm flyin' to Vegas tomorrow. Can't do it," Fay stated.

"Perhaps when you return. This is urgent."

"Nope." Fay paused. "I got an idea. Why not fly to Vegas with me? That'll give us a few minutes to chat. Have your jet follow us, and you can return to Phoenix later in the day."

"If that is what it will take, Ms. King, I'm game," Justine agreed.

"That works. I'll have my assistant call your assistant with the details. Ciao!"

Without waiting for so much as an "okay" from Justine, "Faye King" hung up.

****

By Tuesday afternoon, Cartman County Sheriff's Deputy Doug had pounded more than his share of pavement, searching for information on the dead transient fisherman murder accomplice, Ronald Stanton. He had focused his efforts on the nearby towns of Port Leone and Manatee City.

Doug stopped at Gwen's Manatee City Café for a late lunch, where he struck up a conversation with waitperson Linda. Flirting would better define his encounter with the young and pretty, yet curvaceous, woman.

When Linda next passed by his table, Doug thought to show her Stanton's picture.

Linda studied the photo and handed it back to Doug. "Never seen the guy before. Gotta git!" she said, before dashing off in response to an "Order up!" call.

Doug finished his meal. Then, he waited a few minutes until Linda returned with his bill. He had already calculated the meal plus the tip and handed her a ten-dollar bill. "Keep the change," he told her.

Linda smiled. "Ya know aah do recall seein' that guy in here. Can aah see that picture ah-gain?" she asked.

Doug slipped his right hand into his left shirt pocket, withdrew the photo, and handed it to her. "You may have seen him in here?"

"Yeah." Linda studied the photo. "This here's Ray," she realized. "Aah didn't recognize him without his sunglasses."

"Ray?"

"He's always like wearin' them fancy sunglasses," Linda explained. "Like I mean, the guy's a bum, right? But he's got them expensive designer sunglasses. So's aah call him Ray. You know?"

"I get it," Doug chuckled. "Y'all have a minute to tell me about him, or should I come back when you get off work?"

"Hold on. I'll go see if aah can git me a break. Be right back."

Soon, Linda returned and sat down. "Aah got me twenty minutes. So whadda ya wanna know?" she asked Doug.

"Tell me about Ray," Doug replied. "Does he come here often?"

"A couple times a week. When he comes in, he like

sits in the same spot," Linda said, pointing toward a table. "Near to the door. He orders a coffee and reads whatever section of the newspaper he finds layin' around. From time to time, he buys a donut. He's a real nice guy. Aah kinda feel sorry for him."

"Do you talk to him?"

"Like, Aah mean, just the usual stuff. Like 'hi, y'all, how ya doin'? Nice day. See ya soon.' Stuff like that," Linda explained.

"Has he ever met or talked to anyone else?" Doug wanted to know.

"Naw," Linda replied, shaking her head. "Ray seems to be like a loner, ya know. Although come to think of it, he did sit there with a man one time. That was like last week?"

"You didn't happen to hear what they was talkin' about, did you?"

"No," Linda denied. "But aah do recall Ray seemed like a bit nervous that day."

How so?" Doug questioned.

"Well, like he usually seems relaxed. Laidback. You know?"

Doug nodded.

"But this time he was fidgety… like he was lookin' around a lot and tappin' his fingers," Linda divulged.

Doug asked, "Had you seen the other man before?"

"Never. But the guy was out of place. Aah mean like, Ray is a bum, right? This guy was nicely dressed. Not business-like. More like them Yankee tourists. A snowbird."

"Do you think you could come into the Cartman County courthouse tomorrow to meet with our forensic artists?" Doug asked her. "I'd like to have what we call a composite sketch done up of this man."

"Aah know what a composite is, deputy. It's a drawin' rendered by combinin' various components into a single image. Aah seen 'em do them on the TV," Linda replied, before looking at her wristwatch. "Aah gotta work the mornin' shift tomorrow. Then aah got an online class to take. By the time aah get off at three and get a bus, it would be like five before Aah got on over to the courthouse. Aah can catch up on my classes later. That okay?"

"I'll tell you what. If y'all can be ready to go by three, I'll come by and pick you up," Doug told her. "I'll bring you home when we're done. I might even buy ya supper over to Choctaw Bay Marina for y'all's trouble."

Linda smiled and offered Doug her hand. "Deal." She hesitated, then said, "Ah…Mrs. Doug won't mind your havin' supper with me?"

"Well, first, this is county business. Second, there's no Mrs. Doug," the Deputy replied. "And third, Doug's my first name."

Linda's smile widened. "Okay. See ya here at three tomorrow."

****

"Faye King" received a call from Roman Justine on Wednesday morning. He would not be able to accompany her to Las Vegas due to a pressing matter. Justine did extend an invitation to a party on Friday evening at his Phoenix country estate. He promised a guest list that would include Phoenix's most influential people, as well as politicians from Capitol Hill and Hollywood celebrities. He suggested a business meeting of no more than thirty minutes. The rest of the evening would be hers to enjoy as his honored guest.

Justine was playing right into Fay's hands. And she happened to have the red silk dress Lyza Joe had given to her and the matching red shoes she had purchased in Chicago to wear for the occasion.

One particular potential guest caught Fay's attention, a person who might cause a problem for her: Jade, the international recording star and diva. Jade had sung at three Republican fundraisers when Fay's father had been in office, and she had met Jade each time. Although years had passed, Fay's cover could be compromised. She would either have to avoid Jade altogether or hope her Faye King disguise would be sufficient.

****

At 2:55 P.M., Deputy Doug arrived at Gwen's Manatee City Café and parked his unmarked county cop car around the corner. He was dressed in a soft tan summer jacket and matching cotton slacks.

Linda was waiting, and when she saw him approaching, she smiled.

"Hi," Doug said. "Looks like y'all's ready to go."

"Ready as I'll ever be, Deputy," Linda replied.

"Doug," he insisted.

"Doug," Linda confirmed. She appeared to have spent a little extra time in front of the mirror. She looked much prettier than she had the day before.

"Linda, I'm sorry to take you from your studies," Doug apologized.

"Oh, that's okay. I'm almost done with mah schoolin' anyways."

Doug chuckled. "You're not getting' off that easy, Linda. What are you studyin'?" he asked.

"Geez…it ain't nothin' much. Aah attend FSU

Medical School. Fortunate that aah can do mah classes online classes this quarter."

"Yeah, it's a bit a haul to get from here to FSU, for sure."

Linda giggled. "It ain't so bad. And like aah say, I'm like near to graduation anyways," she replied.

"It's a huge deal, Linda. Are you going to be a doctor?" Doug inquired.

"Naw, maybe one day. Fer now, just a nurse," Linda said with a smile. "Tell ya what though. At least aah can quit my crap job pretty soon."

Doug laughed. "Good for you, kid. Tell me about the man who met with Ray," he requested.

"He was non-descript, he was. I'd say like fifty or fifty-five, maybe? He looked like a tourist."

"A snowbird, you said," the Deputy recalled.

"Yeah. They's in season now," Linda said with a soft giggle. "Oh…Aah don't know. He smoked. He sweated…um…perspired a lot. And he had one of them New York accents."

Doug laughed. "Like from over on Third Street?"

"That kind of accent," Linda confirmed.

"Brooklyn," Doug concluded.

Linda observed, "He did have an interesting way of smokin', though."

"Tell me about that," Doug requested.

"Well, he had a way of gettin' his cigarette from the pack to his mouth," she explained. "He'd flip his wrist so's one cigarette would pop up out of the pack…almost halfway out. Then he'd grab it with his lips…right out of the pack. Aah seen a lot of smokers do that, but this guy had it down to one motion."

"Fluid?"

"Yeah. The guy like drops the pack into his pocket. He used stick matches. You know, the kind with the white tip?"

"Easy strike matches. You can strike them on any surface," Doug said.

"That's them. This guy would use his thumbnail."

"Interestin', Linda. Anythin' else?"

Linda lapsed into silence, thinking. Then she said, "Naw."

Doug and Linda arrived at the courthouse at 4:30 P.M. Cora Coin, the forensic artist, was waiting for them. Doug left Linda in Cora's talented hands and checked his messages at the Sheriff's office. Cora called him forty-five minutes later.

Doug returned to Cora's office. When he entered the room, Cora said, "We're all done, Doug." She held up the sketch. "That's him."

Doug took the sketch from Cora and showed it to Linda. "This him?" he asked.

Linda nodded. "Yep," she confirmed. "A dead ringer for the guy."

Doug turned the drawing over and looked at it once more. He remembered seeing this man before, but not when or where. Then, it dawned on him. "I don't think so. Hang with Cora, Linda," he requested. "I'll have to contact Sheriff Gus."

****

Fay and JP, disguised as Faye and Corazon, arrived at Roman Justine's palatial Scottsdale desert estate one hour before the time indicated on Fay's invitation. She was told Roman Justine was in conference and was shown into the trophy room. JP was directed toward the cabana at the swimming pool.

"Mr. Justine is in a meeting with Senator de la Croix. He will be with you in fifteen minutes, Miss King," the butler assured her.

Fay glanced at her wristwatch. "Please inform Mr. Justine that in eleven minutes, I will be on my way out," she instructed the butler. She made a mental note to avoid the old crow de la Croix.

"Miss King," the butler asked, "may I offer you a drink while you wait?"

"That would be nice," Fay decided. "How about a Blue Wench?"

"A Blue Wench, ma'am?" the butler questioned, uncertain of her order.

Fay smiled. "Tell your bartender a tall glass," she said, holding her hands apart, one over the other, to indicate the size of the glass. "Mix one ounce each of gin, Triple Sec, Blue Curacao, and a splash of lime juice over crushed ice. Got it?"

The butler smiled. "Very well, Miss King. Please, make yourself comfortable." He bowed at the waist and left.

Fay took a look around her. The trophy room was big, with twelve-foot-high windows overlooking a private tropical waterfall and pool. The heads of numerous big game trophy animals adorned the remaining three walls. A big bear, most likely a grizzly, stood on its haunches near the glass wall.

The butler returned with her drink. "One Blue Wench, Miss King," he said, smiling as he handed her the glass. "Will there be anything else?"

Fay returned the smile. "No, thank you."

The butler left the room.

Fay toured the trophy room with her drink in hand,

stopping to admire each and every animal. Roman Justine's collection was impressive, yet she could not help but feel sad for the defenseless animals that had given their lives to satisfy his ego.

She spotted a beautiful white mountain sheep and walked to it. As Fay reached out to pet the doe-eyed sheep, a chill brushed across her neck.

She heard a voice from behind her say, "She's beautiful, isn't she?"

Fay had turned her back on her bald nemesis. It had been foolish of her, doing what Vinny had warned her not to do.

"Yes, she is beautiful," Fay replied, turning to face Roman Justine.

"I was referring to you, Miss King…not the sheep." Justine smiled. "I shot that one on a recent trip to Tibet," he explained, moving closer to her.

Fay's jaw tightened.

"At the time, there were one hundred left in the world," Justine bragged.

"And now there are ninety-nine," Fay assessed. Her gaze again surveyed the room. "They're all females, aren't they?" she noted.

Justine smiled. "Very astute, Miss King. You're correct," he confirmed.

"I could tell by their eyes. The warmth, the strength… the sadness."

"Throughout nature, especially in the big cats and the bears, and I'm sure this is true of the human female as well, the female is more aggressive and more dangerous than her male counterpart," Justine stated. "Mothers protecting their young are particularly ferocious." His gaze swept the trophy room. "Beyond that… the female is nothing more than a sperm receptacle."

Fay's stomach churned. Beyond his total hatred of and disrespect for any female, the sorry bastard had killed a number of them, including a rare mountain sheep, thus ensuring the probable extinction of a rare and beautiful animal. The bastard probably owned stock in the company that imported pad mina into the United States.

She despised the man but, without showing any of her inner thoughts or emotions on her face, Fay extended her hand toward him in greeting. "Faye King," she introduced herself.

Justine grasped her hand. "My pleasure, Miss King."

His hand was clammy, Fay noticed. "Likewise."

"Would you like to see the rest of my collection?" he asked.

No, I certainly would not. Fay knew Justine was talking about little human heads, Adolf Hitler's skull, and Einstein's brain. She hated this.

"Of course," Fay agreed, choking down her disgust. "I would be honored, Mr. Justine. I find this all…captivating."

"Come with me," he said, motioning toward a door on the left.

Fay ran a quick mental inventory of the contents of her pocketbook. Her stomach was still clenching, and should she find herself in need of a place to barf, the handbag was her odds-on-favorite. Downing her drink in one gulp, she followed Roman Justine into his chamber of horrors.

The array of shrunken heads was, as she had

predicted, disgusting - little brown leathery heads with long black hair, straw-sewn eyelids, and straw-sewn mouths. Adolf Hitler's skull and Albert Einstein's brain were each presented in a glass case. Fay looked but didn't see either John Wayne Gacy or Jeffery Dahmer's severed heads, for which she was grateful. It was beginning to look as if her pocketbook would be spared.

"These heads are tiny. How do you suppose they do that?" Fay asked her host, but immediately knew she should not have asked the question. Justine would have a lengthy and gruesome answer for her, and she wasn't in the mood to hear it.

"The Jivaro in South America are active headhunters," Justine began. "Their shrunken head trophies are called *tsantsas*. The process begins when the Jivaro raid neighboring tribes. The prize, the *tsantsas*, brings prestige to the headhunters and traps their victims' souls."

Oh, God. If he tells me how they shrink the heads, I'm gonna puke, Fay thought to herself. *Yeah. It looks like he's gonna tell me.*

"The skin is cut around the top of the chest and back," Justine went on, demonstrating by drawing an imaginary circle around his neck. "Finally, the head is severed near the collarbone. It takes about six days to prepare the head. A slit is made in the back and the skin removed from the skull," he continued, once again giving her a demonstration. "The skin is boiled and by now has been reduced to half its original size. After the skin has been turned inside out, the remaining flesh is scraped away." He seemed to be getting excited. "The head—"

Fay cut him off by waving a dismissing hand.

"Roman. Hold up. I came here to discuss business…not heads."

"Of course. Forgive me." Even as he apologized, Justine's lips conveyed a devious grin. "I tend to get carried away." There was a brief, uncomfortable silence. "How's my friend, the Guppy?" he asked.

Fay clenched her teeth. "Why don't ya take your hand off my ass and cut the crap, Justine," she demanded. "You said ya had somethin' ya wanted to talk to me about. What is it?"

Roman's eyebrows arched, and he smiled. "Let's retire to the other room," he suggested. "I think you'll be more at ease there."

They returned to the trophy room and made themselves comfortable in two high-backed padded leather chairs overlooking the tropical pool.

"Miss King," Justine said. "I'm disturbed by the work slowdown the BAW union leaders have invoked at AmeriCon; you embody the union membership."

Fay crossed her shapely legs on purpose. Her gesture exposed almost half of her thigh in the short red silk dress, and she watched as Roman Justine's eyes swept the length of her leg. "That's right, she responded. "And…?" *Get a good look, you perverted douchebag*, she thought. *You son-of-a-bitch, I'm going to own you.*

"And…" Justine's distracted gaze returned to meet her eyes. "I wished to speak with you regarding your position as it pertains to the work slowdown and the mired labor contract discussions," he stated.

"Why am I talkin' to you and not Don Valley, AmeriCon's CEO?" Fay asked.

Roman eyed her empty glass. "Can I get you another drink, Miss King?"

"I'm good." Fay flashed Justine her new "*ask me another question, and you die*" look. "Like I said before," she replied. "Cut the crap, or I'm out of here."

Justine played it cool. "Miss King. As a major stakeholder and a board member, the health and welfare of all AmeriCon's union workers are my primary concern."

Bullshit. "Concerned? Fay responded. "Since when has management ever concerned itself with union labor? If management was as concerned as you say, Mr. Justine, we would've ratified a contract months ago, and you and I wouldn't be havin' this tête-à-tête."

"Why a work slowdown? Why now?" Justine asked her.

"AmeriCon management has held out against the union's demands that management makes reparations for all unused sick pay. I might add wages are rightfully due labor for sick leave they have not used," Fay explained. "The union has accused management of temporizing while employee morale continues to worsen. The union leadership is concerned. I'm here to either move negotiations forward or to advise the BAW union leaders to call for an immediate strike vote."

Justine's eyebrows arched. "A work stoppage? Miss King. Please. Can we deal?"

"To deal with ya at this juncture, Mr. Justine, would be egregious on my part. I want a meetin' with Don Valley…one on one…no crap." Fay grinned.

Justine said with pleading eyes, "Look, I've got other problems to…" but he caught himself before completing the statement.

Fay knew what he had been about to say. She finished his thought for him. "You've got the Justice

Department preparin' to play lawn darts in your boxer shorts. Correct?"

A sly grin formed on Roman Justine's lips. "You don't miss much, do you, Miss King?" he asked.

"I don't miss nothin'."

"You were the lead attorney for the government in the *U.S. v. Bowman Aerospace* antitrust case. Nice work, by the way," Justine acknowledged.

Fay raised her eyebrows. "And you don't miss much either, Mr. Justine."

"Whatever Joey Stumpanato is paying you, multiply it by five. Add a ten percent bonus should the GFA and the feds go to court and should you win the case," Justine offered.

Fay did quick math. If Joey Stumpanato were really paying her, Justine's offer to jump ship would be in the mid six figures. "You're suggestin' I dump Joey and take on the Attorney General in what could be the biggest case since the Master Settlement Agreement?" Fay asked.

"We're talking a multi-billion-dollar deal here," Justine confirmed.

"I'll consider your proposal after I leave my meetin' with Don Valley, with a ratified contract in hand," Fay decided. "In the meantime, the BAW rank and file needs my full and undivided attention."

"You will consider my proposal?" Justine pushed.

"Like they say, Mr. Justine, 'money talks and bullshit walks.' I think we understand one another," Fay stated.

The party proved to be as outlandish as the people on the guest list. Fay and JP spent a considerable amount of their time watching a flock of thong-birds cavorting in the swimming pool.

Fay had ordered a fresh drink and was sipping it when, suddenly, she felt faint. She excused herself from the gentleman with whom she was talking and retired to the restroom.

****

After his dinner with Linda at the Choctaw Bay Marina, Deputy Doug stopped at the Citrus Tree Retirement Community's main gate. Linda stayed in the car while Doug spoke with the gate guard.

"Hi," Doug said as he approached the man sitting in the small gatehouse. Doug displayed his deputy's badge. "Sheriff's Deputy Dewey. How you doin' this evenin'?"

The guard eyed the badge, then said, "Doin' fine, deputy. What can I do you for?"

"I'm lookin' for Lenny Crane. He workin' tonight?" Doug asked.

"Haven't seen him for a couple of days now. Why? He in trouble?" the guard wanted to know.

"Not at all. I wanted to talk to Lenny regardin' the disappearance of a resident here in the community," Doug explained. "That's it."

"You mean Mr. Joe."

"That's right," Doug confirmed. "Where can I find Lenny?"

"I wish I could tell you, deputy." The guard extended his hand. "Bob Carson. I own Bob's Security Service. We have the security contract for the Country Club here."

Doug shook Bob's hand. "Pleased to meetcha. Y'all say you'd not seen him for several days?" he asked.

"Lenny called me two days ago. Said there was trouble in the family and he needed a week off," Bon explained. "I told him to go ahead. I'd cover for him until he got back."

"How long has he worked for y'all?"

"About a month. Really nice guy too," Bob replied.

"Did he say when he'd be back?"

"No. But I have the feelin' I've seen the last of Lenny."

"Why?" Doug asked.

"I have his paycheck. I stopped by his place over on Palm Street to give it to him. I spoke to the manager and found out that Lenny had moved out," Bob revealed. "I figured if he was plannin' on comin' back, he'd have left his belongings."

During the drive from Citrus Tree to Linda's home, Linda commented, "Doug, since I have known y'all, you've been askin' me a boat load of questions. But y'all missed one."

"I did?"

"Y'all didn't ask me if you could come callin' on me." Linda handed Doug a piece of paper. "So, yes, you can and here is my number."

Chapter 14

She stood there watching as the coffin moved closer to the silver cremator. Even though the deceased's face was obscured by the American flag draped over the body, she knew her well. The flag was removed by a tall man with white hair, finally revealing the woman's face. She was young, maybe in her early forties, and much too young and attractive to be dead. The dead woman's expression indicated she had experienced happiness in her life.

She recognized the woman in the white naval uniform now. In her left eye, a tear pooled. The woman was her.

It was pitch black. She found herself within the cremator, lying on her back inside the same coffin she had seen from afar. She passed from a feeling of inner peace to a state of sheer panic in seconds. Her stomach clenched. She could not move. She wanted to scream for help, but she could not speak.

By the minute, the temperature inside the coffin grew warmer and more uncomfortable. The woman was well aware that the temperature would soon reach 1,600 degrees. Her entire being would be reduced to ashes and bone fragments in less than ninety minutes. Why did they want to treat her like a Christmas turkey and roast her? Did they not know she had much more to live for? This was not her time!

She struggled to escape, praying for the strength to break free from her confinement. Focusing on her legs, she clenched her jaw, and with a mighty thrust, her legs struck out into the total darkness. There was no resistance, yet the night melted into twilight. Fresh air, much cooler than before, engulfed her, refreshing the warm and stale oxygen that had filled her lungs. For a moment, she lay still, gasping. She inched her way toward the source of the light.

Her senses returned. Her mind began to clear; she was lying on her back, not on the cremator's hard steel bed, but on the ground.

As her vision continued to clear, the blurred images surrounding her formed into more definite shapes. The woman's mind began to register their significance. She froze. Terror reclaimed her soul. A large, menacing, twenty-five-foot-tall giant towered over her. A scream formed in her mind but lodged in her throat.

Looking first left, then right, she searched for an escape. Giant men stood all around, looking down at her. Their mouths twisted into sneering grins.

The scream finally came.

****

By late Saturday morning, Gifford Champion had grown concerned. He checked with the attendant at the hotel's front desk. "Faye King" had checked out earlier that morning. She had mentioned to the hotel manager that she and her companion were headed for Tucson. She did not say why, but the manager had assumed they had planned a sightseeing trip because she had asked him for a map of Tucson's monuments.

Gifford knew Fay and JP would have called him if they had decided to leave the hotel, and since they had not, his concern for their safety intensified. He placed a call to their father. Mr. Green had not heard from his daughters either. The two men decided that if they had not heard from them by 2 P.M., they would call in the police and begin a search. As Arizona covered 114,000 square miles, searching for the sisters would prove a formidable task.

****

Realizing her captors were not men but saguaro cacti, she sat up. Assessing her situation, she determined she was sitting in a desert, this disconcerting moment was early evening, and she was suffering from a blinding migraine. On unsteady legs, she stood to survey her surroundings.

Behind her rested a battered white Sports Utility Vehicle. It was inoperable in its inverted position, and the passenger window was broken out. She recalled her dream—the heat, the confinement. How long had she lain unconscious in that torn and twisted hulk? The car's metal and plastic exterior, heated by the hot desert sun, had transformed its leather and plastic interior into an equivalent of a slow-bake oven. Awakened by the unbearable heat, perhaps she had escaped by kicking out the passenger window?

She gazed, over the SUV's airborne tires, to the dark mountain range beyond and toward the glowing reddish sunset. She remembered an old mariner's adage, "Red sky at night, sailor's delight. Red sky at morning, sailor's warning." Was this also a prospector's adage?

A calm evening desert breeze chilled her skin. The overturned SUV would give her adequate protection for the night. She took a step in its direction and crashed to the ground.

"Spider!" a woman called.

She startled awake. It was night.

"Where?" she screamed and recoiled. "I hate spiders." Through blurred vision, she searched to find the one who had spoken to her from the shadows.

"No. You're Spider," the voice said.

She saw a tall woman emerge from the shadow of a nearby tree.

She struggled to stand. She was frightened. "Who's there?"

"It's me. JP."

"Who? I don't know yo…" Her knees buckled and…blackness.

The next day, she awoke to find herself back in the SUV, not knowing how she had ended up there. Her mind and vision seemed clear. But the splitting headache was still there.

As she prepared to scurry from her metal burrow, she paused to examine her reflection in the car's rearview mirror. She could not place the reflected woman's distorted face, but she did recall the woman in her dream. A gash in the woman's scalp, below the hairline, was visible in the mirror. Her hair was matted and streaked with gushing blood. Her bruised and swollen left cheek ached, suggesting she may have suffered a dislocated jaw. Who was she?

She crawled from the SUV, stood, and stretched with difficulty. She refreshed her lungs with morning air.

"How y'all feelin' this mornin'?" A tall, dark woman with raven hair dressed in blue jeans, a white western shirt, black boots, and a baseball cap stood smiling, about twenty feet from her.

"Who are you?" she asked.

The woman's smile faded. Her look of joy was replaced by one of concern. "I'm your sister, JP."

She studied the tall, dark woman. "And who am I?"

Tears welled in the woman's blue eyes and raced down her cheeks. The stranger stepped toward her. "You're Fay."

"Stop," she said and stepped backward, taking a defensive posture.

"Please," the tall woman said in a comforting voice. "You're injured. Let me help."

She relaxed. "I won't argue with you there. I feel like crap."

"You may have a concussion. And now it appears you may have amnesia as well." The tall woman smiled and stepped forward with her arms raised waist high, palms out. "Please let me help you."

"Thank you," she said softly.

The tall woman scanned the western horizon. "The sky is crimson," she observed. "That means we're in for a storm, one that may involve rain. I have to attend to your injuries, but we'll also need water. If we're going to survive this desert, we'll need anywhere between two to three gallons per day." The tall woman searched the area around the SUV, then said, "Come on. Help me find a way to collect rainwater, and I'll patch y'all up."

While the woman who called herself "JP" searched outside the SUV, the woman who did not know who she was searched the interior. Behind the front seat, she found a purse and a suitcase. She found a bottle of whiskey under the front passenger seat. Nothing she found in the car could be used to trap water. She considered the whiskey bottle but using it for water would mean she would have to empty a perfect bottle onto the sand. She thought not and continued her search.

The tall woman's search of the immediate area for a watertight container proved fruitless. So, the two women suspended their search momentarily to think.

The tall woman's gaze settled on a tree about thirty feet away. "There," she said, pointing. She had spotted a barrel cactus near the tree. "I have an idea."

A closer inspection revealed a small cactus, about twelve inches in diameter.

"By cutting off the top," the tall woman explained, "and scooping out the pulp, much like we did when we carved Halloween pumpkins, we'll have a pot. But I need a knife."

Returning to the SUV, they inspected the suitcases and the purses. None contained a knife, but they did discover a derringer in the bag belonging to a woman named Faye King. They considered smashing the whiskey bottle and using the broken glass for cactus carving.

No, not the whiskey.

She said to the tall woman, "Perhaps if we dislodge a piece of the torn metal from the damaged right fender, we could fashion it into a knife."

"Good idea," the tall woman replied. She grabbed the tire iron from its storage compartment in the car's interior wall and went to work on the fender. Thirty minutes of bashing and bending produced an eight-inch blade.

"Good thing this wasn't a plastic car," the tall woman said as she admired the coarse blade.

"Good job," the other woman said as she inspected the knife. "What did you say your name was again?"

"JP."

"Why can't I remember that?" She hesitated. "And who am I again?"

"You're Fay."

She nodded and murmured, "Fay." She smiled. "Good work, JP."

Storm clouds were approaching. They could see rain in the distance as black downward streaking sheets. Using a flat stone, JP honed a sharp edge on the makeshift knife. It was much easier to transform fender metal into a knife than it had been to turn the barrel cactus into a water jug. Several times, her carving hand slipped into the cactus's sharp spines. The whole process appeared painful to Fay.

"Where'd you learn to curse like that, darlin'?" Fay inquired.

There was no verbal response to her question, only a telling glance in her direction. If only looks could kill.

It took about twenty minutes for the tall woman to fashion the water pot.

"This should hold around four gallons, a five-day supply," the tall woman announced. "We better make a second pot."

When it was done, the second pot was more significant than the first.

Fay admired the cactus pots. "Nice work…y'all. Look. I keep forgettin' y'all's name. Mind if I call ya Darlin'?" she asked.

"Darlin' would be fine," came the reply.

There was no way to tell how long the rain would last. Darlin' reasoned they could collect the water on a large surface area, then channel it into their two pots. That way, they would stand a better chance at filling them before the rain stopped.

They searched the car's interior again. The SUV had come to rest on an incline.

"It would be nice if the car were upright," Darlin' said. "I recall that SUVs have a reputation for rolling over when they're upright. It stands to reason an upside-down one should be easy to roll right side up."

From a position on the SUV's uphill side, they tested the car's stability by rocking it back and forth. Even if they could roll the SUV down the incline, there was no guarantee it would land upright. At worst, it would come to rest further down the slope on its top. On the other hand, there was a good chance it would land upright. It was worth a try.

Finding solid footing, both women braced their right shoulders on the passenger door.

"OK. On three," Darlin' said. "One. Two. Three."

On three, they began rocking the SUV. They gained momentum with each rocking motion, aided by the car's rounded roof.

When the SUV was ready to roll, they gave it one more push, throwing all their weight and strength into it. The car rolled over onto its side, gained downhill traction, and rolled upright.

When the SUV tipped onto its right-side tires, Fay held her breath. It seemed the downhill trip was coming to an end. The car rocked back toward them, horn honking and lights flashing, and settled upright.

Darlin' dashed down the incline and deactivated the alarm.

Chapter 15

From the photograph Gifford Champion showed him, the hotel manager could not identify either Fay or JP as the women who had checked out that morning. Champion called Bill Green. Bill called Arizona Governor Nicole Silver, who in turn placed calls to the Arizona Highway Patrol and the Western Army National Guard Aviation Training Site Commander at Marana. All available AHP personnel were dispatched to canvas the numerous motels, restaurants, service stations, and rest stops that bordered the highways leading to Tucson.

At 4:20 P.M., an Arizona Highway Patrol helicopter, with Bill Green and Gifford Champion aboard, touched down at the Marana airport near Tucson. Four Army National Guard helicopters, crewed by WANGAS flight instructors, stood ready. Two Bell OH58A Kiowa and two Sikorsky UH-60A Blackhawk helicopter crews would search the ten thousand square mile desert between Tucson and Phoenix. Each team included a smaller and faster Kiowa and a larger Blackhawk. Each Blackhawk crew included two Army medics and food and water.

****

While the women waited for the storm to arrive, they scanned the car's FM radio frequencies for a weather report. Reported flooding in downtown Phoenix streets confirmed that they were east and a big rainstorm was indeed headed their way.

Even though the rollover had smashed the Ford roof, leaving a small reservoir where rainwater would collect, they needed more. After selecting a large rock, the tall woman used it to enlarge the dent. She pounded a significant dent into the hood for good measure, hoping the storm would deliver enough water to fill their metal reservoirs several times over.

"We'll drain the collected water into our cacti water jugs," the tall woman said.

The noise created by the heavy rock being repeatedly struck against the metal further amplified Fay's persistent and splitting headache. As she sat on the SUV's leather passenger seat massaging her temples, she recalled the purse she had found earlier.

After emptying the purse's contents onto a floor mat, she ransacked the items, searching for aspirin. There was a derringer, a wallet, chewing gum, a handkerchief, lipstick, a small hand mirror, reading glasses, a sewing kit, beer nuts, and matches. She sighed.

"Crap. This woman is a frickin' packrat," she muttered to herself. "A complete 7-11 store in this purse and not one lousy painkiller."

Next, Fay ransacked the suitcase, tossing clothing around in a search for aspirin. Along with toiletries, a cream called "EBLA," and a box of cigars, she finally found the object of her desire.

If there were a ratio to how many aspirin caplets one should consume to the intensity of one's headache, Fay reasoned she would need to take the entire bottle. According to the label on the bottle, the recommended dosage was two. Her throbbing head suggested six, but she was in a comprising mood and so settled on four. She returned to the passenger seat, located the whiskey, and washed the pills down with a generous amount.

A defiant gray thundercloud drooped from the west, masking a large portion of the sky. The brown desert seemed transparent and deathly pale against its massive curtain. The torrent's arrival was announced by blinding lightning, followed by thunder.

****

"How long is this storm expected to last?" Gifford asked the Blackhawk's pilot.

"The Doppler radar indicates a big one, sir. I'd say it should be with us for an hour or more."

From the wind buffeted helicopter, Gifford peered at the black storm clouds engulfing them. "Plenty of rain," he stated.

The rainwater could be a blessing if Fay and JP were stranded in the desert, as everyone connected with the search presumed. "I'm thankful for the rain," Gifford said to the pilot.

"If Commander Green and her sister are down there and if they can trap rainwater, they will do fine. The danger to any desert traveler is a flash flood. Hopefully, they will avoid the washes and remain on high ground."

The pilot looked at Gifford and smiled. "I hope you're buckled in. The ride is going to get rough."

****

Fay awoke with an abrupt jolt, face down in the mud beside the SUV. When she lifted her head, spitting wet sand, she saw a tall woman kneeling next to her.

"What happened?" Fay asked.

"Apparently, the aspirin and whiskey cocktail knocked you out," the woman replied.

"Oh, shit!" Moaning, Fay sat up, wiping mud and blood from her face and hair. "Why do we have cigars in the car? And what is EBLA?"

"You bought the cigars for our daddy and the EBLA is numbing cream Dr. Sue gave to you for your foot."

"Oh. Something tells me I despise cigars, and I almost ate the EBLA," Fay replied.

Realizing it was raining, Fay, with the tall person's help, stood up. She climbed into the SUV's passenger seat that she had not long before fallen out of.

"Next time, you might remember to buckle up before you drink and don't drive," the tall woman suggested.

The metal ponds they had created on the hood and car's top were overflowing with water. After helping her into the SUV seat, the tall woman went to work scooping the water into their cacti water jugs.

With a brief rest, her strength was returning. It was still raining when Fay slipped off her mud-splattered and blood-soaked clothing. Grabbing the shampoo and hand soap bottles from the suitcase, she stood beside the SUV and showered in the heavy desert rain.

While showering, she discovered a red mark on her left breast. Had a snake or spider crept into her burrow and bitten her during the night? The wound did not seem to be venomous. Otherwise, she would be ill or dead.

After toweling dry, she disinfected the wound on her breast with EBLA cream. Then, she pulled on blue jeans, a white T-shirt, and western boots. And, after adjusting the clasp on the back to resize it for her swollen head, she donned a Virginia university brand ball cap.

After moving the water-filled cacti pots to a location next to the car, the tall woman piled rocks around them to prevent them from tipping over. Using the cap from the shampoo bottle as a drinking cup, they enjoyed several caps full of sweet rainwater.

The tall woman admired her. "Y'all clean up real nice." Her gaze focused on Fay's forehead. "Why don't I tend to that gash on your forehead?" she suggested.

While Fay waited for her surgery, she rifled through the wallet that she had discovered in a pocketbook. By studying the picture of a woman on the driver's license inside, it occurred to her that she was the same person she now saw reflected in the Ford's rearview mirror. According to the Illinois vehicle operator license, she lived in Oakbrook. Another document recorded that she was an Illinois State Bar Association member.

I am an attorney? Good grief.

What were Faye King, a lawyer, and another woman doing in the Arizona desert? The mangled Ford and half-empty whiskey bottle suggested to her a drunken Faye King had gone on one too many binges. It had almost cost her her life, a life of which she had no recollection.

The tall woman studied Fay's swollen face, then said, "If we don't treat this gash soon, it will become infected and leave a scar. I saw a handkerchief in your purse, along with a small sewing kit."

The tall woman washed the wound after soaking the handkerchief in whiskey. When the tall woman added too much alcohol to the injury, Fay winced. After she was confident she had done all she could to clean and disinfect the gash, the tall woman threaded the needle.

The tall woman handed Fay the whiskey. "Take a swig to relax your nerves," she advised, after adding a dab of EBLA to the wound. She too took a swig and then proceeded to sew the gash closed.

"Oh, my good Lord, this hurts." Fay took several quick sips of air. Then, she blurted out, "Sue!"

"Sue who?"

"Your name is Sue!"

The tall woman giggled. "If that is easier for you, I am Sue," she agreed. "There, I'm done. Take a look." She flipped down the car's sun visor and pointed to the attached mirror.

Admiring the woman's needlework, Fay believed she might look akin to the bride of Frankenstein. This thought amused her, and she chuckled to herself.

"Sue what?" Fay asked the other woman.

"Ah, Sue Pearce."

"Well, Sue Pearce, I am pleased to meet you!"

****

"Sir," Martin Kato, the Kiowa pilot, yelled over the din to Gifford Champion, pointing to the Kiowa's instrument panel. "Our turbine temperature is climbing. I'm going to return to base."

Champion nodded, gave the thumbs-up signal with his right hand, and yelled, "When can we get another Kiowa out here?"

"A replacement is on the way out, sir."

Gifford considered his options. "Where's the Blackhawk?" he asked.

"Behind us and to our right, sir."

Gifford squinted through the wind-buffeted Kiowa's starboard window. He could see little through the dark and driving rain. "Set it down, Lieutenant," he said to the pilot.

"Sir?"

"Put it on the deck." He gestured toward the chopper's floor with his left hand. "Tell the Blackhawk to pick me up. We'll continue the search."

Lieutenant Kato nodded, gave him the thumbs up, readjusted his flight controls, and prepared to descend.

****

It had been a productive day for the two women. By early nightfall, they had gathered water, bathed, and attended to Fay's medical needs. While they were both gratified by their many accomplishments, they were exhausted.

Two low flying helicopters passed overhead, to the west, going like bats-out-of-hell. Had they had some warning, they might have tried to flag the choppers down. Instead, the women watched until they disappeared into the storm-darkened sky and then Sue turned the SUV's radio on. She found a pro football game. It was halftime; the Cardinals led the Seahawks by a narrow margin. Fay managed to stay awake well into the third quarter, only to reawaken later.

The storm had passed, leaving behind a deafening silence and a splitting headache for Fay. She took four more aspirin caplets with rainwater, and for the first time, she was hungry. While the women were finished the last beer nuts, Fay declared she would be out early the following day searching for some fast food.

Fay noticed a high-flying airliner winking its way across the ebony sky late that night. It occurred to her that if she activated the car's emergency flashers, maybe an airplane would notice the flashing lights and send help.

Fay slept comfortably through the night and awoke refreshed early the following day. Her new friend Sue Pearce had noticed that jackrabbits were more abundant in the early morning and the late afternoon hours. They had fire, wood, a blade to cut and skin with, and they could build a fire pit. The only problem remaining was how to catch one of the wily rodents. Shooting one seemed the best option.

"On the other hand, pear cacti are also edible and easier to catch and clean," the tall woman explained. "Mercy, *nopalito* is sold in every ethnic grocery from San Diego to New York."

While they searched for the cacti, Fay asked, "Who am I again?"

"You're Fay Green. You're a Navy lawyer."

"Oh…yeah. Why can't I remember that?"

"I think you have amnesia."

"You did an excellent job sewing me up, Sue Pearce," Fay thanked the other woman. "How did you learn it?"

Pearce considered her response, before deciding it was best not to confuse the issue any more than it already was. "I'm a doctor," she replied.

"Hey! Don't I have all the luck!" Fay exclaimed. "You'd think I'd recall attending law school." Her eyes scanned the desert. "And if I'm a Navy lawyer, where's my ship? Where's the ocean? All I see is this…this arid sea."

"I'm sure your memory will return."

Thirty minutes of cacti hunting proved fruitless, as jackrabbit spectators by the hundreds would attest.

Sue Pearce wiped her brow with her right hand. "I'm gonna take a hike up that hill before it gets too hot." Pointing toward the hill behind the SUV, she continued, "I might be able to see a town or a ranch from up there."

"You want me to come with you?" Fay offered.

"No. I'll be gone maybe two hours. Besides, if anyone comes along, one of us should be here." Sue Pearce smiled. "You'll be okay. Don't go anywhere. Oh…and if anyone comes along, don't forget to tell them I've gone up the hill to fetch a pail of water." She looked Fay square in the eyes and said in an affirmative voice, "Do not forget to tell them."

"Got it," Fay said with a nod. "I'll write it down. You're going to get water. What did you say your name was again, darlin'?"

"Sue." She pointed to their water supply. "The water is over there." She pointed to the hill. "I'm going up there to see if I can spot civilization."

Fay watched until Sue Pearce had headed up the hill and turned her attention back to finding cacti. Aggravated, she returned to the car and retrieved the derringer, the whiskey bottle, a cigar, and matches. She walked back out into the desert, found a large flat rock, and sat down.

Her recollection told her daylight hours were uncomfortably warm in the desert. There was nothing more endless than a sweltering desert day, and she was hungry enough to eat a jackrabbit…cooked or not.

Soon, a fat jackrabbit appeared. The rodent paused to smirk at the forgetful Fay and to munch on grass.

An image of the White Rabbit from "Alice's Adventures in Wonderland" roasting on a turning spit popped into Fay's mind. She took a hearty swig from the whiskey bottle before setting it on the ground next to her.

"Order in the court," she began. "Ladies and gentlemen of the jury, Mr. Jack Rabbit stands before you. Mr. Rabbit has been accused…has been accused of…mockery. How say you, Mr. Rabbit? Guilty or not guilty?"

She waited for his response. The rabbit wiggled his nose and continued to munch on his grass.

"Have you nothing to say in your defense, Jack Rabbit?"

The rabbit blinked.

"Am I to assume you wish to invoke your Fifth Amendment privilege?"

The rabbit moved several inches to the left, sat back on his haunches, and continued to munch.

Fay surveyed the area behind the rabbit. Spotting a prairie dog, she said, "Mr. Dog. Will you speak on behalf of the accused?"

The prairie dog chose to ignore her and went about the business of being a prairie dog.

"Nothing to say, Mr. Dog?" Her gaze scanned the area once again. "Anyone?"

No sound.

"So be it," Fay declared. "Mr. Jack Rabbit, you stand accused of mocking me, and since you refuse to speak in your defense, I have no other choice but to now pass judgment."

The rabbit moved again to the left, sat back on his haunches, and munched.

"Mr. Rabbit, I find you guilty of the grievous crime of mockery and now sentence you to death."

The rabbit watched with disinterest.

"Now comes Josephine Black." Fay studied the rabbit. "Ms. Executioner, the sentence is death by firing squad. Prepare the prisoner."

She waited.

"Have you any last words, Mr. Jack Rabbit?"

The rabbit said nothing.

"May God have mercy on your soul." Fay removed the cellophane-wrapped cigar from her shirt pocket. After stripping off the wrapper, she bit off the cigar's end and made a face as she spat the tobacco and leaf from her mouth. She placed the cigar back into her mouth, struck a match, and lit the cigar.

Fay puffed, noting the wind direction as indicated by the exhaled smoke. She held her breath to better steady the derringer in her wavering hand. Aiming to the rodent's right to allow for wind drift, she squeezed the trigger. The small pistol popped, and a puff of dust rose to the rabbit's right. The rabbit did not move, as if it was frozen to the spot from fear, unable to move from harm's way.

"Dumb bunny," Fay murmured. Again, she took a hit from the whiskey. After setting the bottle down, she puffed on her cigar several times, leveled the derringer on the rabbit, adjusted her aim to the left to compensate for the miss, and squeezed off another shot.

The gun popped; the rabbit disappeared.

"Damn!" Fay took the cigar from her mouth and set it next to the whiskey. She picked up the bottle and again took a hearty swig.

After setting the bottle back down, she stood and walked to the spot where she had last seen the rabbit. A quick inspection revealed blood, fur, and two ears.

She looked at the derringer. "You blew up the bunny, you piece of crap! It appears you're better suited for killing range cattle than for rabbits." Fay scanned the area, musing, "There must be a cow around here."

When she turned to walk back to the car, she spotted a clump of pear cacti. "Alright!" Fay exclaimed. She slipped the derringer into her right back pocket and walked over to the cacti clump. Not wanting to be surprised by a dozing diamondback rattlesnake, she poked around the cluster with a stick and dropped to her knees. With her blade, she managed to separate five large fleshy pads.

Other than avoiding the hot sun and remembering to drink a sufficient amount of water, Fay's desire for food dominated her morning. By early afternoon, she was again hungry. While searching for a rabbit or more cacti, she spotted a rattlesnake sunning on a rock ledge. She had heard rattlesnake meat tasted like chicken, but she hated snakes more than she hated spiders. Thinking about attempting to pick up a snake made her queasy. However, hunger overrode her common sense, and she approached the snake, gun in hand, and aimed directly at the critter.

She knew a rattlesnake's approach to life was simple. If something was bigger than itself, it was afraid. If something was smaller than itself, it became food. In any case, the snake coiled, rattled, and often struck. Unfortunately, or fortunately, depending on one's viewpoint, the snake must have sensed her coming and slid into a crevasse in the rocks.

I'm hungry. The snake must think he's found a safe place to hide from me. I don't think so, Fay thought.

She searched the ground near her feet for a sturdy poking stick. She found one suitable for her purpose. Within minutes, she was prodding the rock crevasse, searching for the snake.

It was all too easy. When Fay sensed the snake with the stick's tip, she pushed, spearing him. When the squirming and thrashing had subsided, she withdrew her spear. After chucking the branch over her shoulder, she reached her right hand into the crevasse.

"OUCH!" Fay shouted. The pain that shot from her finger and up her arm was unreal. She withdrew her hand to examine her injured finger. "Damn. Broke a nail."

Following a brief recovery period, her prodding hand was back into the rocks, groping for dinner. When Fay located the snake, she withdrew the viper by its tail. Holding the snake by its tail far ahead of her, she realized that the reptile stretched from her waist to the ground. And oh, was the snake fat!

Fay returned to the spot where she had left her whiskey and her cigar. After relighting the cigar and placing it in her mouth, she slipped the derringer into her back pocket and stooped to pick up the whiskey.

"You gonna eat that?" a male voice said from behind her.

Startled, Fay screamed and froze. After catching her breath and calming her shattered nerves, she casually replied, "Yeah, shoppin' for dinner." She held the snake in her right hand, the bottle in her left.

Her situation was tenuous at best. The man had gotten the drop on her. Did he have his weapon trained on the back of her head? Her back was to him; her gun was clearly in his view in her back pocket.

The snake she held in her right hand was beginning to recover. Fay did not want to give up the snake, but she would get bit if she did not either kill it or let it go.

"You should drop the snake," the voice suggested.

She complied by slowly and gently tossing the snake off to her right. "Who are you?" she asked, with the cigar still clenched between her teeth.

"It would make me feel better if you put your gun down first."

Fay followed his instructions by raising her left hand to shoulder height, drawing the derringer from her back pocket, and lowering the gun to the ground.

She stood. "Do you mind if I turn around?"

Chapter 16

Fay turned. A man of average height stood in front of her, a makeshift crutch tucked under his right arm. His long, sinuous white hair fluttered in the faint wind. His warm, dark eyes and sun-furrowed, brown, craggy face suggested he was an American Indian. She estimated his age to be in the seventies. Still, then again, it was hard to estimate age with American Indians. His face exuded a warm, almost spiritual glow. For the moment, considering her physical condition and her predicament, it was like she was looking into the face of God.

"Who are you?" Fay asked.

The man laughed. "That was supposed to be my line."

Fay offered an apologetic smile. "I don't know who I am." She slipped her hand into her pocket and located her driver's license. "But here," she said, offering him her license. "Here's my driver's license."

There was a curious look on his face when he accepted her license. "They call me Two Dogs," the old man replied. He studied the picture on the permit for a moment and then checked her face. "Your name is Faye King, and you don't look good."

"I don't know anyone who takes a decent picture for her driver's license," she protested.

Two Dogs realized she had misunderstood him. "No," he clarified, pointing at her. "I meant you don't look good." He handed her driver's license back to her. "The person in the picture looks fine."

After he had handed the license back to her, Fay glanced at her picture. "I know," she acknowledged. "According to that picture, I've seen better days."

Two Dogs turned to survey her campsite. "You've got a nice place here."

"Ya like it? I decorated it myself," Fay quipped. She pointed to the battered SUV. "Over there's my bedroom and the place where I was born. My kitchen," she said, pointing to the fire pit. "And the rest," she swept her arms around her in a circle, "is my bathroom."

"I'm impressed. I think you should come and sit in the shade," Two Dogs suggested.

After making themselves comfortable under an ironwood tree, Fay pointed toward the cacti water barrels. "Would you like water?" she offered.

"Thank you, I would."

She fetched the water, went to the car, located the cigars, and slipped one into her shirt pocket.

When Fay returned with the water, the man asked, "There are two; where's the other one?"

Fay handed the water to Two Dogs. "OH! That's right." She pointed toward the mountain. "She went up the hill to fetch a pail of water…said to tell you not to leave without her." Fay studied him. "How'd you know there was another?"

His extended right arm swept across his body. "I see two sets of footprints. Only one person," Two Dogs explained. His gaze returned to her. "What are you doing here?"

"I've no idea," Fay admitted. "Two days ago, I woke up in that battered car, and here I am. This is where my life began. The worst thing is, I don't even know who I am or what came before. I am confused."

Two Dogs studied her face. "Other than that, how do you feel?" he inquired.

Fay frowned. "I feel as if I spent my day fighting a large human. My head is swollen to the size of those things over there." She pointed toward a barrel cactus. "My teeth are loose. I think my jawbone is dislocated. My ears are ringing as if I spent the day with Quasimodo in the belfry at Notre Dame. I'm hungry, tired, and cranky; I broke a nail…" Her voice trailed off. "Did I say I was hungry?"

"Interesting that you can remember Quasimodo and not your own name," Two Dogs noted. "Do you like peanut butter?"

She nodded and watched as the old man reached into his backpack. "Whatchya got in there?"

"A peanut butter sandwich," he replied, removing just that.

Fay eyed the sandwich. "Are you Joe Black?" she asked.

"Joe Black?

"You know. The grim reaper, Joe Black. He loves peanut butter."

Two Dogs smiled and shook his head. "No."

"Good," Fay stated. "I'll trade ya a cigar for that sandwich. It says on the box it's from the Dominican Republic. I smoked one a while ago. They're pretty good. And I don't think I even like cigars any more than I like small dogs."

Two Dogs nodded his head in agreement, while at the same time wondering where the heck this crazy was coming from. Smiling, though, he agreed, "Deal."

"Do you have a sandwich too?" Fay asked him. She accepted the sandwich from the old man and handed him the cigar.

"You go ahead. I've got jerky," he assured her.

The two people sat in silence while Fay inhaled the peanut butter sandwich and Two Dogs enjoyed his cigar.

When she had finished washing down the sandwich with rainwater, Two Dogs asked Fay, "Were you really going to eat that snake?"

"Yeah, I was."

The old man made a sour face.

"Two Dogs is an interesting name. How'd ya come by it?" Fay asked.

"You know, I asked my mother that same question."

"What'd she tell ya?"

"She told me that when each of her children was born, it was her custom to name them after the first thing she saw when she left the birthing tipi," Two Dogs explained.

"You lived in a tipi?"

Lapsing into a fake Indian vernacular, Two Dogs said, "All us Injuns live in tipi until after World War Two. The government allows us to move into mobile homes and park six junk cars in the backyard."

"Wow. I'd no idea. Go on. Sorry to interrupt," Fay apologized.

Two Dogs smiled. "My mother said, 'When your sister, Little Fawn, was born, the first thing I saw as I leaving tipi was small deer. Your brother, Soaring Eagle, was named from a large bird I had spotted near the sun.' My mother looked at me, 'Why do you ask, Two Dogs Humping?'" he finished.

Fay slapped her knee and laughed. Holding her right

cheek with her right hand, she protested, "Don't make me laugh. It hurts."

"Sorry."

"Ya know, Two Dogs, that'd make a great joke."

He chuckled. "That was a joke. My Navajo brothers gave me the name. I had told that joke so often, they began calling me Two Dogs Humping. The name seems to have stuck."

She looked around. "Is this Navajo land?" Fay asked him.

"No. This is the Apache Nation. There was a time when a Navajo came to Apache land, it meant war. Nowadays, people can't tell the difference between a Navajo and an Apache. This is my home," Two Dogs explained.

A voice called out from behind them, "Hey, y'all."

They turned around.

"Hi, Sue!" A confused Fay beckoned to Pearce. "Join us!"

Fay rose to her feet as "Sue" (really Pearce) approached.

"This is Two Dogs, our new friend," Fay said, making the introductions. "Sue, this is Two Dogs."

Two Dogs stood and extended his hand to JP. "It is a pleasure to meet an American sister," he said.

"Yes! Likewise! Good to meet a brother."

"Sue?" Two Dogs inquired. "Is that Sue 'Sue' or Sue 'Sioux?'"

Pearce laughed. "That sounds like something I'd say. My name is actually Janshe, by the way. Everyone, except for my sister for the time being, calls me Pearce," she explained. "I am myself from the Seminole Tribe. How about you?"

He stated, "Navajo."

Fay was listening to the conversation but, to Pearce, she appeared to be perplexed.

"I see you and my sister have met," Pearce said.

Two Dogs shook his head. "I'll have to explain it to you one day, but it's been interesting, to say the least."

"Do you have a name, Two Dogs?" Pearce asked.

He extended his right hand toward her. "Charlie Thunderbird. Pleased to meet you."

Pearce extended her hand to shake his. "Are you referring to the car?" she asked.

Charlie explained that the car was actually named after the bird.

At this point in the exchange, Pearce felt the need to sit. She could hardly contain her laughter.

Fay smiled. "Pleased to meet you, Charlie Thunderbird." She glanced at Charlie's makeshift crutch, then asked, "Did you injure your leg?"

"I'm an Army veteran," he explained. "I injured my hip in Afghanistan."

"Why didn't ya have the government repair it for ya?" Pearce asked. "The Veterans Administration has hospitals."

"I tried, Janshe, but the VA never seemed like they were interested in helping me. After several frustrating years, I gave up fighting with them," Charlie replied.

"And you walked here, sore hip and all?" Fay asked.

"No. I rode here on my horse," he clarified. "Unfortunately, the horse died along the way. I made this crutch and walked the rest of the way."

Filled with concern, Fay asked, "What are ya doing here, Charlie?"

"Two men stopped by my ranch about twenty-five

miles from here two days ago," he explained. "One man said there had been trouble and they were going for help. I did not talk to the second man. He stayed in their truck. These two guys didn't look like they belonged in the desert, so I was suspicious. I decided to have a look for myself, so here I am."

"But your horse died. I'm sorry."

"He was old. It was his time." Charlie's warm eyes searched Fay's face. "We need to get you to a hospital," he said.

"How are we gonna do that?" Fay asked. "Your hip won't endure a twenty-five-mile trek through the desert. And if I tried to walk outta here alone, I'd get lost or forget where I was goin' before sundown."

"True," Charlie agreed. He searched through his backpack. "I'm a little rusty, but I could build a fire and send smoke signals."

"No kidding?" Fay was amazed.

"I have a cell phone," Charlie went on, producing a small black phone. "I'll call nine-one-one."

"Nine-one-one?" Fay queried.

"Tell you what," Charlie offered. "I'll call the U.S. Forest Service. I know the number."

In a short time, Charlie was speaking to the Forest Service. He clicked off the phone, then told the women, "They've been looking for you."

"Who?" Fay asked.

"The Navy, your father, half the population of Arizona," Charlie explained. "A chopper is on its way. They should be here in thirty minutes. You still hungry?"

Fay shook her head. Her appetite had gone the way of the carrier pigeon. "But I bet Sue is."

****

"Sir," the chopper pilot said to Gifford Champion, "we've received a call from a forest ranger. A reservation sheriff has found Commander Green and her sister."

Champion's eyes brightened at the news. "When? Where? Are they alive?"

"They're alive, sir."

"Thank God. Has anyone contacted Bill Green's chopper?"

"Affirmative, sir."

****

Twenty-five minutes later, Charlie Thunderbird observed two helicopters searching an area two miles south. "I must have miscalculated our position," he said.

Fay had fallen asleep with her head resting in Charlie's lap.

Charlie immediately began talking on his cell phone. Soon, the two hovering choppers reared up, pointed in their direction, and were hovering nearby within seconds.

As the two choppers settled to the ground, Fay, Pearce, and Charlie shielded their eyes from the dust and flying rocks. Army medics burst from the larger chopper's open door and rushed toward them, with two stretchers and medical equipment in hand.

Charlie observed a tall man with white hair exit the smaller chopper, supported by a soldier. His eyes widened. He gave his new friends look of admiration. "You are the daughters of William Green, the great man," he said.

"Who is William Green?" Fay asked.

Chapter 17

Dr. Gelis, Tucson General Hospital's neuropsychologist, told Pearce that the restoration of her sister's memory would be a slow, frustrating process for both her and Fay. "Don't expect miracles but be thankful for small gains," the doctor advised. "Expect to repeat things to her again and again. Her long-term memory is gone, but I expect it will return."

"Will she remember anythin'?"

"Her experience in the desert will be easiest for her to recall. We don't expect her to recall her life before that," Dr. Gelis admitted. "Amnesia is unpredictable. While we can't envisage a timetable for her recovery, we can expect to recover her memory in time. With your help."

"What should I do?" Pearce pleaded.

"Be supportive. Expect your sister to be irritable. She may forget what you told her a minute before," the doctor cautioned. "Be patient, repeat, and reinforce. Her memory will gradually return, and as it does, her memory of her ordeal in the desert will fade."

Pearce sighed. Tears welled in her eyes as sadness swept through her soul.

Dr. Gelis reached over and grasped Pearce's left hand. "Are you ready for this?"

Pearce nodded.

"It's going to be tough," Dr. Gelis warned.

Pearce insisted, "I'll do whatever it takes, Doctor."

"I've conducted a thorough neuropsychological evaluation. I've tested Fay's cognitive abilities, sensory-perceptual skills, motor speed and coordination, attention, concentration, and mental processing speed. I've tested her right hand and left hand performance, assessed her language functions, assessed her non-verbal skills, and tested her verbal and non-verbal memory," Dr. Gelis relayed. "I finished my evaluation by assessing her executive functions and cognitive flexibility."

"I'm not sure I understand it all, Doctor Gelis, but it sounds comprehensive," Pearce replied.

"We've been thorough, for your sister's sake. Should litigation ensue in the future, we need to be documented for the lawyers."

"I hadn't considered the legal aspects," Pearce stated.

Dr. Gelis responded, "I think your sister is fortunate. Her brain has been injured, but I expect a complete recovery."

"Thank you, Dr. Gelis." Pearce smiled, although worry was still evident on her face.

Dr. Gelis smiled in return. "Why don't you go say hello to her?" she suggested, standing up. "And remember, she won't know who you are at first. She may even be abusive toward you. That will pass. Be patient."

Pearce nodded. "I will."

"Your sister will have a much bigger challenge ahead once she's dealt with her memory loss."

"What do you mean?"

The doctor's expression suggested concern. "When she was admitted, the hospital gave her a complete physical. It's standard procedure." She hesitated for a moment. "As you know, your sister took several severe blows to her head," Dr. Gelis went on. "Her head injuries were inflicted by blunt force. She was beaten by a fist or with a club."

"I thought the car crash…I don't understand…" Pearce said, her voice trailing off.

"She was assaulted. Four or five hard blows to her face. Two more blows to the right side of her head."

"She was assaulted?" Pearce exclaimed. "By whom?"

"If we knew, there would have been an arrest made," Dr. Gelis replied, her eyes conveying her deep sympathy. "Fay's lucky she did not suffer optic nerve damage. Her skull is intact, although her jaw was dislocated, meaning she won't need reconstructive surgery."

"Thank God," Pearce murmured.

"There's one more problem." Dr. Gelis stopped talking and sighed. She knew that the best way to relay this information was to be upfront. "Let me get right to it. When we examined your sister, we found a bite mark on her left breast and another on the left side of her neck," the doctor stated.

"Animal?" Pearce asked.

"No. Human," Dr. Gelis clarified. "We questioned that. Further examination revealed she had been sexually molested. To be blunt, it appears your sister was raped."

"No!" Pearce cried.

Dr. Gelis maintained her sympathetic look and nodded.

"Wow," Pearce whispered. "How do I…I guess I should…break it to her?"

"Why not wait until she has fully recovered?" Dr. Gelis suggested. "If you tell her now, she won't have the strength to deal with it. And she probably won't remember you told her anyway."

"No point in telling her again and again," Pearce decided.

"Right."

****

Deputy Doug visited the office of Bob's Security Service. Lenny Crane's employment application indicated that he had served in the Navy and had retired after twenty years. He had held several security jobs before his employment with Bob's. Company policy had required all employees to be fingerprinted. An identification photo was included in Lenny's personnel file.

As Doug perused the file, Marci, Bob's accountant/office manager/receptionist/gofer, watched. "Lenny's a real nice guy," she offered.

"Do you know him well?" Doug asked.

"No. Not really," Marci admitted. "Lenny was a quiet one. But I could tell he was a decent guy."

"Why?"

"Well, when he first came to work here, I already knew he was a single man, so I asked him if he would like a home-cooked meal. He declined my offer, but I insisted he come by the house that Friday after work," Marci explained.

"Did he?" Doug inquired.

"He did. He was reluctant, but I figured he was shy. He brought a bottle of wine. We had a nice dinner. The next thing I knew," Marci said, "it was morning, and I had one helluva headache to show for it."

"You fell asleep?"

"Yeah, right after dinner. We ate dinner and bam.

The next thing I knew, it was time to go to work," she explained. "But that's how I know Lenny's a decent guy."

"How so?"

"Well," Marci said, "he could have taken advantage of me. But he didn't. And while I was sleeping, he cleaned up the dishes. Only a decent guy would have done that."

"Did you meet him ever again?" Doug asked.

"No." She sighed. "He didn't seem to have the time after that. He up and left."

Doug thanked Marci and hurried to his car to call Sheriff Gus.

****

Pearce left Dr. Gelis's first-floor office and proceeded to Fay's fourth-floor private room. Like Dr. Gelis, the entire staff at Tucson General seemed nice. As Pearce approached the open doorway, she saw that a nurse was leaving the room.

"She's sleeping," the nurse said as they passed each other.

Pearce slipped into the room and said "hi" to the rent-a-cop sitting inside the doorway. She sat in a chair next to her sister's bed.

Several minutes had passed before Fay, with her eyes closed, said, "I'm awake. What do you want?"

"Hi, Spider. How ya feeling?" Pearce responded.

"Like crap." Fay sighed. "Worse than crap. Why, you another doctor?"

"Can I get anythin' for you?"

Fay did not respond. She opened her swollen and blackened right eye slightly and closed it again. "Who are you?" she asked.

"I'm JP, your sister," Pearce replied.

"I have a sister?"

"Yeah," Pearce affirmed. "Me."

Fay opened her right eye again, gave JP the once over, and closed it. "Oh. I didn't know."

Pearce reached toward her sister and grasped her right hand. "Your hands are dry. Can I rub hand lotion on them?" she requested.

Fay did not respond.

"You asleep?"

"No." Fay opened her eyes. After studying Pearce for a moment, she commented, "You're pretty. If I'm to have a sister, I'm glad she's pretty." She closed her eyes. "Where did you get the tan? And how did I end up with an Arab for a sister?"

"Gotta be the Injun in me," Pearce answered. She smiled and reached for hand lotion placed on a stand near the bed. After squirting a small amount into the palm of her right hand, she asked, "Can I put the lotion on your hands?"

"Go for it, Sacajawea." Fay opened her eyes, observing JP, and then was silent for a moment. "An American Indian Indian. Or an India Indian?" she asked.

"The American version."

Fay pinched a lock of her blonde hair between her thumb and forefinger. Drawing her hair to within a few inches of her eyes, she examined it. "And you said you were my sister?" she inquired.

"Same father, different mother," Pearce explained.

"Sounds confusing."

Pearce grinned. As she applied the lotion to her sister's hands, she said, "Dad was here a while ago. Did you see him?"

"A tall, distinguished lookin' guy with silver hair?" Fay asked.

"Yeah."

"No. I didn't see the guy." A slight smile formed on Fay's lips. "He's my father?" Her short laugh was filled with amusement. "I think I was trying to flirt with him last time he was in here," she admitted.

"William Green," Pearce explained, continuing to massage her sister's dry hands with the hand lotion.

"Now I'm feeling creepy," Fay said. "You say he's my father…and I thought he was my doctor, and I had a crush on him." She rested for a moment. Her chest heaved as if breathing had become difficult for her. "So, I have a family," Fay went on. "A pretty Indian princess sister and a tall, distinguished father."

"Yes, you do. And you have a brother too. But do you want to hear the real jaw-dropper?" Pearce asked. "That silver-haired devil is the President of the United States. Or used to be, anyway."

"How about a mother?" Fay asked. "Do I have one of those?"

"We did. But Mom died about twenty years ago."

"Too bad."

"Yeah. Too bad," Pearce affirmed.

Fay re-opened her eyes and studied Pearce. "Who did you say you were again, darlin'?"

"Sacajawea. Your sister."

"Oh, yeah, yeah, yeah… that's right…my sister. Tell me. How do I get out of this place?" Fay asked.

"Well, you have to recover first. And we'll see about gettin' y'all released from here," Pearce replied.

"Y'all…where y'all from, Precious?"

"Florida," Pearce explained. "We're both from

Florida."

"Too bad."

"Why?"

"I'd be from a warm place. Like Hawaii," Fay decided.

"Florida is warm," Pearce replied. "Hey! Are ya hungry?" she asked.

"Hey! Yes! I'm starving!" Fay struggled to sit up. With a hopeful look on her face, she asked, "Can you get me some fast food? They got a fast-food place here in the hotel, don't they?"

Pearce grinned. "This is a hospital. But yes, there's a fast-food restaurant near the waitin' rooms." The expression on Pearce's face changed from joy to sorrow. "I don't think they'll let ya have any fast food, Spider," she said.

"Spiders? Goddamn spiders. That's all I need right now." Fay dropped her head back onto her pillow and slapped at her bed covers. "Damn!" she murmured. "A hospital." Louder, she said, "You gotta help me get outta here!"

****

"Did Lenny Crane ever turn up?" Virgil Gus asked Doug.

"That's why I'm callin', Sheriff," Doug explained. "I left the office of his former employer. He checks out. Former Navy, honorable discharge. The fingerprints from Bob's match his service record. I'm runnin' a prior with the FBI right now. I'll let you know what turns up."

"From the sound of your voice, little buddy," Virgil said, "something else is bothering' y'all."

"I don't know if this is anythin' or not, Virgil," Doug admitted, "but when I was talkin' to the lady here at Bob's, she says Lenny Crane came callin'."

"Oh?"

"She invited him over to supper. But she fell asleep right after they ate. Next thin' she knows, it's the next mornin' and time for work," Doug relayed.

"She fell asleep, you say?"

"Yes, sir. Sounds odd, don't it?"

"Good work, Doug," Virgil said appreciatively. "It's beginnin' to look like Lenny is involved. Keep lookin'. I've got a meetin' with the Arizona Gila County Sheriff and his detectives in a few minutes. The detective spoke with a rancher, a former Indian reservation sheriff who found Miss Green and her sister in the desert. I've got Lonny flyin' in to help me out. I want you to hold down the fort for a while longer. You're doin' a good job down there, Doug. Keep it up."

"Thanks, Sheriff. I appreciate hearin' that," Doug replied.

"Oh, hey, Doug, you still seein' the medical student?"

"I am boss. All is well. Thanks for askin'."

****

As the days passed and with her sister's patient coaching, Fay regained her memory. She reasoned that if she could master the names of all the former U.S. presidents, she stood a good chance of getting out of the place she had grown to hate.

Fay began to notice the fresh flowers that were always by her bedside. She asked why they were there. She was told her friends Joey and Vinny made sure she had a fresh bouquet every day. Nice guys, it was too bad she did not recall who they were.

It seemed whenever Fay opened her eyes, anyone in

the immediate area would proceed to ask her a raft of questions, the most common ones being, "How do you feel? Do you know what day it is? Who is the President of the United States?" She would tell them the President was her father. And they believed her! *Yeah, right!* If she got those three questions right, she would be on her way home…wherever home was.

The days turned into weeks. Fay had mastered all the U.S. presidents' names, plus two other men who were not presidents. For some unknown reason, Jimmy Hoffa and Jeff Davis kept slipping into her lineup. Her sister would remind her Hoffa and Davis were former presidents but of a whole different kind.

People would visit her. Most she could not remember from one day to the next. Fay did look forward to her daily visits from her friend, Charlie. After dark, when the daily hospital hubbub had subsided, Charlie would come to her room. Charlie was great. Each night, he would sing to her. Or perhaps he was chanting? Whatever it was, it made her constant headache go away. She came to regard Charlie Thunderbird as her medicine man.

One day, Charlie stopped coming. When Fay asked the pretty woman with the black hair (*her sister?*) about it, she was told Charlie had been admitted into the hospital for hip surgery. Their father, the tall, distinguished guy with the silver hair, had arranged for it. Fay missed Charlie, but she was happy his hip would be repaired.

Later in the day, as she was half-asleep and listening to her favorite gospel singer on her MP3, Fay overheard someone having a conversation with the rent-a-cop at the doorway. She opened her eyes, and there he was! The

King! Elvis himself had come to visit her in the hospital.

She must be the luckiest woman in the whole wide world. Imagine that! The King…right there in her hospital room. And he had explicitly come to call on her. There was another man with him. A guy named Lonny? Or Boyd? Or maybe he was from Brooklyn, and his name was Bird? She was having a tough time keeping people and their names straight anyway.

Fay, Elvis, and Boyd chatted together for the longest time. Then, Elvis and the other guy left. They were going to visit with Two Dogs for a while, they said. Before he left, the King promised her that they would go fishing on his boat one day soon. *Fishing. Yeah, right.* About the only fishing that would happen that day was…well, she didn't want to think about it now.

****

Virgil and Lonny visited with Charlie Thunderbird in his hospital room. After talking to the Gila County Sheriff and his detective, Sheriff Gus was curious to learn more about the men who had stopped at Charlie's ranch.

"How's Fay doing, Sheriff?" Charlie asked.

Virgil shook his head. "She's still in the ozone, Charlie," he said. "She asks often about you and has been callin' me Elvis."

Charlie gave him the once over. "You look like Elvis. I can see how she might be confused," he acknowledged. "But didn't he die a long time ago?"

"The Sheriff's responsible for about seventy-five percent of all Elvis sightings in the Florida panhandle," Lonnie offered.

Virgil laughed. "Yeah. Half the time, they want my autograph…or Elvis's autograph. It's flat out weird at times."

"I guess people refuse to let the man die," Charlie said.

"Hey, Charlie, I've got a question for you," Virgil said.

"Anything to help, Sheriff."

"Two men stopped by your place and your conversation with them prompted you to venture out into the desert, right?" Virgil asked.

"That's right," Charlie confirmed. "I'd seen two cars pass by my place earlier in the day. I noticed the make and the cars' color but not much else. It's hunting season, so I get a few hunters passing by." Charlie motioned with his right hand toward a water glass placed on the table near his bed. "Would you mind, Sheriff?" he asked.

Virgil handed him the water.

"I spent all my life in the desert and never got thirsty. Now they got me laid up in this damn air-conditioned hospital, and I can't drink enough water," Charlie grumbled.

Both Virgil and Lonny laughed.

"Okay. It's the two men you want to know about," Charlie went on. "As I said, I saw two cars pass by my place in the morning. About two hours later, one car came back along the road and pulled into my place. There were two men in the car, but only one got out. He said they had run into trouble about twenty-five or thirty miles up the road and needed to use my phone."

"Your phone?"

"Yeah. I wondered about it," Charlie continued. "These days most everyone has a cell phone, but not this guy. Anyway, I took him inside my trailer, showed him to the phone, and went back outside. I wanted to keep my eye on the other guy. The one in the car."

"What was he doin'?" Virgil wanted to know.

"He sat there and waited for his friend," Charlie answered. "My refrigerator is stocked with beer, so when the guy was done using the phone, I asked if they wanted a beer for the road. He took to the idea. I pulled two beers out and walked to the car with the man."

"I'd imagine you got a good look at the two men, Charlie," Lonny said.

"I could pick them out in a lineup if I had to," Charlie asserted. "These two were odd ones. I could tell by the way they were dressed they were not hunters. They weren't tourists either. It got me to thinking about what they were up to."

"I read your interview with the Gila County deputy," Virgil said. "You mentioned the second man was older."

"He was older than the man who used the phone. He looked to be in his mid to late fifties. But it's hard to tell with you Caucasians."

Virgil grinned at the sarcasm and continued with his questions. "You told the deputy the man was a cigarette smoker?" he asked.

"I mentioned it because he had an unusual way of lighting his matches," Charlie offered. "They were the 'light anywhere' matches. He used his thumbnail to strike the match. I thought it odd. Most people use a lighter or book matches. But this guy used stick matches."

Virgil reached into this jacket pocket and withdrew a folded paper. He unfolded it and handed it to Charlie. "This is a composite sketch of a man I'm lookin' for. Is this the man you described to the deputy?" he inquired.

Charlie took the sketch from Virgil. He studied it for

a moment and then handed the drawing back to him. "That's him," he confirmed. "Seems like you know who he is."

"His name is Lenny Crane," Virgil explained. "Lenny was last seen in Citrus Tree, Florida. He disappeared not long after two men were murdered."

Charlie scratched his head. "As I recall, the guy who used the phone called him Ron."

****

The following morning, Fay opened her eyes, surveyed her surroundings, and declared, "What the hell?" She sat up. The room was deserted. According to the digital alarm clock on the stand near her bed, it was 7:10 A.M.

"Hey!" she barked. No response. Again, she surveyed the vacant room. *Will you look at those flowers*! Fay noticed the IV tube attached to her bruised right wrist. She clenched her teeth and winced as she successfully removed the IV with her left hand and fought a brief but losing battle with the metal containment railing running the length of the right side of her bed.

That completed, Fay threw off her bed covers, crawled to the foot of the bed, and hopped to the floor. Standing on the cold floor in her bare feet, her gaze swept the floor, searching for slippers or shoes. Seeing neither, she crossed the room to the closet and threw open the double doors. While the clothing selection within was sparse, she did find a bathrobe and slipped it on.

She wished the startled rent-a-cop a spirited "good morning" as she whisked past him in the hallway near the door to her room. She continued on to the nurse's station further along the hall.

"Morning," Fay said to the nurse, whose attention was focused on a computer monitor. When the nurse looked up at her, her jaw dropped. Fay offered her hand. "Fay Green." She jerked the thumb of her opposite hand back over her shoulder. "Room four-twelve."

"Miss Green…" the nurse stammered.

By now, the rent-a-cop had caught up with her and stood several feet from her. Fay looked over her right shoulder at him. She read his nametag, said, "Hey, Pete," and turned her attention back to the nurse.

"Why don't you go back to your room, Miss Green, and I'll call Dr. Gelis for you?" the nurse suggested.

"Is Dr. Gelis the one I need to see to get me out of this place?"

"Dr. Gelis is your doctor. And yes."

"Where is he?" Fay demanded. "Right now, I mean."

"She," the nurse clarified. "Dr. Gelis is with her patients right now. If you please go back to your room, I will see—"

Fay waved a dismissing hand. "No, no, no. You tell Dr. Gelis I'm having some fast food in the lobby," she insisted. "When she's got a minute to spare, she can find me there."

Fay turned and walked barefoot toward the elevator. She stopped, turned, and looked at Pete the rent-a-cop. "You comin', Pete?" she asked him. "I seem to be short on cash at the moment. I need you to buy me breakfast. I will pay you back," she promised.

Chapter 18

One week later, in the office of AmeriCon attorney Aaron Morton

"Faye King," "Corazon Garza," and a man of Asian ancestry, introduced as Mr. Ho, faced attorney Aaron Morton and his client Don Valley.

"Don," Aaron Morton cautioned, "be careful. This one has a ruthless reputation. She'll fillet us both like fish."

"What's your stake in this, Ms. King?" Valley asked.

"I, like you, Mr. Valley, have to contend with my demons," Fay responded. "I've got everyone, including the IRS, FBI, CIA, DEA, and the JD, lookin' up my dress. I had to cut a deal with the Feds. I deliver Roman Justine to them or spend my life cleanin' toilets for every bull dyke at the Women's Federal Prison Camp in Pekin, Illinois. I heard they make the lawyers clean the toilets with their tongues. So, I'm motivated, like you should be."

Mr. Ho, who had not said a word since they had first entered Morton's office, directed an icy stare toward Aaron Morton.

Morton got the message. He looked from Mr. Ho to Fay, to Pearce, and back at Ho again; all three appeared cool and stoic. He shifted his attention toward Don

Valley. "Don, if you've never taken my advice, this is the time to do it. Play ball with these people," Morton urged. "If you don't, I suspect three of the five people in this room will walk away under their own power. And I don't believe you, or I, are on the list."

A tad melodramatic, Fay thought, but she liked the spin Mr. Morton put on it.

"What do you want me to do?" Valley said with a dramatic sigh.

"Wear a wire," Fay responded. "Glue yourself to Roman Justine. We want to know everything there is to know about the GFA's inner workings."

"I get caught, I die anyway," Valley protested.

Fay recalled a story Gifford had told her about a GFA CEO who had approached him about exposing the GFA. The woman had ended up "accidentally" drowned in a boating mishap. The incident was likely on Valley's mind now. He needed more encouragement.

Fay shot a piercing stare at Valley. "You tried to kill me, you piece of shit. That pissed me off. The way I see it, you've got no choice," she growled. "If that's not enough reason, why don't I start with accessory? Bid shoppin', conspiracy, debauchery?" She handed a manila envelope to him as she spoke. "Embezzlement…by the time the government works its way up the alphabet, you'll be tied up in court until you're penniless, or better yet, dead of old age. Or, if that is not enough to get your attention, how about I bite your face off? We'd save us all a crapload of time."

Valley opened the envelope and withdrew three photographs. The color drained from his face.

"When the government gets to the S's, there'll be two, Mr. Valley: solicitation and statutory rape." Seeing the quizzical look on Valley's face, Fay responded, "I'm referrin' to Marla Dent, age fifteen. Photo number two." She pointed to the photos he held. "Math isn't my strong suit, Mr. Valley, but by my count, and correct me if I'm wrong, it makes Marla a minor." She smiled at Don Valley. "They call it 'jailbait.'"

Don Valley swallowed and shifted in his chair but remained silent.

"Mr. Morton believes that if you refuse me, you die, right here, right now. He may be right." Fay smiled, being careful not to threaten Don Valley. She had used Morton's words, not her own. Her voice softened as she said, "Humor me, Mr. Valley. If you wear the wire, you may die. On the other hand, you may be able to plea-bargain with the feds. If I were a bettin' person, and I am, I'd go with the odds on this one."

Valley nodded and lowered his gaze. "Still…I need time."

"Fuck that shit!" Fay barked an immediate response. She glanced at her wristwatch and added in a calmer voice, "In four hours, Corazon and I will be aboard my jet on our way to the Cayman Islands, if you agree to this." She softened her tone even further. "Follow my lead, Mr. Valley. Take an early retirement—negotiate a golden parachute. Get out before the shit hits the fan. Don't be a pussy. I need to know your answer…now."

Valley sighed.

"Look, Valley," Fay continued. "Mr. Ho is an impatient man. I am sure he would be able to persuade you. But in the end, I think if you play your cards right, you'll come out clean."

"What she means, Don," Attorney Morton counseled, "is that Mr. Ho is more than likely Triad. His method of persuasion goes without saying. If you play ball with the feds, I will ensure that the Justice Department, or the Federal Trade Commission, will reach an agreement with AmeriCon. A court order will be issued to refrain from initiating a suit against us, if we consent to cease activities which could be the subject of antitrust action." Morton's gaze shifted from Valley to Fay. "She's got you - check that – she's got the entire GFA membership by the balls. If the feds take her down, she will take us all down with her."

"I'll wear the wire," Valley said.

"Smart move." Fay turned to Mr. Ho and said, "Mr. Ho, with your permission, Corazon and I are gone. He's all yours." She stood, straightened her skirt, and picked up her briefcase and purse. Pearce followed her lead.

The two women had reached the door when Fay hesitated and turned to face the three men who were watching her in awe. She smiled in Mr. Ho's direction.

"Take good care of him, Mr. Ho," Fay stated. "It's been nice knowin' y'all." She pointed her right index finger and thumb at Valley as if she were pointing a pistol at him. She winked, dropping her thumb as if she had pulled the trigger.

As they walked along the hallway to the exit, Pearce whispered, "I think you'll be one of the five people nominated for an Oscar this year."

"Was I good?" Fay whispered back.

"Good? Ma'am, you were great. You had me so convinced, I almost wet my pants. I'm sure Valley and his lawyer did." JP was grinning. "Where'd y'all learn to cuss like that?"

Fay chuckled. "From sailors, like y'all, darlin'. But if it makes any difference to ya…I wasn't actin'. And

Jangho's Triad impersonation was beyond Academy Awards quality. Well," she added, "we have a jet waiting at Sky Harbor International. Where do you want to go?"

"We were fortunate Jangho was visiting the States and could help us," Pearce reflected.

Fay agreed. "And it was good to see Colonel Kim again."

"I should help Bart return our borrowed jet to the DEA. We could drop you off at home on our way," Pearce offered.

"Sounds great!"

They continued walking; Fay stopped. She looked at Pearce with a questioning gaze in her eyes. "Where's home?" she asked.

Pearce gasped. "You—"

Fay laughed and continued walking. "Only teasing! Home is Bremerton, right?"

"You often worry me, ma'am." Pearce shook her head.

"Before I go home, I've unfinished business to attend to," Fay stated.

"Ma'am, you're not thinkin' about goin' after your kidnappers?"

"I am. I've got a score to settle."

"Promise me you won't act until I return," Pearce pleaded.

"You got it."

The two women reached the building's elevator. Fay punched the "down" button.

"On second thought, Sacajawea," Fay said to her sister, "when we get to Sky Harbor, file your flight plan for the Grand Cayman. Have Bart contact Luke Air Force Base Flight Ops. I want to park the jet there until tomorrow night. I've got more unfinished business to attend to."

A concerned look came over Pearce's face. "Don't tell me you're goin'…"

"No. I'm not," Fay interrupted her. "I want to say goodbye to Charlie Thunderbird. And I want to call Joey and Vinny to thank them for the boatload of flowers."

****

Charlie Thunderbird watched from his porch as a distant dust cloud worked its way up the dirt road leading to his ranch. He had a visitor. Perhaps hunters? He stood there, watching as the car drew closer. A brown utility vehicle pulling a horse trailer turned into his driveway. Charlie shot a confirming glance at the rifle propped near his front door. He continued to watch until the car came to a stop in front of his house. It was hunters, all right.

The driver's door opened, and to his surprise, out jumped Fay. She smiled and waved. "Two Dogs!" she called.

Charlie relaxed and gingerly stepped from his porch to greet her.

"Hi, Charlie. How y'all feeling?" Fay asked.

He responded by patting his hip. "Almost as good as new," he said, with a giant smile on his face.

"I'm heading for home. But I wanted to stop by to say goodbye."

Charlie looked past her. His gaze settled on the horse trailer. "You plan on riding back to Washington state on horseback?" he asked.

Fay turned and looked back at the trailer. "No," she laughed. She seemed excited. "Close your eyes. I've got a surprise for you."

Charlie closed his eyes.

"No peeking until I say so, Charlie," Fay called.

Charlie counted the minutes until he heard, "Okay, you can open your eyes now."

Standing before him was a beautiful black and white pinto.

Fay motioned for him to come closer. "Come on. Come meet her."

Charlie approached the horse. He patted her on the muzzle and stepped back to admire the beautiful animal. She was standing at full attention, her ears pricked forward, observing her new surroundings.

Fay handed the lead rope to him.

A large grin formed on his lips. "How? Why?" Charlie spluttered.

"It happens I had an extra five-thousand dollars I didn't know what to do with." Fay pointed at the trailer. "I got a good deal on a horse and a trailer. I was hoping I could leave her here for a while. She won't be a problem for you. I bought a three-year supply of feed at the feed store. They'll deliver it too." With a hopeful expression on her face, she asked, "So what do you say? Can I leave her here?"

Charlie considered her proposal, then nodded. "If you promise to visit her."

Fay turned from Charlie and reached up and patted the pinto's neck. "They told me she's a bit spirited," she said with a sigh. "She's got spirit, Charlie, and I seem to have lost mine." Fay continued to pat the horse's neck. "When I was a child, my mother told me I was a thoroughbred. I protested, 'Mama, I am not a horse!' My mother laughed and said, 'No, darlin'. It means y'all have spirit.' You see, my mother was a true Southern lady. At the time, I did not appreciate her concept. But, as I matured, I came to know what courage and strength truly were."

Fay turned to Charlie. "I can assure you I once had more than my fair share of spirit," she continued. "I'm no longer that thoroughbred. Now I seem to do what I have to do to get by. I'm ashamed to say it, but I no longer find passion in my purpose." She smiled at Charlie. "Forgive me, Charlie. This is a happy occasion! I didn't mean to cast a cloud over it."

"Faydra, I am Indian. My people know the spirits," Charlie replied. "I will talk to my people about it. We will talk to our spirits. We will get your spirit back for you."

Fay stepped forward to hug Charlie's neck. "Thank you, Two Dogs. You have proven to be a wonderful friend." She released him from her grasp and stepped away from him. "Deal. I'll be back to visit," she promised.

Fay looked with affection at the pinto and frowned. "Sad. She doesn't seem to have a name."

Charlie's gaze swept the horse from head to tail. "Her name is *Ne-ahu-jah klesh at-tad*."

"Navajo?" Fay asked.

He nodded and grinned. "It means 'pretty snake girl.'"

Chapter 19

Bremerton, Washington, five days later

Fay awoke with a start, a strange hand pressed over her mouth. Fay had been assaulted, according to Pearce, but she had no recollection of it. But that would never happen again! This was not her preferred way to obtain sex. She could not see her attacker because the room was dim, but she knew he was a man. She struggled; it was futile to resist.

"Don't struggle, and I won't hurt you," the man warned in an almost soothing whisper. "I'll remove my hand if you swear not to scream."

Fay considered her options.

"You'd be dead by now, Commander Green, if my intent was to kill you."

She nodded her head in agreement. The pressure of the man's hand eased from around her mouth. "Who are you?" Fay croaked. "What do you want?"

The man snapped on the nightstand light. Through her dilated eyes, the man's face came into focus. What she assumed to be a blade was pressed against her throat.

"Remember, don't scream," the intruder warned.

Inching her hand up under the pillow, Fay searched for the derringer she had placed there before she had retired for the night. "Back for seconds, Doctor? Was I good in my beaten state?" she taunted.

He did not respond.

"What?" Her hand continued to feel for her derringer. "You raped me, you low-life bastard."

"Rape?" He seemed unsure.

"You don't recall raping me?" Fay asked scornfully.

"I didn't rape you, Commander Green." The man's gaze shifted to the right, then back at her. His voice was soft. "Your weapon is in my pocket."

"How do you know me? How did you even find me?"

"I might be an assassin, Commander, but a rapist I am not."

"Not included in your job description?"

"Commander Green, I want to talk to you for a minute, then I'll go," the intruder asserted. He removed the knife from against her throat.

Fay shifted upward to a sitting position, pulling her bed covers under her chin. "Go ahead, I'm all ears."

"When I dumped you in the desert, I thought you were dead," the man began.

"Apparently, you were wrong. What was that supposed to be?" Fay mocked. "Oh, right, I drove my sister and me out into the Arizona desert in a drunken stupor and crashed. Shame on me."

"I picked you up from Roman Justine's home."

"What was I doing at Roman Justine's home?"

"You attended a party," the man explained. "Mr. Justine doesn't feel the need to explain his actions or the actions of his guests to low-life bastards like me. I do what I'm told."

"Which includes disposing of people in the desert."

"I do what I'm told," the man insisted. "Justine pays well."

"You couldn't pay me enough to murder anyone," Fay retorted. "Enlighten me. How does one get into the business of killing another human?"

"I was a SEAL, ma'am," the man responded. "The Navy, my employer, and your employer paid me to serve and protect my country, and yes, to kill people. After fifteen years of legal killing, it wasn't hard for me to make the transition. Same job, different employer, better pay."

"Justine is your employer. I don't think it's the same thing," Fay shot back.

"I'm not trying to justify what I do. And I'm not proud of it," the intruder insisted. "But it's what I do."

"I would imagine you're good at what you do."

"I came here to warn you, Commander."

"Warn me?" Fay asked derisively. Her eyes widened, and her jaw dropped. "You get a conscience suddenly?"

"Maybe," the man replied. "As I said, when I dumped you in the desert, I thought I was dumping a mob lawyer. My orders were to sever your head and torch your car."

A chill ran up her spine. "My head! What in God's name for?" To quench her dry throat, Fay pointed to water glass on her nightstand. "Will you hand me the glass?"

The man handed her the glass. She sipped at the water. "What were you going to do with my head?" Fay demanded.

"Justine wanted it. He said he would shrink it; he would send it to Joey Stumpanato," the intruder divulged. "I don't ask questions."

"I know, you do what you're told," Fay repeated.

She felt her neck. "My head is still attached. What happened?"

"I was looking at your face, thinking how beautiful you were." The man shook his head slightly. "I attended the meeting where the PI introduced your surveillance to Justine. I had never seen you before. Your disguise was convincing."

"My head was swollen like a watermelon. I can imagine how beautiful I looked…but thanks for the compliment," Fay replied.

"I picked up your purse. I removed your wallet and looked at the picture on your driver's license," the intruder continued. "It took a minute, but I recalled who you were. I had met you before."

Fay studied the man's face. After a few moments, she realized that she recognized him, but she could not recall where from.

He must have read the puzzled look on her face. "The Pollywog. Last year," he prompted.

"Right!" Her photographic memory kicked in. "I spoke with you at the bar," Fay recalled. "I asked you if you knew Paul Charma, whom I later learned you had assassinated. You told me you were a Marine. The MEU, I think you said?"

"That's right, Commander. You introduced yourself to me as Faye King at the time. I remembered the name," the man explained. "My name is Jon Shaman. And I, like you, have a photographic memory."

"That's why I still have my head?" Fay asked.

"That's right," Shaman confirmed. "When I realized you were not a mob lawyer, I knew there would be no way your disappearance and death would go unnoticed. As far as I knew, it was too late to do anything about your death."

"You created an accident scene because something that looked to be an accident would not attract a criminal investigation," Fay said, filling in the blanks. "Hence, you inadvertently saved my life."

"I stopped at a ranch while leaving the desert. I told an Indian who lived there that there had been an accident and I was going for help," Shaman resumed.

"Two Dogs," Fay said softly.

"Two Dogs?"

"Oh, it's a long story. The Indian found me. The Indian mentioned two men had stopped. Two Dogs found us and called for help," Fay recounted. "What did you tell Justine when you didn't return with my head?"

"I told him I heard a car coming along the road. So, I split."

"He believed you?"

"Why wouldn't he?" Shaman asked.

"And you didn't tell him my true identity?"

"I didn't mention it."

"Why not?" Fay wanted to know.

"He didn't ask," Shaman answered. "Justine pays me to clean up his messes, not to gather information."

Fay chuckled. "So, what's the problem? Justine thinks I'm dead, and he doesn't know my true identity." The expression on Shaman's face told her otherwise. "He knows I'm alive. How?"

"Valley told him you were still alive," Shaman revealed.

"Valley, that weak assed pussy. He sold me out. Did he mention anything else?"

"No. Only that you were still alive and on your way to the Cayman Islands."

"Huh, so he will start his hunt there," Fay surmised. "Which brings us to why you are here."

"Once Justine knew you were alive, he put his PI on your trail and told me to stand by…which could only mean he still wants your head," Shaman explained. "He's on a trophy hunt, you being the trophy."

"Mercy," Fay said in a dry whisper. "I'm to be added to the trophies on his wall."

"Given enough time, his PI will find you, whether you're Faye King or Fay Green," Shaman warned. "To be forewarned is to be forearmed."

"Thanks, I think." Fay averted her gaze away from Shaman. Drumming her fingers on her bed while she hatched a plan, she returned her gaze to him. "I need to get Justine before he gets me," she resolved.

Shaman nodded. "A good defense is to have a great offense."

Fay nodded as well. "It works the same way in the courtroom too. I don't suppose I could ask you to help me? For old time's sake?"

"When Justine finds you, he will ask me to kill you," Shaman told her.

"Will you kill me, Mr. Shaman?"

"I'm in a difficult position, Commander," the man explained. "I'm still an asset to Justine. I know a lot about his business dealings, both legal and illegal. If I refuse an assignment, I become a liability. If I decline the assignment, he will hire another person to kill you. Either way, you're dead. And your killer would come after me."

Fay considered Shaman's words. "I suppose I'd rather be killed by you than by a stranger."

A slight smile formed on Shaman's lips. "My advice is not to let Justine find you," he replied.

"The best defense is a good offense. How did I get from the party to the desert?" Fay asked.

"Your drink was spiked with *GHB*."

Fay struggled to recall the night that she had attended Justine's party. "I recall feeling faint. The last thing I remember, I was in the restroom splashing water on my face," she recounted.

"You passed out there," Shaman explained. "A secret panel opened. Justine's people took you out. Your clothing was removed and given to a body double. She returned to the party. Later she drove your car to your hotel, packed your clothes, and checked out."

"Body double or not, my sister would have known she was not me," Fay asserted.

"I don't know."

"How were you involved, Mr. Shaman?"

"Another man and I were in the house. Justine asked us to come to his master bedroom suite. He showed us to the bathroom, where two bodies were lying on the floor. One body was wrapped in a blood-soaked sheet," Shaman said.

"My sister and I?" Fay guessed.

Shaman nodded. "Justine told us there had been an accident. Two guests had overdosed. He wanted them removed and placed in the desert. Nothing more was discussed."

"But he told you to cut off my head?"

"When we got to the dumpsite, I called Justine to let him know we had arrived. That is when he told me to cut off your head," Shaman replied.

"Wait a minute. You stopped at Two Dogs' place to use Two Dogs' phone," Fay recalled. "You had a cell phone. Why stop at Two Dogs' place to use his phone?"

"I didn't use his phone," Shaman admitted. "My reason for stopping was to tell him where to find you."

"Mercy. What did you think when you saw a body wrapped in a blood-soaked sheet?" Fay inquired.

"Justine has been known on occasion to beat his prostitutes after he's partied with them. I assumed he got carried away and killed one," Shaman stated. "He told us one was a mob lawyer. Whoever it was, it didn't matter."

"You said he beats his prostitutes. What about the others?" Fay asked.

Shaman shrugged his shoulders. "I do know a few are sent to the oligarchs, in Russia, in exchange for business favors."

"He trades them to the Russians?" Fay gasped.

"It's what I understand."

"Why would those women agree?"

Shaman rubbed the fingers of his right hand together. "Coin," he replied.

Fay frowned. "What happens to the women when the oligarchs are done with them?"

"They're sold to the Russian Mafia. The Mafia, in turn, sells them into slavery."

"Slavery?" Fay repeated.

"Sexual slavery is big business in many Eastern European countries," Shaman explained.

"How sad," Fay mused. "How many women has Justine traded to the Russians?" Her astonishment was escalating.

"Thirty-seven," Shaman stated definitively.

Fay remarked, "You seem certain about the number."

"He keeps a ledger. Get the ledger, and you got him." Shaman stood, tossed her derringer onto the bed, and walked toward the door. "Good luck to you, Commander."

"Shaman," Fay called.

He stopped and turned toward Fay, who was now pointing the derringer at him.

"What's the bounty?" Fay asked.

"Five hundred large."

"That's it? I'm disappointed," Fay replied. "Tell Justine you found me. You can take the bounty and retire, Shaman."

A slight smile formed on Shaman's lips. "Where did I find you?"

"Vancouver, B.C.," Fay decided. "I'll take it from there."

"You got it, ma'am."

"Shaman…a medicine man, or doctor. Right?" Fay speculated.

"Something like that."

"Mr. Shaman, when Justine sends the replacement killer, who will it be?"

"Ron Stanton is the man's name…if it makes a difference to you," Shaman answered.

"If you didn't kill Alvin Joe, it had to have been Stanton," Fay concluded. "Alvin must have found out about the GFA's bid-rigging scheme. He intended to expose the GFA. But before he could, Justine sent Stanton to kill him. Is there a way for me to contact you?"

"Hardly," Shaman replied. "And by the way, your weapon is not loaded." He again turned to go but stopped short at the door. "Call the Fillmore Hotel in Los Angeles," he said, without looking back toward her. "Leave your message for Doctor Samuel Carlin. I will get back to you." He disappeared through the doorway.

Fay listened until she heard the entry door to her condo click shut. She waited for a full minute to be sure she was alone and then reached for her cell. Quickly, Fay punched in the number.

The phone rang once and then she heard, "Gus."

"Virgil, where are you?" Fay asked.

"I'm in Phoenix. Why are you whisperin'?" Virgil whispered back.

"I had a visitor," Fay explained. "Roman Justine's hitman was here."

"Are you okay?" Virgil had to know.

"I'm fine. It's a long story. I'll tell you all about it later. But I do have a name for you," Fay offered. "I think the man who killed Alvin Joe is Ron Stanton."

"Ron Stanton is also known as Lenny Crane," Virgil revealed.

"What? You know who Stanton is? Chief Crane? Holy crap!"

"Stanton was stalkin' Alvin Joe," Virgil explained. "He assumed the identity of the real Lenny Crane, a transient. We assume Stanton paid Crane two grand to swap identities with him. Stanton, posin' as a security guard, spent about a month watchin' Mr. Joe… learnin' his habits. He had, more than likely, searched his office."

"For the reasons we suspected?" Fay asked.

"Alvin Joe uncovered the GFA's bid riggin' scheme. He had been documentin' it. No tellin' how the GFA found out what he was up to."

"Maybe he confronted them with his suspicions?" Fay offered.

"If he did, it cost him his life," Virgil stated bleakly.

"What about the real Lenny Crane? Where is he?"

"Dead," Virgil replied. "After Crane retired from the

Navy, he drifted from job to job. By the time he had arrived in Manatee City, Stanton had found him and bought his soul. Lenny became Stanton's accomplice. Stanton killed him after he helped dispose of Alvin's body. We buried who we thought was Ron Stanton."

"The fellow I met, Jon Shaman, had nothing to do with Alvin's death," Fay informed Virgil.

"I don't think so," the Sheriff replied. "What do you want me to do about Jon Shaman?"

"Nothing for now," Fay requested. "As absurd as it may sound, Shaman came here to warn me."

"About Stanton?" Virgil guessed.

"Yeah. Shaman says Justine knows Faye King is still alive, and he wants her head."

"Your head?" Virgil repeated, shocked.

"Yeah, Justine wants it shrink-wrapped and sent to a guy in Chicago named Joey Stumpanato…as sick as that sounds," Fay replied.

"Well, at least he hasn't discovered your true identity," Virgil said. "Sit tight. Now that I know Stanton is connected to Justine, I'll track him through Justine."

"Be careful, Virgil," Fay warned. "These guys are lethal."

Chapter 20

The air around the Seattle waterfront had a distinct chill to it. A hint of salt, creosote, and rotting sea vegetation pervaded its unique odor. "Faye King" stood in the shadows below the twin-level waterfront freeway, watching the fog roll in from Elliott Bay, its arrival announced by the lonely sound of a foghorn. Terminal Thirty and the vast Ming & Yang cargo container storage lot were located across Marginal Way South.

The waterfront was not the safest place for a lone woman at 01:15 hours. The area was frequented by vagrants, transients, drug addicts, and drunken merchant mariners. When the occasional car did pass by, Fay pulled back into the shadows of the massive freeway pillar.

The ground around her feet was littered with newspapers, empty wine bottles, fast food wrappers, cigarette butts, and the stink of urine. Fay flipped up the collar of her black wool trench coat and tried to shake off the penetrating cold. Her black knit watch cap was pulled down to eyebrow level and was doing an excellent job keeping her head and ears warm. Her feet were toasty in black, fur-lined, knee-high leather boots. Now, if only Justine would show. She repeatedly looked at her wristwatch. He was late.

In her right coat pocket, Fay gripped her derringer, her finger at ready on the trigger. Steam streamed from her nostrils each time she exhaled. She had thought long and hard about meeting Roman Justine alone. But despite the danger, she had decided to meet him by herself. This was her problem, her vendetta. There was no point in involving anyone else.

As an afterthought, Fay had called Seattle Detective Frank Farmer. He was out, but she left a message for him on his answering machine. Pearce was sitting in a car three blocks and a cell phone call away.

Fay was startled by a noise behind her. Peering into the darkness, she saw nothing. She took a small flashlight from her left pocket, flicked it on, and directed the beam in the direction of the noise. Two red eyes were reflected in the beam. It was a rat the size of an Afghan hound. Holding the light on the ugly rodent, she bent and scooped up a small rock, stood, and threw it at the rat. It disappeared into the darkness.

Fay clicked off the flashlight when she heard a car arrive across the street…a white town car. The passenger got out, slammed the car's door and stood at the curb as the car drove off. *Justine*. She watched to be sure he was alone. He disappeared through a doorway into a vacant warehouse.

Fay waited five more minutes before crossing Marginal Way South. She entered the warehouse through the same door. The basis for the meeting with Justine was to exchange his list of the thirty-seven prostitutes whom he had traded to the oligarchs. "Faye King" had agreed to dissociate herself from the BAW union affairs and the Stumpanato family. She did not trust him, but with her sister no more than a phone call away, there was a measure of comfort. Justine had chosen the location.

The cavernous warehouse was dark. Fay drew a flashlight from her pocket. She clicked it on and swept the light around the immediate area but saw nothing. Roman Justine had told her he would meet her in a second-floor office at the far end. She kept the light trained on the floor. Her boot heels clicked on the concrete floor as she walked toward the warehouse's far wall. Her finger remained on the derringer's trigger, the weapon still resting in her right coat pocket.

She heard a noise behind her. Fay snapped off the flashlight, spun around, and dropped to one knee. It sounded like someone had come through the door. She remained silent, straining her eyes and her ears in the darkness…nothing. She exhaled the breath she had been holding, stood, snapped on the flashlight, and turned back toward her destination.

When she reached the wooden staircase which led to the next floor, she stopped. She directed the flashlight's beam up the stairs to the door at the top. After climbing the stairs, she paused at the top to listen. No sound. Her heart pounded in her chest, loud enough for her to hear. The door's hinges groaned as she pushed it open using the toe of her right boot.

The doorway led into a dark hallway. Fay swept the beam down the hall, counting three doors on the left wall. Justine had said the third door. She tiptoed along the hallway to the third door and paused.

"I'm at the door, Roman. Are you alone?" Fay called.

"I'm here…alone," came the answer. "Come in."

She released her grip on the derringer, removed her right hand from her coat pocket and turned the knob. Fay put her right hand back into her pocket and grasped the derringer. She pushed the door open with her left foot. The room was dark. "I'm not coming into a dark room."

Justine struck a match. She watched the disembodied flame travel a short distance through the air, and soon the soft glow of an oil lamp lit the room in an eerie light. Justine's demonic face was reflected in the oil lamp's glow.

Fay entered the room. "A bit melodramatic, don't you think?"

"Ms. King, it's so nice to see you again," he said smoothly.

"Cut the crap, douchebag! I agreed to meet you here. I didn't agree to be sociable."

"Fair enough. Come in." Justine rose from a hard-backed wooden chair placed next to a table. Pointing at a similar chair set at the opposite side of the table, he offered, "Have a seat."

"I'll stand. Did you bring it?" Fay asked curtly. Removing her derringer from her coat pocket, she revealed it to Justine for the first time.

His gaze shifted as he noticed the weapon. A slight smile formed on his lips, but he remained silent.

"This can be quick and painless. Toss me the list, and I'm gone from your life," Fay demanded.

He reached inside his jacket.

"Slowly." She pointed the derringer at him.

"No problem," Justine replied. He removed a small notebook from his jacket and tossed it onto the table. Nodding in its direction, he said, "Transaction complete."

Fay stepped further into the room, keeping her gaze on Justine.

"What now, Ms. King?"

In dealing with snakes, I know three things, she silently reminded herself. *They will eat anything smaller than they are. They fear anything more significant than they are, and they will defend themselves if threatened.* With this in mind, Fay growled, "You beat me and raped me, you poor excuse for an asshole."

"That was unfortunate," he responded.

"Unfortunate? And the three days all-expenses-paid trip to the Arizona desert was thoughtful…although a bit tacky, I must say." Fay paused; a venomous sneer formed on her lips. "But what really pissed me off is you ruined my favorite dress."

"But you survived, Ms. King. I'm impressed," Justine responded.

"I survived you twice, Justine," Fay retorted. "Once when you beat me to within an inch of my life. The second time when you left me to die in the desert. I figure you've got almost no chance surviving me one time, cockroach."

Justine shot back, "I love it when you talk dirty to me, bitch."

"You know, Roman, I'm not a bad person once you get to know me. In fact, I've been known, on occasion, to take an ice pick to my heart, chip off a little piece, and give it away. But I have to really, really like someone before I'm willing to endure that sort of pain," Fay stated.

Justine grinned. "In another place, another time, you and I would have made a dynamic duo, Faye."

"Hardly."

Justine's gaze shifted away from her and seemed to refocus behind her. His slight, constant smile grew more prominent. The flickering lamplight distorted his features, making him seem eviler.

It was an old ploy. Fay had seen it a million times in old Western movies. The trick was to make your opponent think someone was behind you. You lost your concentration for an instant, and your opponent was on top of you. She sensed the hairs rise on her neck. "You there, Shaman?" she called.

Justine's eyebrows arched. "You two know one another?"

"Don't move another inch," Fay commanded.

"Am I to believe you would shoot me, Ms. King?" Justine moved several paces toward her.

"Stay put too, Shaman," Fay ordered as she lowered her aim, pointing the muzzle at Justine's groin, "or I'll blow his goddamn nuts off." Her memory rebooted to a scene back in the desert, where she'd held a jackrabbit at bay. She blinked her eyes. Standing before her was Roman Justine and not a jackrabbit. Now disoriented, she said, "What say you, jackass. Guilty or not guilty?"

"Kill her, Shaman," Justine ordered.

"Guilty," Fay said as she squeezed the derringer's trigger.

Three shots rang out. She sensed a sharp pain. Her vision blurred, and she sank to her knees. Roman Justine likewise dropped to his knees, holding his chest, disbelief etched into his face.

For a moment, the two people held each other's gaze. Both fell forward. Fay lay motionless on the cold wood plank floor. She could see a pair shoes approach from the shadows.

"Shaman," Fay moaned. She heard a click. It sounded like a gun hammer cocking. Her world faded to black.

****

Frank Farmer was standing at the entrance to the warehouse when he heard the three shots. Without waiting for a confirmation, he clicked on his radiophone. "Officer down! Officer down!" he radioed. "My location…Ming & Yang warehouse, Marginal Way South and South Atlantic Street."

Within minutes, every available cop and EMT in the city would converge on this location. He pushed through the door and lumbered toward the far end of the darkened warehouse.

When Farmer reached the staircase, he stopped, breathing hard. He flashed the flashlight's beam on an open door at the top of the stairs. Satisfied it was safe to proceed, he raced up the staircase, taking two steps at a time.

At the top, he paused at the door. He eased his head around the doorjamb but saw nothing. He swept his light the length of the hallway. Two forms lay still on the floor.

Farmer eased his large torso through the doorway and into the hallway. He drew close to the first of the two lifeless forms and knelt down beside a tall man. Frank estimated him to be early forties in age. The man's throat had been slashed. He appeared to be dead.

Frank stood and moved over to the other body. He again knelt next to the victim. The second figure, a smaller and older man, had been shot in the back. He was dead. Farmer rose and inched his way toward the open door at the end of the hallway.

When he reached the door, he called, "Fay?" No answer. He eased his head past the doorjamb and peered into the room. His heart sank. In the flickering oil lamp's growing light, he saw Fay's motionless body sprawled across the floor. "Where's the EMT?" he barked into the radiophone.

****

The first face Fay saw when she awoke was Frank Farmer's. "Where am I, Frank?" She tried to sit up.

He gently held her down. "Harborview Hospital. You were shot."

"No kidding! Where?" Fay gasped.

"Your left side. A doctor has already attended to it. He said you'd live."

Fay responded with a weak smile. "Frank, I killed Roman Justine."

"There was no one else in the room when I found you," Frank replied.

"No, Frank. I shot him," she insisted. "Check my weapon. It's been fired."

"You fired your weapon. We don't know what you hit," Frank asserted.

"He was there. I heard shots."

"I heard shots as well," Frank reported. "I found a man shot dead in the hallway."

"It was Justine. I shot him," Fay repeated.

"No. The man's name was Ronald Reagan Stanton."

"Stanton?" Fay asked.

"I found him about fifteen feet from where I found you," Frank explained. "Stanton was carrying a knife, not a gun."

"The other shots, Frank? I heard more than one." Fay struggled to sit up. He did not try to stop her this time. "One shot was from the gun of a man named Jon Shaman, one of Justine's hit men. He was standing behind me," she explained. "How could he have missed me? His shot was point-blank."

"I think Shaman's shot was dead on target," Frank responded. "He shot through you. His bullet was meant for Justine."

"Shaman shot me, and I shot Justine?" Fay asked.

"Shaman's bullet passed between your left arm and your torso. A fraction of an inch either way, and you would have lost an arm or three ribs."

"Shaman shot Justine. And a result, he saved my life. A second time," Fay stated.

Frank nodded. "Your guardian angel. I found the second man in the hall. His throat had been cut. Stanton had slashed this man's throat and left him for dead," he guessed. "The second man shot Ron Stanton as he reached the door leading into the office where I found you."

"Justine hired Stanton to kill me," Fay divulged.

"Lucky, he came up fifteen feet short." Frank placed a comforting hand on Fay's right shoulder. "Thanks to Sheriff Gus."

A quizzical look formed on Fay's face, then faded to horror. "NO! Frank." She wailed. "No. Not Virgil." Tears flooded her eyes. Her head dropped back onto her pillow. "No. No. No," she moaned. "Virgil's dead? No, Frank, no!"

Frank waited until Fay's sobbing had subsided. He removed a handkerchief from his jacket pocket and dried the tears that had streaked her cheeks. He snatched several tissues from the box on the table next to her bed and handed them to her.

"Where's my sister?" Fay pleaded.

"JP is in the waiting room with my wife. She wanted me to talk to you first. Fortunate for us, Gus is not dead," Frank informed her. "However, he is here in the hospital.

He is now in surgery and not expected to make it."

When she had finished drying her eyes and blowing her nose, Fay reclined and stared at the ceiling. "Why, Frank?" she whispered.

"I gather Sheriff Gus had been tracking Ron Stanton. He caught up with him at the warehouse," Frank speculated.

"It's my fault. I called Virgil and gave him Stanton's name. If I hadn't done it, Virgil would be alive now," Fay asserted.

"And you would be dead." Frank again reminded Fay, "Virgil is in life-threatening condition. Time will tell whether it's time for him to meet his maker."

"I don't care!" Fay exclaimed. "God! Why Virgil? His soul was good."

Chapter 21

Tahoma National Cemetery, Kent, Washington

Fay stood beside the coffin containing the man she had fallen in love with. He had had no relatives, according to his obituary. She had chosen to manage the arrangements related to his death as executor of his estate. But, as Fay looked around at the hundreds of first responders in attendance, his family was extensive. She had chosen Tahoma National Cemetery, as opposed to the cemetery in Virgil's hometown in West Virginia, because it was closer to her. Virgil, a former Naval officer, was eligible for burial at Tahoma.

During a previous phone conversation, Virgil had indicated that when the GFA operation was completed, when things had settled down, he would have liked to pursue a serious relationship with her. Fay knew that included marriage. She had not been opposed to the notion. But now, under the current circumstances, it was not to be.

She waited until the procession had passed by the casket to pay their last respects to their fallen brother. Fay approached the coffin. Tears streamed down her cheeks. At the funeral home, she had placed a bottle of cola near his right hand. No telling how long his journey to heaven would take. He would need a refreshment along the way.

As the casket lowered into the ground, John Denver's "Country Roads" played in the background. In his will, Virgil had requested his beloved boat, *Mountain Mama*, be donated to the Cartman County Sheriff's Department. The funds from his life insurance policy were to establish Cartman County's first harbor patrol. Deputy Doug would head the harbor division. Virgil's entire estate was left to charity and to the department…except for his trusty .44 Magnum, which Fay kept, along with a photo of him in his white dress uniform. This would be her lasting memory of Virgil Gus.

Fay began her eulogy with, "Virgil, you gave me my life in exchange for your own. No matter where you may journey, I vow I will follow. Not the highest mountain or deepest sea will keep me from you, my love. My dear prince, may you now be at peace…and rest assured in knowing I will follow."

Fay, dabbing at a tear, glanced at a tall man wearing sunglasses dressed in Western boots and a dark business suit, who had remained a distance from the crowd. She smiled; he smiled in return. The man waved and turned away.

The funeral was expensive yet simple. It must have cost the feds a ton of money. All the actors had played their parts to an Academy Award standard. The funeral had to be beyond convincing. Virgil Gus was now dead, while Carson James was about to begin a new life. The U.S. Marshals Service Witness Security program would assure Mr. James the security, health, and safety of a government witness whose life was in danger, as a result of his testimony against organized crime members.

****

One month after Roman Justine's stunning disappearance, one of the country's wealthiest citizens, Louisiana Senator Lois de la Croix, opened an inquiry into the Galaxy Friendship Association's corporate practices. The Justice Department subpoenaed the acting director of the GFA and the CEOs of twenty defense contractors on the same day. No one seemed to notice that Senator de la Croix had, in the past, received hundreds of thousands of dollars in legal campaign contributions from the GFA and Roman Justine. No one seemed to care. For Senator de la Croix, it was damage control time.

The news media would record the Senator's outrage during the coming weeks. Her constituents had been duped; these horrible people known as the Galaxy Friendship Association had defrauded her country.

In the end, the GFA and its twenty member companies were ordered to reimburse the federal government the estimated tax money lost by the taxpayers due to the GFA's scam. Nineteen of the twenty GFA CEOs suffered the shame and embarrassment of getting caught. Each received jail time ranging from six months to two years. Each company paid one hundred million dollars, the maximum fine for corporations convicted of violating antitrust laws. AmeriCon CEO and federal informant Don Valley retired. He walked away from the proceedings unscathed.

****

That same day, in the Czech Republic, a nineteen-year-old American woman was preparing to service her seventh man of the day. Kristi Larssen had met man number seven, like the hundreds before him, in the club's lounge. She had the impression this man was different. She told him that he seemed gentler and kinder than all the others. And for a change, he was an American. When the door to her room had closed behind them, he spoke to her in English. Only then did she know he was indeed different from the other men.

He introduced himself as Jon Shaman. He told her he represented the American Red Cross. It was the only lie he would say to her that night. As he handed her the black jogging suit and black wool watch cap he had concealed under his full-length black leather coat, he encouraged her to hurry. A car was waiting for them around the corner from the club's entrance. He told her not to worry; no one would bother her when she left the club. He assured her the bartender and bouncer had been paid to look the other way. Besides, he had arranged with her owner to gain her freedom. Kristi would never know the arrangement included the man's death.

After she had dressed, she left the room with Shaman behind her. As she reached the door, she hesitated.

"Hurry, we don't have much time," Shaman urged. He noticed the scar on her right wrist but said nothing.

"Wait, Jon," she whispered, her voice hollow. She returned to the nightstand next to her bed. Opening the drawer, she removed her black leather-bound *Holy Bible*. "My salvation," Kristi murmured. She turned back toward the door and hugged Shaman. "Thank you, thank you, thank you, Mr. Shaman."

Together, they left the room.

Shaman explained to Kristi that a Marine helicopter was waiting to fly her to a hospital in Dresden, Germany where doctors would care for her. When she had fully recovered, the American Embassy would arrange for her passage to the United States.

Outside and around the corner from the entrance to Club Hawaii, two women, also dressed in black, sat in a black sedan with the engine running. No one would notice the sedan. It blended in well with the other black sedans waiting for their passengers—the rich Czech and German men frequenting the numerous brothels in this small Czech border town.

The women watched the Club Hawaii entrance for any signs of trouble. They communicated with Shaman via the short-wave transmitters commonly used by CIA operators. This would be extraction number eight of what would prove to be twenty-four more young American women freed from their servitude. As the two women waited in the dark alley, Navy Petty Officer Jansche Pearce and Commander Faydra Green agreed Jon Shaman was good at what he did.

Fay would not condemn Jon for the things he had done in his past, for what he had become. After all, who was she to express disapproval? Although his body had never been found, Fay believed that her alias Faye King had killed Roman Justine. Was she no better than Shaman? Like Jon, her participation in the grim and dangerous op had served as her attempt to set her heart and soul straight with her country, her maker, and herself.

Shaman's current efforts did not go unnoticed by the U.S. judicial system. In their eyes, he was repaying his debt to society. For his part in rescuing the sex slaves, he would remain free from prosecution for at least two contract killings and for abducting Faye King and Corazon Garza, all by the order of his employer, Roman

Justine. How he faired with his maker, only time would tell.

Two klicks beyond the edge of town, two U.S. Marine helicopters waited in a night-shrouded field. One helicopter, complete with Marine medical staff, stood by to whisk Kristi Larssen away from her living hell to the hospital in Dresden. The second helicopter, large enough to transport the black sedan in its belly, stood ready with six E-Team commandos aboard. Six men cut from the same cloth as Jon Shaman prepared to respond with force, if necessary, should the two women need them.

The following spring, J. Pearce married Egan Fletcher, the handsome Navy captain she had met a year and a half prior when she and Fay had been investigating the murder of Paul Charma. The nation buried President William Green four weeks later. He had suffered from an ongoing illness. Fay confided in her trusted friend, Gifford Champion, that her dad had hung around long enough to see Jansche, his baby girl, married. That one-month stretch in Fay's life proved to be both the happiest and the saddest. It was difficult for her to lose Virgil, a significant man in her life. It was much more difficult for her to lose her father less than a year later, especially since they had rectified old arguments and were speaking again.

It did not end there for Faydra. There was the President Green Library and the various funds and organizations needing her attention. Her father had not finished writing his memoirs. Fay called on Gifford and his NCC journalistic skills to help her finish them. He agreed.

Gifford speculated when the Navy named its newest aircraft carrier to honor her dad, it was perhaps the proudest moment in Fay's life. The U.S.S. *William R. Green* was christened six months following his passing. Fay, together with her sister, brother, Egan, Frank, Vern, Charlie, and Gifford were all on hand to break the traditional champagne bottle across the ship's bow. To her chagrin, Fay had to make a speech on national television.

"I consider myself a recluse. Having to make the speech terrified me, Gifford. I was so proud and so sad, I could barely speak," Fay told him after the ceremony.

She had not fully recovered from her assault. While the headaches seemed less intense and less frequent, she claimed her heart was still heavy. She forgot things from time to time…like time. She was forever losing track of the day, or the year. She seemed to have forgotten much, but she had not forgotten the man who had not only saved her life but had also stolen her heart: Cartman County Sheriff Virgil Gus. Yet, now and again, Fay would catch a glimpse of the tall, dark gentlemen for a split second. He would smile and vanish. She took comfort in knowing she and Carson James would cross paths again one day. Yet, every year on her birthday, she would receive twenty-four sterling silver roses - no card.

Roman Justine never did materialize. Either he had slipped out of the country to start a new life, or he had died, as Fay believed. She told her sister, "I do not care what kind of man Roman Justine was, or what he did to me for that matter. I have killed another human being. And I am, and will always be, profoundly remorseful for my selfish act."

A word about the author…

Except for time spent in military service I live in the Pacific Northwest with my legal-beagle son K-K. and seven large tropical fish from the Amazon River. I am a second-generation Seattleite (that's what they call those of us who dwell in the shadow of Mr. Rainier). I have had the opportunity to travel our planet many times over. My stories are created from my memories of my personal experiences, the places I have visited, and the people and friends I have known.

Thank you for purchasing
this publication of The Wild Rose Press, Inc.
For questions or more information
contact us at
info@thewildrosepress.com.
The Wild Rose Press, Inc.
www.thewildrosepress.com

Milton Keynes UK
Ingram Content Group UK Ltd.
UKHW021345170524
442873UK00045B/1016

9 781509 241323